THEY CALL ON THEIR ANIM

Ginny Mallard is a personal concierge with an elite client list. Bar owner Teddy Tonica mixes, pours, and listens to his regulars. She's a dog person; he's attuned to felines. So what qualifies this odd couple as the best crime stoppers around?

Maybe it's Ginny's knack for sniffing out the hard facts. Maybe Teddy has a way of getting strangers to divulge their dirty secrets. Maybe it's the snappy banter they sling back and forth, like characters out of Gin's favorite noir movies.

Or maybe it's their furry companions—a shar-pei named Georgie, and Penny, the bar cat—who really know the score.

Praise for

COLLARED

First in the delightful Gin & Tonic mystery series
from L.A. Kornetsky

"Charming. . . . Vivid descriptions of Seattle's Ballard neighborhood are a plus in this cozy tale."

—*Publishers Weekly*

"The plot moves quickly, enhanced by smart dialog and good characterizations. . . . A strong beginning to what should be an entertaining series."

—*Library Journal*

ALSO BY L.A. KORNETSKY:

Collared

FIXED

A *GIN & TONIC* MYSTERY

L.A. KORNETSKY

G

GALLERY BOOKS

New York London Toronto Sydney New Delhi

Gallery Books
A Division of Simon & Schuster, Inc.
1230 Avenue of the Americas
New York, NY 10020

First Gallery Books trade paperback edition October 2013

Interior design by Renata Di Biase

Manufactured in the United States of America

10 9 8 7 6 5 4 3 2 1

Library of Congress Cataloging-in-Publication Data is on file.

ISBN 978-1-4516-7165-0
ISBN 978-1-4516-7167-4 (ebook)

For Deborah and Neil,
the Labradors of Doooooom, and Miss Thing

1

The dogs were gossiping.

The gray tabby paused, halfway down the fire escape, and surveyed the sidewalk below her. It was late afternoon, the sun cool and fading, dappling the pavement with shadows. The humans she could see from her vantage point were walking faster than they did in the evening, heading somewhere important. And the two dogs out in front of the Busy Place, one a shaggy black mutt of dubious Labrador ancestry, the other a fawn-coated shar-pei, were paw-to-paw, sprawled next to the bike rack, which tended to hold more leashes than bikes.

Dogs gossiped about everything, very little of it interesting. But she had a vested interest in one of those dogs, so she made her way down to the street and joined the conversation.

The smaller dog acknowledged her with a sniff at her ears, which she allowed only because it was Georgie, and she allowed Georgie things other dogs would get hissed at for. The larger dog ignored her utterly, still talking. "They don't like it. They don't like it at all."

The tabby thought that the Labrador sounded more like a hound, mournful and worried.

"They never like anything," Georgie said. "Do they know what they don't like?"

"Who doesn't like what?" the cat asked, inserting herself into the conversation.

"There's something happening at the Old Place," Georgie said, as though that explained everything.

It took Penny a minute to remember: the old place was the shelter Georgie had been at, before her human took her away. The Labrador had been there, too, apparently, or at least knew enough to spread gossip.

"You keep track of what happens there?" She couldn't fathom why.

"Mmmm." Georgie put her head down on her paws, her square-jowled face level with Penny's. "The dogs there are unhappy. Not that anyone is ever really happy there, it's not a happy-place, but this is different. Things aren't right. They're . . . wrong."

"A little more detail, please?" Anything that bothered Georgie bothered Penny, but "wrong" wasn't helpful.

Dogs weren't built to shrug, but both the Labrador and Georgie managed it.

"Wrong," Georgie repeated. "Smells wrong, sounds wrong. For months now, it comes and goes and comes back. That's what they're saying, anyway. But it's not where they are, it's happening somewhere else in the building, so they don't know."

"No way to know. But everyone's upset." The Lab definitely had hound in him, somewhere.

"So?" Penny looked at them, then sat down and began washing her paw, waiting for them to figure it out. When they just stared at her, she paused mid-groom and twitched her whiskers at them, half annoyed, half superior. Dogs. *"So if you need to know something, and you can't sniff it out, get someone who can open doors."*

Georgie lifted her head, one ear flopping over while the other stayed upright. Her wrinkled face didn't really have expressions, but Penny could see comprehension gleaming behind those dark brown eyes, finally.

"Humans," the shar-pei said to her canine companion with the air of solving the problem. "Humans can do it."

"Humans?" The Labrador looked confused but excited. Then again, Penny thought with a sniff, they usually did.

"Our humans," Georgie clarified. "They sniff things."

"Humans sniffing?" The confusion turned to a dubious disdain for human noses.

"Human-sniffing. And door-opening. They go anywhere, look at anything. We just have to figure out how to get them to look." Georgie turned her head to look at Penny. "How do we get them to look?"

Penny finished grooming her paw and swiped it over her ears. "Leave that to me."

On the other side of the windows, inside the shaded confines of Mary's Bar & Grill, another conversation was taking place, this one slightly more heated. Two men were leaning on opposite sides of the bar, at the far end where it curved back into the wall.

"He's insane." The older man was emphatic about that, while still managing to keep his voice low enough to not disturb the few early customers seated at the tables, indulging in a little late afternoon libation.

"He's not insane," Tonica countered calmly, not pausing

in his arrangement of the speed rail's condiments. The new afternoon bartender, Jon, had rearranged them during the previous shift, which meant that during a rush someone might reach for an olive and end up with a lemon. Not cool. "You're overreacting. He's just being an asshole. I mean, more of an asshole than usual."

The galley chef and general handyman squared his shoulders and scowled at the bartender, and regardless of the thirty-year gap in their age, he looked more than ready to take the other man to the mat to win the argument. "He's an insane asshole, Tonica, and I swear, I'm going to quit."

"You know you're not going to quit, Seth. They'll take you out of here feet-first."

Seth scowled at that, too. "Bah. If he gives me grief one more time about the menu, or anything at all, I swear, Teddy, it's going to be him going out feet-first, and I don't care if he is the boss. He's gone insane." He turned and scowled at the blond woman sitting at the bar, for good measure, and then stomped off into the galley kitchen, his body—still showing the musculature that had made him a boxing contender in his youth—shaking with indignation.

Ginny Mallard tried very hard not to laugh, but Tonica's heavy and extremely theatrical sigh broke her.

"Is Patrick really being that bad?" she asked between giggles, not even pretending that she hadn't been eavesdropping.

"He's gone insane," the bartender admitted, giving up on the condiments and turning so that he faced where the blonde was sitting, a few stools down at the bar. "He was always a pain in the ass, but recently, it's gotten . . . worse." He ran a hand over the top of his head, as though the argument might have somehow disordered the dark brown brushtop, and sighed again. "But he's the boss. Whatever bug got up his ass, I hope it crawls out soon. Seth may not quit, but the rest of us might. And I just got everyone properly trained." He shook his head. "Seriously—if Pat's not careful, he's going to ruin my bar."

Two months ago, Ginny would have laughed off that claim; Tonica was just a bartender at Mary's, if admittedly the one who worked the most shifts and seemed to organize everything. But he wasn't the owner, or even the manager. Calling the cozy neighborhood bar "his" would have sounded like ego overstepping reality. But it was simple truth: Patrick, the bar's owner, might not want to give him the title of manager, but Tonica managed it anyway, from filling in for folk who were out sick to writing up shift schedules and shuffling paperwork Patrick couldn't be bothered with. And that, she figured, gave Tonica the right to consider Mary's "his."

She knew all this, because last month their casual acquaintance and trivia-night rivalry had become something else, when she'd had to ask him for help.

Mallard Services was a private concierge company: she did for others what they didn't have time—or inclination—to do themselves. Usually that meant arranging formal parties, from choosing invitations to arranging the caterer's run-through, or shepherding visiting relatives to and from the airport. But a good concierge was adaptable, and so she'd agreed to take on an assignment to find her client's uncle, who had disappeared with time-sensitive business papers that needed to be filed.

That was when she'd convinced Tonica, with his people-shmoozing skills, to help her. That was when they'd gone into what she called "researchtigations," which was almost like being investigators, but without a license. Or, according to Tonica, a clue.

And the man they were looking for had died, their client had been arrested for money laundering, and they'd gotten warned off poking their noses in anywhere by the federal agent who showed up. Not one of her better jobs.

Anyway, out of all that, the one thing she knew for certain was that Theodore Tonica was more than just a bartender, even one who, it turned out, had a poli sci degree from Harvard.

"So what're you going to do?" she asked. "I mean, short of locking Patrick in the storeroom and forging his signature on all the orders."

"I already do that," Tonica said. "The signatures, anyway. But I'd have to soundproof the storeroom before locking him in there. Nah. Too much work. I'll come up with something else."

"Well, if you need any help . . ." She wasn't sure what she could do, but it was the best she could offer. Mary's was becoming her office-away-from-the-home-office these days. She didn't want anything to change, either.

Thinking about that made Ginny acutely aware that

they hadn't gotten another client for their little sideline of not-quite-investigations. She could blame part of the delay on the fact that she'd been spending one night a week with a dog trainer—Georgie had bitten the guy who tried to attack them, and the cops had suggested it would be better for everyone if she could prove that the shar-pei had proper training in the event it happened again. The problem was, between that, and keeping her private concierge business afloat, and trying to stay in touch with her friends, it was hard to find time to do anything about *finding* those clients.

And part of it, Ginny admitted, was that she had absolutely no idea how to find more clients of that particular sort. The two of them weren't licensed, so they couldn't exactly advertise, and really, what could they say, anyway? "Inexperienced researchers for hire, two-drink minimum?"

Although that was a catchy tag, now that she thought of it.

And it wasn't as though Tonica was helping drum up business, either. Far as she could tell, he was still treating it as a one-off, not something they *did*. And yet . . . when they were in the middle of it he'd been as hooked on the challenge as she was. He just needed a push, that was all.

That thought brought her back around to the current discussion, and her immediate worry. "You wouldn't quit, would you?" Tonica had worked at other bars before Mary's, and just because he'd been here for two or three years didn't mean he would stay, always. "I mean, you said this is a good place to work, better than anywhere else in town. You wouldn't leave?"

He tilted his head and looked at her again. Whatever was showing on her face seemed to worry him. "Relax, Gin. I'm not going anywhere. Whatever's gotten into Patrick, he'll settle down eventually and go back to being the absentee boss we all know and ignore." But his face had lines and shadows that hadn't been there even a week before, and Ginny didn't feel reassured.

He gestured at her drink. "You want that freshened?"

She looked down at her martini, which was only half gone. "No, I'm good."

She paid for her first drink, then Tonica "refreshed" it, and then she paid for the next, if she had a third. It was one of the little, unlooked-for bonuses to their working together, like having the best table by the window reserved for her, and she didn't feel guilty about it at all.

All right, she admitted, maybe a little.

"Oi, boss!" Seth called from the other side of the bar, bent over something. "Some help, will ya?"

"Excuse me," Tonica said, and went down to help Seth carry an oversized crate of something out of the back room. She watched for a moment as they discussed something in low tones, the ambient noise of the other customers making it impossible to eavesdrop this time.

One of the things that she liked most about Mary's, besides the staff, was that they didn't have a jukebox, or live music, ever. There was a radio at the bar that sometimes played jazz, just softly enough to be soothing, but you could always hear who you were talking to. If you wanted a noisy pickup joint, there were a lot of other places to go both locally and downtown. Mary's was where you came to be heard, more than seen. It was where you came with friends, took someone on a third date, came on your own when you didn't want to be alone.

Ginny scanned the bar again, letting her gaze flit over the sparse crowd. This early in the evening—it was barely five o'clock—it was mostly folk who worked out of home offices, like herself. She knew three of the men and one of the women set up at the tables, less for who they were or what they did than what dogs they owned, since she ran into them at odd hours while walking Georgie.

The thought made her check out the front window, to reassure herself that her dog was still comfortable and not needing a walk. The familiar fawn bulk was still hunkered down next to the other dog, exactly where she'd left them an hour ago. Plus, she noted with amusement, the addition of a smaller form, currently draped over Georgie's fore-legs. Mistress Penny-Drops: the feline resident-at-large of Mary's, and her dog's best friend, if you could assign animals relationships like that.

Maybe you could, or maybe she was being silly, but there was no denying that they seemed to enjoy each other's company. Dogs were pack animals—so what if Georgie's pack was feline? The rest of it walked on two legs, and that didn't seem to bother Georgie at all.

Dogs . . . just kind of *accepted* things.

Someone came up beside her but didn't call across the bar to get Tonica's attention. They were, apparently, waiting to be noticed. Ginny turned around on her stool to see who it was, and the woman took that as an invitation to speak. "Hi. You're Virginia Mallard?"

The woman wasn't anyone Ginny knew, either personally or as a seen-around-town local. That of itself wasn't wildly odd—Mary's was a neighborhood bar, tucked into the tail end of a side street—but Ballard, retaining an independent neighborhood vibe separate from the city that had annexed it, had enough local interest that strangers still wandered in occasionally, especially tourists.

This girl didn't look like a tourist, though. She was classic Ballardian: her clothing looked like what Tonica constantly disparaged as "hipster light"—chinos and a dark green pullover just worn enough to be acceptable, but had been very expensive not too long ago. Her hair was done in shoulder-length brown braids, about a dozen of them, with the tips touched with just enough purple to be noticeable but not so much to be flashy.

A new client? Normally they approached her via a phone call or less often an email, not the personal approach, and the woman didn't look like the sort who would normally hire—or could afford—her. Still, it never hurt to be professional.

"Hello, and yes, I am." Ginny shifted a little, in case the woman was looking to claim the bar stool next to her. It was early enough that the bar itself was empty, except herself—the half-dozen people who had come by after work had chosen tables, instead—but she could understand why a woman alone would sit at the bar. That was what she'd done, too, the first few times she came here.

She'd been new to the neighborhood, hadn't known anyone, and figured that talking to the bartender was better than sitting alone at a table, looking like fresh pickup meat, or worse.

But the woman didn't sit down. Instead she stood in front of Ginny, her head tilted to one side, her eyes squinted half shut as though she were staring into the sun.

Ginny had the sudden, uncomfortable thought that she was about to be hit on.

"You're the woman who did that thing last month?"

Well. That had not been what she was expecting, at all.

"That thing?" Ginny asked slowly, not sure if she should say yes or no.

"The real estate thing. Where the guy went to jail and all."

The "and all" covered a lot of territory, including fraud, assault, burglary, and a man she'd known, however briefly, dying. Ginny still didn't believe it had been suicide.

"Yeah," she said, putting down her drink and giving this woman her full attention, trying to figure out what was up. "I am."

"Oh." The woman's brown eyes opened wider, and she looked even more nervous. "Oh, good. Um. I, ah, um."

Ginny waited, wishing that Tonica was here to say something, but not wanting to look away from the woman to see if he was still busy, or if he could be called down. She was the better researcher, totally, but he had the ninja people skills. And right now she really could use those.

"I heard about you. I mean. Everyone's heard about . . . it was, people talk."

Ginny hadn't known they were being gossiped about. It wasn't surprising, she supposed: they hadn't exactly hidden what they had done, and some of it had gone down right here at Mary's. Had she known, though, she could have used it for cheap advertising . . . assuming that they were saying good things, that was.

"My name's Nora," the woman said in a rush. "Nora Rees. I work down at LifeHouse. I mean, I'm a volunteer there, I don't have—I'm a student, but I work there, volunteer work."

The girl was borderline incoherent, but Ginny picked up the essentials. LifeHouse was the name of the local animal shelter where Ginny had gotten Georgie last summer. She'd been innocently minding her own business, doing some window shopping, when they'd ambushed her with a row of animals up for adoption, and she'd ended up going home with a gangly, half-grown, mostly shar-pei puppy.

"I know the place, yeah," she said now. "I got my dog there."

"The shar-pei mix outside, yeah, I know. Um, I checked the records, when . . . I mean—"

"When you came looking for me?" Ginny asked.

"Yeah. I mean, when—"

This woman was never going to get to the point. "And?"

"And I want to hire you. To investigate. The shelter, I mean."

* * *

Teddy had been checking the taps when the Greenie-hipster child approached Ginny. He noted it out of the corner of his eye, not really paying attention, the way he kept his eye on everything that happened at his bar, and Stacy monitored the tables during busy evenings. At first he didn't think anything of it—with her curls and curves, Ginny got attention, even if she didn't always notice it. But when she got that look on her face—the one that usually meant her brain was firing on all thrusters—he casually moved back down to that end of the bar, just in case. In case of what, exactly, he didn't let himself think about. He was just listening. That was what bartenders did.

"You think there's something wrong at the shelter?" his sometimes partner was asking the girl.

"Yes. I don't know. Maybe."

The girl was not exactly inspiring confidence. He took a closer look. Definitely a Ballard Baby, he decided: too crunchy-granola for Downtown, too poor to live in Fremont these days. Mostly harmless.

"Something funny's happening," the girl was saying now, her hands emphatic. "Not funny hah-hah, funny wrong. Money-funny. Not counterfeiting, um, no. I, it's just. . . ." She took a deep breath and started again. "It's about our finances. We're working in the black—the shelter's founder sank a lot of money to get us started, and donations and adoption fees keep us going, plus all our professionals donates their time, but we rely a lot on grants."

Ginny nodded, indicating that she was following along so far.

"And I'm not an accountant or anything, I don't handle our books, but we have this one grant, specifically, that funds our ability to offer low-cost neutering. It gets renewed yearly, and all the paperwork has to be just so, you know? We're coming up for renewal, and Este, she's the one who founded the shelter, her and her partner, she wanted me to go over the paperwork, make sure everything was in order."

"And everything wasn't?"

"I . . . don't know."

Teddy got the feeling that this girl, Nora, was used to having the answers ready to hand, that people had always told her how to behave to save the earth, be a good citizen, be a good daughter, and it had always made sense to her. This was the first time she was running into something that didn't make sense.

He shook his head. She'd get used to it, eventually.

"There's a lot of paperwork, not just going forward but to back check previous grants," the girl went on, "and I'm not sure, this isn't my thing, really, but I don't think all the funds this year are accounted for properly. I think someone's been taking it. I thought at first maybe I'd miscounted, or missed a receipt somewhere, one of the payment records, or there'd been a misallocation, but I checked all that, twice. And the only thing left is that someone's been stealing it." She sounded horrified, and her face twisted in confusion. "Who would do that? Steal from a shelter? Steal from animals?"

"Animals are less likely to call the cops." He joined into

the conversation now, leaning over the bar, his elbows planted in the standard bartender pose that Ginny joked could convince a hardened felon into spilling their guts. "How much money are we talking about?"

"I don't know. Maybe two thousand?" She didn't seem at all surprised that he had joined them; he didn't know if she'd been expecting him, or her world assumed that everyone was interested in what she had to say. "It's not a lot of money, really, but the grant allows us to fix any animal that's brought in, not just the ones we're hosting. Going to the vet could cost you a hundred dollars or more—we can do it for half that, because the grant covers the rest of our expenses, the supplies our vet uses, all that stuff. But if we run out of money, we have to turn animals away until the grant's renewed. And if we can't account for everything, the grant might not be renewed."

"The grant money's all been in cash?" Teddy asked.

Nora nodded. "It's set up so that we get a check from a special account every quarter and that gets cashed so we have the money we need on hand, instead of throwing it into the main operating fund and figuring out what goes where every month. That's supposed to allow us to pay for supplies and stuff more easily. Or something?"

Or if someone wanted to muddy their tracks, if you were being cynical. Teddy tried not to be cynical, but money tended to bring it out in him. Penalty of growing up with too much of it, probably. That was one of the reasons he was on this side of the country, and the rest of his family was on the other side.

"So if you think the money's been stolen, why not go to the cops and report it? Why come to us?" Ginny asked. It seemed a logical question to Teddy, too. That would start the official process, and insurance would cover whatever was missing, right?

The girl shook her head, her colored braids twitching slightly with the movement. "Oh, no. We can't afford to. If the cops get involved—if we get any kind of negative publicity at all—never mind the grants, we might lose our permits! There's all this paperwork that you have to get approved before you can run a shelter, and they can yank it if they even think you're doing something wrong. I couldn't risk that!"

"And even if they didn't, I bet you're right: a hint of misused funds, even a small amount, and you could forget about ever getting another nonprofit grant," Ginny said. "From them, probably from anyone. And there's no way public donations can keep a shelter going."

Nora's braids practically danced this time as she nodded emphatic agreement. "Este and Roger funded the shelter, to start. It was all their own money that bought the building and got us set up. But there's no way they could keep us going on their own. And if we lose any of the larger grants . . . we'll have to shut down, and the animals will all be sent to a shelter that isn't no-kill.

"Please. Say you'll help? I can't pay much, but . . ."

She included both of them in her plea, looking back and forth between the two with absolute assurance that they would say yes.

"We need to discuss it," Teddy said, before Mallard could jump in and commit them. "We'll get back to you."

The girl fished into her bag, a bright yellow canvas courier bag, and pulled out a business card. She held it in her hand a minute, clearly unsure of whom to hand it to, and then placed it down on the bartop between them.

"That's the shelter's number. It goes directly to the back office, not the reception desk, unless nobody's there to pick up. But I answer the phone in the office most days; if I'm not there, they'll know how to reach me."

"I take it nobody else knows about this yet?" he asked, based on her earlier words.

"No. And they don't know I've come to you. You can't say anything!" She suddenly went from worried to panicked, like he was about to take out an ad in the trades.

"If we take this job, our discretion is assured," Ginny said, moving smoothly back into the conversation. "We simply need to discuss this between ourselves."

"Okay. I'm, I'll wait until I hear from you, then."

Nora turned and walked out of the bar without pause, her back straight and head high, as though she was aware that they were watching her, an audience of two.

Teddy picked up the business card, smoothing one finger over the slightly crumpled edge. Ginny swung around on her stool to look at the card in his hand.

"You think she's even twenty-one?" she asked, sounding somewhere between depressed and amused.

"Maybe. Barely. I wasn't going to card her unless she asked for a drink."

Ginny's mouth quirked upward, then firmed again, all business. "This is the shelter I got Georgie from."

He looked to his left, through the plate glass window that fronted Mary's, a remnant of its earliest life as a dry goods store, and saw the dog in question, sleeping in her usual spot. He'd talked Patrick into adding a rubber mat under the bike rack, better for sleeping dogs and tires alike than plain sidewalk. The local newspaper had done a write-up about them, for that. He didn't know if it had gotten them any more business, but it hadn't hurt.

And now Patrick was talking about changing things, cutting corners on the menu, focusing on foofy drinks and bringing in a band for the weekends, like that would be a good thing. . . .

"Yeah, I figured," he said to Ginny, putting his worries about the bar to one side for a moment. "That's why she came to you?"

"I don't know. Apparently, people are talking about—" She stopped, and he understood why. Other people might talk about it, but they didn't. They'd been there. Their erstwhile client had been tagged by the feds for money laundering—thankfully after paying them and nobody had been around to sniff at that money, or tell them they had to give it back—and what more was there to say?

"Reputation?" he said, to fill in the uncomfortable silence. "We have a reputation?"

Ginny frowned at him, and he guessed that it wasn't because she didn't get the joke, but because she was thinking about their new case. *Potential* new case, he clarified, to soothe his nerves. They hadn't agreed to take it, yet.

"The shelter's pretty new; it's only been around a few years. They're no-kill; they keep the animals until they can find a home for them."

"So they're probably always strapped for cash."

"Yeah, I think so. They had about a dozen dogs, when I found Georgie, and more cats." Her frown deepened. "They're the only shelter in the area that takes in pit bulls and pittie mixes. If they close . . ."

Teddy wasn't much of a dog person, for all that he'd gotten fond of Georgie, but even he had read about the trouble finding homes for pit bulls, deservedly or not. He didn't like to think about what would happen then.

"They can't pay much, if they're strapped," he said.

She raised an eyebrow at that, or tried to, anyway. Both went up, making her look more surprised than disapproving. "You're in this for the money?"

Now it was his turn to frown at her. "You know I'm not. I'm just not sure this is a good idea. I told you that." He meant the entire venture, not merely this particular potential job, but he'd take it one battle at a time.

"We'd be doing a community service." Her voice had a singsong tone to it he was starting to recognize.

"We'd be snooping," he said bluntly. "In financial records. And she's not the owner, not even the manager. She has no right to ask us to do this."

Ginny waved that off with a hand. "But she was the

one who was asked to handle the grant paperwork. Which means she has access to all the records we need."

"Access doesn't mean authority, Mallard."

"Well," she said brightly, "then it's a good thing we're not official PIs with licenses that could get pulled, isn't it?"

"Damn it, Gin." He pulled back from the bar and crossed his arms, staring at her.

"Look, just think about it, okay? If you don't want to do it, fine. I won't ask again."

There was that voice again. "But you're going to do it, anyway?"

She gave an elegant half shrug and took the business card out of his hands, tucking it into the case of her cell phone, as usual set on the bar next to her like a digital IV.

"Ginny Mallard. Are you taking this case?"

"I don't know," Ginny said. "I'm going to think about it, too."

He wasn't convinced, but short of calling her a liar, there was nothing he could say.

Four and a half years ago, the owners of LifeHouse Shelter had taken over an abandoned warehouse down by the old docks, buying it for pennies on the dollar, and set up shop. Lacking the money to gut the building entirely, they had to adapt the existing structure as best they could, which meant that on the outside it still looked like an old warehouse, although what had been the loading dock area was now fenced and turned into a dog run.

The kennels were at one end of the building, the clinic at the other end, so that the smells of sick animals and chemicals were kept away from the adoption areas. In between there was a reception area, and behind that was what remained of the building, split into two areas by a Plexiglas wall inserted floor to ceiling, the remaining space filled with old sofas and remnant carpets, and climbing structures for the cats, where humans met with animals and scoped each other out.

LifeHouse was certified by the state to house twenty dogs and up to thirty cats. They'd been near or at capacity since they opened their doors, proving that the founders had been right: there had been a real need in the community.

The shelter opened early in the morning so that volunteers could come in to care for the animals, but visitors weren't allowed until much later. According to the sign by the front door, open adoption hours were from noon to 5 p.m., five days a week, Wednesday through Sunday.

At 4:30 that afternoon, the shelter was filled with light and activity. There were humans bustling about, cats sprawling and prowling, dogs being exercised in the fenced courtyard off the parking lot or wandering freely in the meeting areas, being socialized with each other. The receptionist at the front desk monitored the humans as they arrived, while volunteers kept an eye on the animals. A family with two preteen children were in one of the socialization rooms, sitting on the carpeted floor and letting kittens tumble over them, waiting for the right one to show itself.

At 5 p.m., the shelter's doors closed to the public, and

then the slow shutdown began as the animals were fed and exercised one last time, and then the dogs were placed in their kennels for the night, the cats rounded up and placed in their own cages. The sounds of barking and the patter of paws on floors and endless scratch-scratch of claws on carpeted surfaces faded, the murmur of human voices slowing likewise as the volunteers ended their shift and went home.

At the other end of the building, in the clinic, the vet tech made final rounds, ensuring all the cases were locked and equipment put away. There was only one dog in need of care that night, a new arrival still in twenty-four-hour isolation before being let into the general population. The tech paused to give the older hound mix an affectionate ear-pull and make sure that he was comfortable before turning off the lights and locking up.

At 8 p.m., the lights were out all over the shelter, pale red emergency lights glowing in each hallway, reflecting off linoleum floors and metal fire doors.

An occasional bark or whimper came from the canine quarters and was answered by another, then most of the animals, knowing the routine, settled down to sleep. Pale red and yellow lights shone through the windows, alarms activated on every door and window. The security company's patrol started after 10 p.m., swinging by the building twice an hour to pass a flashlight beam through the parking lot and make sure that there were no disturbances.

A little after midnight, a noise broke the silence, a low, unhappy yowl, followed by something else less identifiable, then the sound of heavy thumps. Throughout the shelter, heads lifted, ears picked up, and low whines rose from throats. No barks, no howls, nothing that might draw attention to themselves, merely the sound of anxious worry, waiting.

If the security guard heard them during his pass, concrete walls being no barrier to a determined dog's voice, he didn't react; one howl was much like another, and the alarms were unchanged, no sign of activity outside the walls. His job was to prevent disturbances from the outside, not to investigate possible disturbances within.

He never considered the thought that someone might have come in through the narrow windows set high in the clinic walls, the glass carefully cut and removed, and bodies lowered on ropes into the space while others busied themselves outside, in the parking lot, black-clad shapes blending into the shadows when he passed by.

Eventually, when nothing more was heard, and no one came to investigate, most of the heads went back down onto paws, cats recurling themselves. Most, not all. Along the rows of kennels, noses were pressed up against the mesh, nostrils flaring, ears alert. Older cats and streetwise newcomers rested in alert pose, the tips of their tails barely twitching, waiting. Listening.

At 5 a.m., the first sound of human voices returned, the clatter and clank of wheels and doors, a man's familiar low voice calling out greetings to the first animals on his route.

Only then did the sentinels relax.

2

"We'll talk about it tomorrow,' you said," Teddy muttered to himself, slapping the rim of the steering wheel in frustration. "Brilliant. Because now it's tomorrow, genius."

It was tomorrow, noon already, and he still hadn't made a decision. And Ginny would be here soon, expecting an answer.

He got out of his car and checked the parking lot out of habit: an old beater Ford he didn't recognize, but otherwise empty, and the trash bins had been emptied last night, the lids left open. All was as it should be.

There was an entrance into the back of the bar off the parking lot, but Teddy instead went around the building and leaned against the front wall, waiting for Ginny to walk down the street, her stride probably hampered by Georgie's slower pace and constant need to stick her doggy nose into something.

He didn't know why he was even dithering; he knew how this was going to go down. There would be that look on her face, the one that said she knew something he didn't and was going to tell him about it. And, in the telling, change his mind. Which he hadn't made up yet.

"No, Ginny." He tried saying it out loud. "Absolutely, no."

Even the air, damp and cool, seemed skeptical.

"Shit."

He looked down the short, tree-lined block one more time, but it remained empty of anything other than a few midday shoppers and one jogger in professional-grade orange running gear, clearly not Ginny. He checked his watch: five after noon. She was running late, and he was, technically, on the clock.

Mary's front door was an old wooden beast, painted a bright red, and currently wedged open by a straightback wooden chair stuck between door and frame. Teddy stared at it, then sighed. After the bar had been robbed, and then would-be killers had gotten in a few months back, he'd suggested to Seth that maybe they should keep the door closed when the bar wasn't actually open for business. Obviously, that suggestion hadn't made a dent in the old man's habits.

"Seth!"

There was a clatter in the tiny kitchen, in response. Teddy shook his head, amused. Seth's bad moods were by now a source of comfort rather than concern.

Normally he'd have come in early and immediately gone behind the bar to check that everything was in shape before his shift started, obsessively prepping everything so that he was ready the moment the clock ticked over, no matter if it was a lazy afternoon shift or a hot-from-the-start Saturday night. Today he ignored the bar entirely, pulled one of the small tables out from the wall and dropped himself into one of the chairs, stretching his legs out in front of him and contemplating the tips of his boots.

Teddy wasn't sure when meeting for lunch had turned into a semiregular thing, but Tuesday through Thursday, the three days during the week he took afternoon shift, Ginny would come downtown and grab lunch with him before Mary's opened for business. Sometimes she brought Georgie; sometimes Seth or Stacy would join them if they were on shift. Sometimes the conversation was serious, but more often it was casual. Mainly, Teddy thought, Gin used it as an excuse to get away from her desk for a while, force her to stop working for an hour.

He wasn't sure what he got from it, himself. Bad enough he was dragging himself out of bed earlier to get here in time. But he admitted, at least to himself, that he enjoyed the new routine. It wasn't that they'd become close friends, exactly. The competition that had formed between them over a year's worth of trivia nights was still as fierce as ever. Things had somehow shifted while they were working together on the Jacobs job, though she was still an occasionally irritating workaholic know-it-all.

"We're missing a case of tonic water," Seth said, coming out of the kitchen, and clearly cranky.

Then again, Seth's normal state was cranky. Teddy sometimes thought the older man had been born muttering "get off my lawn." He certainly looked the part. Seth had been a half-decent boxer in his youth, before he decided that getting beaten up for a living wasn't a good long-term strategy, and his body reflected that, even in his sixties. He routinely wore baggy pants and a gray hooded sweatshirt, and could have come from the set of *Rocky 14,* as the down-but-not-out trainer for a promising street kid. Nobody looking at him would believe that he could take a galley kitchen and a limited budget and turn out surprisingly solid food. "Was it not delivered, or did it go missing, after?"

"Wasn't me who took possession," Seth grumbled. "Talk to that useless boy."

Useless Boy was the unofficial name for Clive, the recent grad who was supposed to be helping Seth out with the general chores after school and on weekends. That was a new development, and one Seth still wasn't entirely on board with.

"You're supposed to sign off on anything that comes in during his shift," Teddy said, exasperated. "He's still too new to know what to look for." Besides, the kid was barely twenty-one, and while he might be legal to work here, he wasn't what Teddy considered reliable enough to be signing for anything. The moment he got a real job, he'd be gone, and Teddy doubted he'd bother to even give notice.

Seth made a rude gesture that summed up Clive, and then scowled at the table, out of its usual place. "Suppose you'll be wanting food, too. And her, too?"

"If it's not too much of a bother."

Seth muttered something under his breath about trouble and disappeared back into the kitchen. A few seconds later, more rattling of pans and slamming of cabinet doors could be heard.

"What're you grinning about?"

He looked up to see Ginny silhouetted in the doorway, the midday sun filling in behind her. She wasn't his type, particularly, but made a nice silhouette, he had to admit.

"Seth still thinks you're trouble."

"What did I ever do to him?" she asked, taking the other chair opposite him. She was wearing a brown top, with a deep V-neck that he'd have to be dead not to appreciate. Her hair was pinned up, the shoulder-length blond curls tamed for once.

"You're female," he said. "Seth naturally assumes all females are trouble, two-legged or four." The old man wasn't too fond of Mistress Penny-Drops, the bar's unofficial adopted cat, either. Teddy realized, with that, that he hadn't seen Penny in a day or two. Not that he kept track of her, but she usually showed up for the evening shift, at least long enough to wind around his legs and collect some attention before disappearing to do whatever it was cats did.

He took a second, closer look at Ginny's attire, noting that she was dressed more formally than usual. "You had a meeting this morning?"

"Yeah. Kinda." She looked evasive, which was unusual for her. "Breakfast meeting, so I just killed time downtown for a while. Georgie is going to sulk when I get home."

"New client?"

"No, it was personal."

He raised an eyebrow. "Oh?"

"Not that kind of personal, Tonica. I had to meet with a lawyer." She made a face, as though the lawyer left a sour taste in her mouth, and reached up and started unpinning her hair, as though his comment had reminded her of the combs and pins. Once the curls were loose, she shook her head and let out a sigh of relief. "Oh, that feels better. I swear, one of these days I'm going to get a haircut like yours."

"You could probably carry it off," he said, "but every femme from here to Portland would be lining up at your door like a lovesick puppy."

She took that as a compliment, smiling as though to say "of course," and he shook his head, wondering why he'd thought otherwise. Ginny had a lot of issues and hot-buttons, and he was learning how to punch some of them, but as far as he could tell, sexual politics didn't faze her a bit. Then again: Seattle. He'd grown up in a more conservative part of New England, and the cultural learning curve had been tricky his first year here.

Seth came out of the kitchen and stood there, hands on his hips, staring at them.

"I got grilled cheese with tomato," he said, finally, grudgingly, as though telling them that was the worst part of his day.

"And a salad?" Ginny asked.

His mouth twitched, as though he were going to respond, then he simply grunted and turned back into the kitchen.

"You know how he feels about green salads," Teddy said.

"I know. It's just so much fun to see his head spin around. Is Stacy working today?"

"Later. She's got a gig today." Mary's sole waitress and bartender-trainee was also an artist's model. Teddy didn't get it—she wasn't particularly pretty—but apparently good bones were more important. It brought in enough money that she could afford to work at Mary's the rest of the time, though, and for that he was thankful.

"So. Did you decide?"

Ginny's dog might not be a bloodhound, but Gin herself was rarely distracted from anything for very long. Teddy sighed and leaned back in his chair, making the wooden frame creak.

"You remember what Agent Asuri said? That we shouldn't stick our noses into things we're not trained for? We got lucky last time, Gin. You know that, right?" Asuri was the fed who had responded when he put out a friend-of-a-friend call for help, when they'd realized they needed more info than even Ginny could dig up. The agent hadn't been much impressed by them.

"We were lucky to figure things out, and we were lucky nobody got—" He almost said "killed," but someone had died, even if the jury was still quiet on if it had been murder or suicide. "What makes you think we'll get lucky a second time?"

"First, we weren't 'lucky' "—and she used air quotes to emphasize the word—"to figure things out. That was basic logic, deduction, and a bit of your mad people-shmoozing skills."

"A bit?" He mimed being wounded, slapping one hand flat against his chest.

She made a face at the theatrics. "All right, a lot."

They argued, mocked, battled, and occasionally outright fought, but from the first, he'd liked Ginny Mallard. If he were called on it, he'd admit that she was at least as smart as he was, good-looking if you liked curvy blondes, and could keep up in a battle of wits. Could win them, a fair percentage, too.

He wouldn't lie and pretend that he'd never thought about getting her into bed, but mostly it had been early on, the passing sort of thing you did when a new woman showed up. As far as he could tell, she'd never thought of him that way at all. He didn't buy into the "friend zone" thing, but they seemed to have slotted each other there, or something like it, without conscious effort. He guessed that was a good thing, since they were working together now.

"And it's not likely anyone's going to do violence over a few thousand dollars," she continued, obviously still determined to convince him to take the job. "I mean, yeah, people say they'd kill for a couple of thousand, but here? I doubt it. More likely someone's just skimming off the till to pad their vacation fund or something. They probably are telling themselves they'll put it back before anyone notices. You'd investigate something like that here, wouldn't you?"

"No, I'd line everyone up and read them the riot act," he said bluntly. "And the next time, I'd call the cops."

"No you wouldn't," Ginny said. "You like everyone here too much."

"I would, too," he said. "I can like 'em all I want, but if I don't report a theft, that's my job and my reputation on the line."

Ginny frowned, and tapped her fingers, three sharp clicks. "But what if you couldn't? If reporting a theft meant Patrick would have to close Mary's down? Because that's what would happen at LifeHouse."

"It's not the same thing, Gin." But before he could explain why, Seth came out again, carrying a tray loaded with plates. Rather than bringing it over to them, he set it down on the bar. "This ain't no damn restaurant," he growled. "And I ain't your damn server. Come get your own damn food."

"Think of the kittens, Tonica," Ginny said, getting up and following him to the bar to grab a plate. "The sweet, homeless animals! Think of the amazingly good karma you'd rack up!"

Seth had already grabbed his food—sandwich and salad—and gone to the table, pulling another chair up to join them.

"More animals?" he asked, coming in on the tail end of the conversation. "You're not bringing more animals into this place, are you? Bad enough that cat, and her wrinkled excuse for a dog. What's next, a parrot?"

"This place could use a parrot," Ginny said, and then added, "and where is Mistress Penny?" She sat down with her own plate and looked around, as though expecting to see the little tabby appear out of thin air.

"I haven't seen her for a while," Teddy said. "She may be sulking because you didn't bring her girlfriend along."

Penny might or might not be his cat—opinions varied on that, with his firmly in the "no" category—but Georgie was definitely Penny's dog, as much as she was Ginny's.

"And no," he said to Seth. "No more animals. And no, Mallard, we don't need a parrot." He wasn't a pet person, and Mary's was a bar, not a refuge for wayward critters. Although, thinking about some of their regulars, he had to admit that there were nights . . .

"The shelter animals need us, Tonica," Ginny wheedled. "We're their only hope."

"Hrmph. You two should just keep your noses tucked into your own business," Seth said. "Last time, we near all almost got killed."

"Oh, let it go already," Teddy said, exasperated, even though he'd been making the exact same point earlier. "You weren't even in the bar when it happened." That was half the problem—Seth had been taking out the recycling when the goons tried to use force to get them to talk. By the time he came back, the excitement was over, and he was still peeved about that.

Ginny interrupted after she took a bite of her food. "Oh man, Seth, this sandwich is good. Please tell me you're going to put this on the menu?"

Seth looked pleased, but then he scowled again. "Too expensive. Good cheese, have to charge more'n seven dollars, and Patrick's new 'cheap bites' idea puts the kibosh on that."

"He's probably not wrong about a nine-dollar sandwich, with this crowd," Teddy said. He took a bite, and his eyes almost closed in satisfaction. That was good cheese, yeah, and good bread, and the tomatoes were nearly perfect, even though they were off-season.

"You offer people good grub, they pay for it. You offer 'em crap, and they'll go somewhere else. That dumb sonofa—"

"Not while I'm eating," Teddy said, and took another bite. The sandwich—thick with cheese, tangy with tomato, and crunchy with toast—deserved his full attention, not to be ruined with a rant about what a dick their boss was being.

Ginny studied Tonica's face, listened to the tone of his voice, and decided that she'd let him eat in peace instead of pushing the pros of this job at him. She might not be the shmoozer he was, but she could read *him* pretty well. His brain was turning it over, had probably been turning it over all night, and the fact that he hadn't said no—or anyway, hadn't said no in the tone of voice that said "final decision"—meant that he hadn't decided yet, so there was still a good chance at yes.

Besides, she hadn't eaten much at breakfast, too focused on business, and Seth had seriously outdone himself with the sandwiches. When she was a kid, she would never have believed a simple GC&T could taste so good.

When she'd cleared her plate of the last chip and crumb of sandwich, she wiped her mouth and fingers with her napkin, put the paper onto her plate, and looked across the table at Tonica.

"So?"

He sighed, and bused their plates back to the tray on the counter, for Seth to take back and wash. "You're going to do this, aren't you?"

There wasn't much point in denying it. "Yeah." She'd made up her mind on the way back home last night, watching the happy wag of Georgie's tail.

"Christ." There was a lot packed into that word, and she didn't think all of it was directed at her. So she just sat and waited while he thought, one elbow leaning against the bar, his gaze looking somewhere past the far wall. Tonica was more of a seat-of-his-pants decision maker, usually, but he was still harboring doubts that this "pseudo-PI" gig was a good idea. With someone else, she might have tried to do a soft sell—or a hard one—but Tonica liked to think that he was making up his own mind.

There was a soft thump above them, and then a delicate-boned gray tabby cat dropped down from her usual perch on top of the bottle display, onto the surface of the bar itself, as daintily as if she'd stepped from limo to curb.

Ginny had no idea how Penny got into the bar without anyone seeing her—the vents, maybe? Some hidden crawlspace only cats knew about?—but she came and went with a quiet that Ginny, accustomed now to Georgie's nosier entrances, could only marvel at.

"Oh there you are, you," Tonica said, looking sideways at the cat. "Where've you been, lady?"

As though responding to his question, the tabby padded the length of the bar, her tail held high, to sit next to Tonica's elbow.

"Sweetie, down," he said to her, and then turned his attention back to Ginny. "I don't know. I—" He broke off as Penny lifted one paw and pushed on his arm. It wasn't a pat, or a pet; it was a very definite shove.

"What?" he asked her, as though she was going to answer, and Ginny hid a grin. Once you start talking to the animals, she knew firsthand, it was all over. Tonica could claim that Penny wasn't his cat all he wanted: he was her human.

Possibly irritated that he hadn't gotten the point the first time, Penny reached up and swatted his arm again, claws out but not digging into shirt or skin.

"Ow! What?" he asked again, but the cat, her message apparently delivered, merely sat there blinking peacefully at nothing in particular, a soft rumbling purr coming from her body.

"See?" Ginny said, unable to resist. "Even Mistress Penny thinks it's a good idea, to help the shelter out."

"Well, I don't think it's a good idea," Seth said, even though nobody had asked him. "Whatever it is, if Blondie came up with it, it's trouble."

Good sandwich or not, that nickname really pissed her off, calling up every "dumb blonde" joke she'd ever been subjected to. "One of these days I'm going to teach you not to call me that, old man."

He snorted at her threat, then got up and re-piled the dishes on the tray as though Tonica had done it wrong, and started carrying it back toward the kitchen.

"Careful, Seth," Tonica warned him as the old man walked by. "You're tougher, but she's meaner."

He snorted again and disappeared through the kitchen doorway.

As though annoyed by their distraction, Penny pushed at Tonica again, and used claws this time, based on his yelp.

"C'mon, Teddy." She was laughing now. "You don't stand a chance against her."

"She just wants me to refill the kibble bowl," he said, scooping the little tabby up and petting her. Penny rested her head against his arm and seemed to loosen all her bones, melting against him.

"Yeah, you keep telling yourself that. Look, I've got to get back to work, clients wait on no lunch break, and you guys need to open. I'll call later and we can discuss a plan, right?"

"Yeah." He was reluctant, still, but he'd go along and they both knew it. Curiosity might be a feline trait, but humans had it, too, in buckets. "Yeah, all right. But if we're doing this, I'm taking lead. You may know more about research, but getting people to admit to possible wrongdoings—or even knowing about wrongdoings—is different from sorting through records. There's more chance of offending someone or pissing them off so much they shut us down, and talking to people is still my strong point, not yours."

"Absolutely," she said with a straight face. That had been the hook she'd used to get him on board in the first place; the fact that he now thought it was his own idea meant she'd done her job right. "I'll call our client and let her know we're on the job."

On that note, she left, putting an extra swing of confidence in her walk. At least until she was on the other side of the door, and walking down the block toward her apartment. Only then did she let some of that confident front fade. She'd known he'd give in. They were alike that much, at least: the idea of something unknown, something hidden, was too tempting to resist. But this was Tonica, and for every way she knew to manipulate him, he knew as many ways to manipulate her, and she thought sometimes they spent more time trying to figure each other out than they did actually conversing. She never knew where he was going to fall during an argument.

Of course, she admitted with a faint smirk, that was also half the fun.

* * *

Humans looked down, and they looked side to side, but they rarely if ever looked up. Penny went high, not so much following Georgie's human home as accompanying her, unseen. While the human went into the building where she lived, Penny went up a less direct route, finally leaping down onto the fire escape outside the apartment window just as the front door opened.

Penny waited until the human finished greeting Georgie and went into the smaller room, and then let her paw scrape at the window, once.

Georgie was at the window instantly. "Hi."

"He agreed," she said.

"Good!" There was a pause. "To what?"

"Georgie . . ." Penny stopped to think. No, she hadn't told the dog what she had overheard the humans saying in the Busy Place, the night before. Rather than explain, she plowed on as though Georgie had simply forgotten. "A human came to see them yesterday, asked them to look at the shelter. They are going to investigate."

"Humans know there's something wrong, too? Of course humans would know."

Penny was less confident in human knowledge, but in this case it seemed they were all on the same scent. "They know something's wrong, but not what."

"Well, neither do we," Georgie pointed out. "Yet." All they knew was that there were people in the shelter when there shouldn't be, and things—noises and smells—that made the residents uncomfortable.

"We need to find out," Penny said. "We need to talk to the ones in the shelter. Rumor isn't enough; it can get mangled and chewed

along the way." Georgie couldn't do that; her human didn't let her wander alone. That would be her job, then.

"We can be helpful?" Georgie liked that idea. "We can help save the Old Place, too!"

There was a noise from the other room, and Georgie trotted off to investigate, sticking her head through the doorway. Her curling tail wagged once, shaking her entire backside, and then she came back to the window.

"She's on the phone," the shar-pei reported. "Talking to someone else. A meeting, tomorrow. About the Old Place."

"Good." Humans would do what they did, and she would do what she could, to keep them on the right trail. "You need to make them take you with them, listen to what they say," Penny said, thinking hard. "And let me know where you go, and when." Last time she had not been able to put a paw on them for hours at a time, and she hadn't liked that.

Georgie tilted her wrinkled head and widened her eyes in confusion. "How? The things I'm learning with the trainer are good, but how can I tell you we're going somewhere I don't know?"

That was a good question.

Georgie perked up, like she'd just heard someone call her name. "If you let him collar you, put on a leash, maybe you can come, too!"

Penny didn't even dignify that with a response.

"Go with Herself," she said instead. "Listen to everything they say, and remember it!"

"What are you going to do?"

"Theodore's at the Busy Place tonight," she said. "I'm going back there."

With that, Penny put her paw up at the window screen, touching Georgie's nose through the mesh, and then leaped gracefully down the fire escape landings onto the sidewalk. Back on the ground, she paused briefly to groom her tail, her ears cocked to anything happening around her, or if Georgie might call her back for some reason. Then, satisfied everything was as it should be, she headed back downtown to keep an eye on her own human.

They were not going to get in trouble without her, this time.

After confirming with their new client, Ginny called her partner. He didn't answer, of course: Mary's would be open by now, and he didn't answer the phone when he was working.

The recorded message telling her to leave a message beeped at her, and she started talking. "Teddy." It still felt odd calling him that, when she still mostly thought of him as Tonica. "Hey, it's Ginny. So, I spoke with Nora and she wants us to come in tomorrow morning, meet her at the shelter before it opens. I know you don't do mornings but it was either that or wait a couple of days until you were off shift, or me go on my own, and neither one of those sounded ideal, so suck it up." She could almost see his expression at that. "So I'll see you tomorrow, ten a.m. sharp, at the shelter?" She paused, and the answering machine beeped to indicate that she was out of time before she could think of what else she wanted to say.

"Damn. They should have a 'please hold while you gather your thoughts' option on these things."

Part of her wanted to dive into researching the new job right away, but they really needed to talk to Nora first, to get a better sense of what was going on; blind searches could turn up interesting things, but she wouldn't know if they were useful yet, not without some background info. Besides, she had other things that needed attention now, no matter what new gigs fell into her lap. She was in the final phase of one job, helping a single dad arrange a birthday party for his seven-year-old twins. Not exactly a mental challenge, but a job was a job, and the guy was paying for 100 percent of her skills and time. Normally she was good at ignoring distractions, but today . . . Maybe it was the thought of the dogs in the shelter, at risk because someone got greedy, but she couldn't stop thinking about this job.

"Enough. Focus."

Silence fell on the apartment save for the soft clicking of the keyboard, Ginny's pen scratching on paper, and the muffled sound of Georgie moving around in the other room. Part of her awareness identified the distinct sounds of dog-nails clicking on hardwood floors, sighs and thumps and the occasional rattle-slurp when Georgie hit the water bowl, or looked for new treats miraculously appearing in her food dish. These were familiar, comforting sounds now, a steady accompaniment while she worked.

After a few hours, Ginny pushed away from the desk, stretching her arms over her head until she heard her back crack properly. She glanced at the display on her computer, and frowned. It was almost five o'clock—she'd gotten her focus back, and then some, apparently. On the plus side, the birthday party was wrapped up, and her in-box was, at least for the moment, at zero.

"Hey Georgie-girl," she called. "Do you need to go for a walk?"

The usual happy clatter of claws on the bare floor didn't meet her query. Ginny frowned. Usually Georgie came and slept under her desk while she worked, but the dog hadn't come in with her. Except for poking her head in briefly a while back, in fact, she hadn't seen the dog since she came back from Mary's. That was unusual—it was a decent-sized apartment, but not *that* large.

"Georgie?"

She got up and walked out of the second bedroom she used as an office, into the main living area. Georgie was at the window, her paws up on the sill, looking out intently.

"Are there squirrels on the fire escape again, baby?"

When she walked over to the window, there was nothing on the fire escape except the remains of this summer's failed attempt to grow herbs, and Georgie was looking up at her with those big brown eyes that always made Ginny feel like she was Best Human Ever.

She knelt down and kissed the top of Georgie's square head. The dog's fur felt like peach fuzz, warm and bristly. "Keeping the homestead safe, huh? I love you, puppy-dog."

A blue-black tongue licked the tip of her nose in reply, and Ginny laughed, hugging the dog. "What did I do without you? Come on, we'll have a walk and get some fresh air. And tonight we've got training session! You going to be good for Bobby?"

Georgie didn't bark, but she managed a low woof that Ginny took to be agreement.

"Getting you from that shelter was one of the best things I've done in years," she said, resting her chin on top of Georgie's warm, blunt head. "I won't let them get into trouble now. I promise."

Georgie woofed again and leaned against her, as though to give either comfort or support.

3

Ginny had, once upon a time, stayed out late most nights, and then relied on an alarm clock to wake up. Now, more often than not, she was in bed before midnight and woke up a few minutes before 6 a.m. under the weight of a heavy doggy stare, Georgie's paws perched on the edge of the bed, her brown eyes intent on Ginny's face until the human's eyes opened. Then the stubby, curled tail would start wagging, and a blue-black tongue would wash Ginny's face until, defeated by cute, she was willing to get out of bed and take Georgie for a walk.

That Friday morning was a textbook case of Life, Now.

"All right, all right," Ginny said, pushing the dog away halfheartedly. "Enough with the tenderizing. I'm awake, I'm getting up, see?" She swung her feet over the side of the bed and hit the floor, trying to decide which need was more pressing: the bathroom, or the coffee machine. The bathroom won.

Georgie had quickly learned that the bathroom was a human-only space—mainly because there wasn't enough room in there for both human and dog. But she was waiting when Ginny came out, and accompanied her mistress to the kitchen, where caffeine waited.

"Georgie, at ease."

That was the command Bobby had been working on with them last night. Because of Georgie's protective instincts, and her solid build, the trainer decided that the shar-pei could benefit from a few commands beyond the basics. "At ease" was supposed to keep Georgie from wandering off or getting distracted, without being as imperative a "do not move" command as "stay."

It all seemed horribly complicated to Ginny, and Georgie hadn't quite gotten it yet, so Ginny kept an eye on her as she went about making breakfast. For the moment, at least, the dog was perfectly content to sit and watch her.

Her cell phone, which she'd left on the counter to charge the night before, was blinking. She had a message. Pouring the coffee one-handed, she tapped the screen to see what was up.

Time-stamped 2:10, the text was from Tonica, confirming the appointment with Nora, and saying he'd swing by to pick her up at 9:45 a.m. Ginny, her brain still not entirely awake, stared at the message and then shrugged. Since his apartment was a couple of towns away, she figured it made sense for him to swing by, and arriving together would make for a more professional appearance. Fifteen minutes should be enough time, barely, to get from here to there in time for a 10 a.m. meeting.

"He'd better not be late," she said out loud. At the sound of her voice, Georgie gave up on "at ease" and made an impatient dance, the sound of her claws on the wooden floor conveying her impatience.

"All right, sweetie," Ginny said, putting down her phone. Getting up from "at ease" if Georgie felt the need was part of the training, so she didn't repeat the command. Besides, the dog was right: it was walk-time. "Half a cup so I don't walk into anything, and then we can go. Get your leash. Leash!"

Georgie disappeared to get her leash from where it hung on a peg by the door. By the time she returned, pink lead in her mouth, Ginny judged that she could get dressed and leave the apartment without being a menace to herself or the rest of humanity.

"Good girl," she praised Georgie, snapping the leash to her collar. "Now stay here a minute, let me just throw on my sneakers, and we'll go."

Georgie might not have the largest vocabulary, but she knew that "sneakers," like "leash," usually meant something good. She sat down on the floor, her backside quivering in excitement, and waited.

Ginny threw sweatpants and a long-sleeved tee over the tank and shorts she slept in, shoved her feet into socks and sneakers, and collected Georgie at the front door.

The air was cool and damp, promising that November was well and truly here, after a warmer-than-usual autumn. Human and dog both shivered and made short work of the morning obligations. Up and down the tree-lined block of her neighborhood, Ginny could see other human-and-canine pairs doing the same thing. She knew most of them by now—there was nothing like sharing a morning poo-walk for breaking the ice among neighbors—but nobody seemed in a mood for conversation today. It was too cold and damp, and still a workday morning. TGIF only went so far, and didn't start this early.

Back in the apartment, Ginny unhooked the leash and put it back on the peg, and laughed as the dog made a beeline to the kitchen. Georgie knew what came after her morning walk. Ginny followed at a slower pace, filling Georgie's food dish and adding fresh water before escaping into a hot shower to finish the process of waking up.

Ginny normally dressed well when she was spending the day in the office, under the theory that clothes were part of the professional mind-set, but knowing that they were going on a client call today made her go for lightweight wool slacks and a silk blouse that were a little nicer than usual, although still not too nice if she had to run, sit on the ground, or play with a shelter dog. Not that she expected to have to do any of those things, but better to be prepared than look like an idiot. She stared at herself in the mirror after gelling her curls into some kind of style, and decided that today some foundation would not be amiss. More than that, though, was above and beyond the call of duty.

In the kitchen, Georgie was scraping at her dish as though the sheer force of her tongue could somehow produce another scrap of food. The rattle of the dish against the tile floor made Ginny remember a phone call she'd been putting off for almost a week now.

When it came to business, she sat down and did it. When it came to this, there were few who could procrastinate better.

"Oh, hell. All right, do it now, it's done," she muttered, and—after checking the time—called her mother.

"Virginia?" Her mother, as always, answered on the first ring. "What's wrong?"

"Nothing's wrong, Mom. I was just calling to see what you wanted me to bring for Thanksgiving."

It was a yearly tradition—her mother would then insist that Ginny didn't need to do anything, that she had it all handled, etc., and in the end would call her a few days before in a panic with a list of all the things that still needed to be done. Since it was only the three of them, it usually wasn't a big deal, but . . .

"Oh, Thanksgiving, oh, I didn't tell you?"

Those were words that never ended well. "Tell me what?"

"Your aunt and uncle. They're coming out. For Thanksgiving."

Her aunt and uncle lived out of state, and the two families weren't particularly close. She hadn't seen them, or her cousins, in years. Literally years. "Why?"

Her mother sighed. "I don't know. But it's not going to be anything good."

Ginny usually cringed at her mother's blunt commentary—especially when it was directed at her—but in this case she had to agree. Their family communicated in emails and occasional birthday cards, not actual visits, and she was perfectly okay with that.

"So we'll make more of whatever we make, and hide the booze. It's only one day, right? They're not planning to stay with you?"

"No, no." Her mother sounded as though the idea would send her into a panic. Her parents had a nice apartment, but it wasn't really set up for four people to stay there more than overnight. "I just . . . I don't know what to *do* with them!"

Ginny sighed silently, knowing already where this was going. "Yeah, it's okay, Mom. I'll handle it. I'll get a list of things they might want to see or do, and arrange it all." She did it for other people, she could do it for family. Anything to keep her mother from freaking out.

"Oh, Virginia, I couldn't—" her mother started, the relief clear in her voice.

"Mom, it's what I do for a living," and never mind that her parents still weren't happy with that decision. "It's okay. And I have to go now, okay? Client meeting this morning, gotta get ready."

She ended the call, aware that her mother's preoccupation with this invasion had saved her from the usual interrogation about her own life. A small gift, but she'd take it.

She loved her parents, but there were days she wished she hadn't been an only child. Maybe a sibling would have been able to give them the married-with-a-real-job happiness they kept trying to urge her into.

She'd done the real job thing, and the job had disappeared under her when the company was bought out.

Being her own boss suited her fine now. As for marriage . . . first she'd have to find someone she wanted to date more than a few times. The current guy seemed like he had potential, but she wasn't going to assume anything yet.

Cutting those thoughts off at the knee, Ginny poured herself another cup of coffee and went into her office. If she hustled, she'd be able to clear out her in-box, file the paperwork from yesterday's meeting with her lawyer, and maybe sort out last month's expenses before Tonica arrived.

"Mallard. No."

She hadn't actually intended to bring the dog, but the moment she'd put her shoes and coat on to meet Tonica downstairs, Georgie had fetched her battered leash and sat by the door so patiently and expectantly that Ginny didn't have the heart to leave her home.

"It gives us a reason to be there?" she said in response, not meaning for it to sound like such a question. Tonica, thankfully, only sighed and waited while she convinced Georgie, once again, that the back of the coupe would not eat her.

Once they were all settled, and he started the car and pulled away from the curb, she asked, "So, you want a background, or do you want to play it blind? Not that I have much yet."

"Blind, I think. We can compare notes after."

Ginny got twitchy when she met someone cold, but that was how he worked and she wasn't going to screw with it, not so long as it worked. She tapped the screen of her tablet and studied her notes, but didn't share what was there. She hadn't lied, there really wasn't much. Animal shelters weren't big news, and nobody who worked there seemed to have much public profile. All right, she'd try to play this Tonica's way.

Most of the early morning commuters were already in downtown, and there wasn't any local traffic, so they pulled into the six-space parking lot in front of the old warehouse at exactly 9:58. Their appointment with Nora was for ten o'clock. The three of them—Tonica, Ginny, and Georgie—extracted themselves from Tonica's beloved vintage Volvo coupe and looked around. The old warehouse looked like it dated back to Ballard's heyday as a lumber town, and was a set on a corner lot, with a newer brick building pressing up against it on one side. It might have been renovated from its earlier use but didn't look very impressive even now.

The lot was empty, but Ginny had spotted a beat-up sedan and an SUV in the equally small parking lot around the corner of the building, probably the employee lot.

In the distance they could hear dogs barking, not very well muffled by the walls. Georgie lifted her head slightly but otherwise showed no interest.

"Think she remembers being here before?"

"Dogs don't have much long-term memory," Ginny said. "Being hurt creates a basic fear of the source—a man, a car, the smell of the vet's—but they don't have specific long-term memories the way we do." She paused. "That's what our trainer says, anyway. So, no, I don't think she associates this building with where she lived before she came here. Might be different once we go inside, though."

"Only one way to find out." Tonica gestured for her to precede him, his muscular torso looking oddly different in a dress shirt and dark blue sport coat, rather than his regular sweatshirt or sweater. He was wearing the usual jeans and lace-up black boots, though, so she had decided not to rag him about it, especially since she had dressed-to-impress-with-competence, too. "Puppies first."

Despite her words, Ginny hadn't been sure exactly how Georgie would react to coming back here. Ginny had only been to the shelter once before, herself, to sign the paperwork that made Georgie hers. She had first encountered the half-grown shar-pei pup during one of Ballard's summer weekend street fairs, when the shelter held a "sidewalk parade," accosting innocent passersby with pitiful-faced puppies and adorable kittens. Ginny hadn't intended to acquire a dog that day—or, in fact, any day—but twenty-four hours later she had been standing in front of this same building, more or less ready to change her life for the sake of big brown eyes and a ridiculous tail.

"C'mon, sweetie," she said now, tugging on the leash.

"You had better be talking to the dog, Mallard," Tonica grumbled. "I'm not your sweetie."

"I only leash the things I love," she shot back. Their back-and-forth used to be sharper; she put it down to the early hour. Tonica really wasn't a morning person.

The front door of the shelter was thick glass, with the name painted on it in white. No cute animal cartoons or slogan, just the name. Inside there was a small foyer, just enough room to let someone close an umbrella—or a dog to shake off the rain—and then another door, this one made of heavy, polished wood.

The receptionist, a chunky young woman with hair done up in a multitude of blond dreadlocks, looked up when they came in, and smiled. "Hi there! We're not open for animal visit yet, but if you'd like to make an appointment, I can arrange that!" She exuded a sense of professionally perky that bordered on the annoying, but when her gaze went from Ginny to Tonica and then down to the dog standing alertly between them, her poise slipped a little. "Oh. Hi. She's beautiful." The tone of the girl's voice went from welcoming to slightly accusatory in those short sentences. Ginny blinked, wondering what they'd done wrong, and then realized what had happened.

"Isn't she though?" she said brightly, stepping forward and using the half excuse she'd suggested to Tonica. "I adopted her from the shelter last year, and I thought I'd come down and show off how well she's doing."

Perky, and a little extra, swam back into the other woman's voice now that she knew they weren't here to abandon the dog. "Oh, that's so nice. We have a board for photos of our graduates; it would be great to add her. What's her name?"

"Georgie. Oh, she was originally named Lena."

"I didn't know that," Tonica said, slightly startled.

"Yeah. She just didn't seem like a Lena, to me, though. A Lena is . . . delicate."

Georgie, almost on cue, let out a solid burp.

"Yeah, Georgie's a lot of things, but delicate ain't it," Tonica agreed, grinning.

"I named her for George, in the Nancy Drew books." Ginny said. "She was always my favorite."

Tonica's eyes narrowed. "Those are detective stories, aren't they?"

"Shut up, Teddy," she said, embarrassed, and then, "Oh," directed to the receptionist, almost like an afterthought, "and Nora said to let her know when we came by?"

During their phone call, the client had suggested that they play it casual, rather than setting up an actual meeting, to keep anyone from suspecting anything. Ginny thought that Nora was being more than a little paranoid, but the first rule of being a concierge/problem solver was that the client was always right—to their face. You could do things properly once they were appeased.

"Oh." Perky thought for a moment. "I saw her going into the back office this morning. Let me buzz her, and then I'll go get our camera. Hang on."

Ginny, suspecting that this might take a while, went over to sit on one of the two battered sofas, Georgie obediently lying down at her feet, muzzle resting on her paws, eyes alert. If the dog had any hesitation going into the building she'd left a year ago, she didn't show it. In fact, reaching down to pet Georgie's head, Ginny thought she looked almost . . . pleased.

★ ★ ★

Teddy, feeling restless and not sure about the cleanliness of the sofas Ginny was sitting on so calmly, walked over to a corkboard up on the far wall, curious. It was filled with photos and rap sheets of the animals currently available for adoption. He scanned the papers, paying more attention to how they were posted rather than what was posted. It was well organized and professionally presented: someone was clearly doing there job here, at least. All the photos were well lit, with the animals looking directly into the camera, the sheets all generated on a computer form, but with handwritten notes in purple ink calling out specific comments—all positive—about each animal. There was a red dot at the top right corner of some of them, a yellow dot on others, and a green dot on yet others, and some of them had a mix of colored dots, while a handful had no dots at all. He puzzled over them for a while, before the receptionist returned, armed with a camera.

"Nora will come out in a minute. Why don't we bring gorgeous Georgie over here, and I can get a good shot of her? No, that's all right, I can manage her, can't I, girl?" she said to Georgie. Then, to Ginny, "You can stay on the sofa."

Teddy closed his eyes and waited for the explosion. You didn't just tell Ginny Mallard to stay on the sofa, especially where Georgie was concerned.

Ginny, surprisingly, didn't say anything. But Georgie did. A short, soft bark that had Teddy turning around, surprised. Georgie was the quietest dog he'd ever met—she didn't bark much, and never without provocation. But this was clearly a warning noise.

The shar-pei, still at Ginny's feet, had lifted her blunt-muzzled head and uttered her warning, her entire body language shouting "back off." The receptionist, clearly not a fool, had frozen with her hand outstretched, obviously having intended to take Georgie's leash. He suspected that not every dog that came through here was as easygoing as Georgie.

Then again, easygoing Georgie had bitten someone who threatened her mistress. Even sweet-tempered dogs had teeth. He needed to remember that.

"Georgie!" Ginny sounded surprised, but not entirely disapproving. "Baby, what's wrong?"

"Oh." The young woman recovered some of her confidence, once assured that this was an unusual occurrence. "I was working with kittens this morning, maybe she smells them?"

Teddy almost laughed at the hopeful suggestion.

"No, I don't think that's the problem," Ginny said, still busy soothing her dog, the leash safely wrapped around her wrist.

No, not likely. Georgie's best friend was a cat, and Teddy didn't care if that was anthropomorphizing: anyone who had seen Georgie and Mistress Penny together would agree. It was weird, but it was. Something had clearly spooked the normally mellow dog, though.

"Oh." The girl scrunched her face up in thought, sitting back on her heels. "My perfume?"

"I think she's afraid of your hair." He couldn't help it: the way the dreads moved around her head, they looked like snakes, and if he were a dog, he'd be freaked out by them coming at him, too.

"My . . . oh." The girl touched her head protectively, and Teddy held his breath for half a second, worried he'd put his foot in it badly enough to get them kicked out. Women could be touchy about their hair: he'd gotten smacked enough times by his sisters to know that.

Then the receptionist laughed and said to Georgie, "Is that it, sweetie? You want me to tie them back?"

Apparently, that was all it took: once the woman's hair was gathered in a scrunchy, and no longer swinging over her shoulders, Georgie was happy enough to have her photo taken by this strange woman.

And taken, and taken. First, lying down, then standing up, then a side profile, made more difficult by Georgie's need to turn her head and see what this strange person was doing. Finally, the woman seemed satisfied, and Georgie was returned to Ginny's care, just as Nora came down the hallway, looking slightly more professional in khakis and a pale green shirt than she had in the bar the day before. Compared to the receptionist, Nora's color-dipped hair looked practically sedate, but Teddy wondered if some variation of braids was a requirement for working here.

"Hi. Sorry for the delay, I was just finishing something up. C'mon back. Este wants to meet you."

They left the receptionist slotting the memory card into

her computer, promising to have the picture up by the time they came out, and the four of them, Teddy, Ginny, Nora, and Georgie, walked down the hallway to a sliding panel door. Once inside, the panel closing behind them, they were in what was clearly the heart of the operation: a large room with three oversized secondhand metal desks and chairs, none of them anywhere as nice as what was in the lobby, and a laptop on each desk, chained with a security lock.

"We all work here," Nora said. "Open floor plan, mainly because we didn't have the money to put up internal walls. It can get pretty chaotic at times, but it's nice, too."

She led them through the bullpen, to where two doors were set into the wall, both of them closed. Teddy looked up to where the wall met ceiling and decided that these had been original to the building, not part of the renovation.

Nora knocked once on the far left door, and then opened it without waiting for an answer.

Inside, the office was more comfortable, if no less shabby. The woman behind the desk stood up and offered her hand to the newcomers. "My name is Este Snyder. And this must be Lena!"

Their surprise must have been obvious, because the older woman laughed. She had a good laugh, full and soft, and smiling softened the severe lines of her face, making the pale gray strands in her dark hair seem brighter, somehow, less like signs of age and more . . . Teddy wasn't sure, but he felt himself warming to her, immediately.

"She's Georgie now," Ginny said. Her voice was slightly stiff, but not unfriendly, as she shook the woman's hand.

"Of course. A new life needs a new name. Hello, Georgie. You're looking quite well." She looked up at the humans then, and her face lost some of its animation.

"Nora told me what she had done, this morning."

And she didn't approve, clearly. Teddy was glad he'd listened to his gut and dressed well today. Ginny had worn a slacks-and-sweater combo that managed to look both casual and stylish, flat shoes showing under the hem of the slacks. Together they should be able to calm any fears of scammers or con artists. Or maybe they looked like scammers and con artists trying to look reputable, and were about to get tossed out on their ear.

Thankfully, convincing the woman to trust them was Ginny's job, not his.

Tonica had that look on his face, the one that meant he was assessing the person in front of him, trying to suss her out purely from body language. Ginny took the lead, distracting the older woman so he could do his thing. "So now you have official awareness that the money is missing."

"I knew it was missing." Her tone was matter-of-fact: Ginny couldn't tell if the woman was irritated at having to admit to that knowledge or not. "I had hoped that whoever it was who had taken it would reconsider, and return it before I had to take official notice. But that has not happened."

Resigned, but not annoyed, Ginny decided. Maybe.

The woman sat down again and indicated that they should sit, also. There were two chairs in front of her desk:

Nora perched herself on the sill of a window that had been blocked up with bricks on the outside, creating an alcove that had been filled with several anemic-looking plants.

Using the moments of distraction while they settled in to do her own assessment, Ginny knew that the woman was in her early sixties: the narrow face and silvered hair were offset by a lean, muscled body that reflected care and exercise rather than age. That matched with what little had been available in public records about the shelter's founders: Hester "Este" Snyder had retired at fifty-eight from a boutique PR firm that specialized in corporate image repair—although they called it "Facilitating Corporate Relations"—and started the shelter that same year with her long-term partner, Roger Arvantis. After that, they had become quite private, leaving no Internet footprint that Ginny could trace, not even the usual animal-related local charity events you might expect someone in their position to take part in.

That, to Ginny's mind, was the sign of someone either pathologically shy or with something to hide. A former PR person was probably not shy—Este certainly didn't hold herself that way. Something didn't fit, here, and when things didn't fit, it usually meant there was something very important missing from the picture. But was that something criminal, or even slightly questionable, or had Este just burned out? Ginny admitted that she had an active imagination, but she didn't see this woman as being a criminal, and there was too much public history for her to be in the witness protection program.

Ginny would have loved to have gotten Tonica's take, but there was no graceful way to speak to him privately, now. She pulled her tablet out of her bag and, as discreetly as she could, started jotting down notes.

"First off," Este continued with a nod of acknowledgment at Ginny's tablet, "I want to reiterate that I did not authorize your hire, and you are not being paid by the shelter itself."

Probable translation: we are not your employer, you will not be answerable to us, and we will probably ignore and disavow anything you discover if we don't like it.

"However—"

Ginny amended her translation to include "but the money used to pay you came from my pocket, one way or the other, and therefore I will feel free to interfere."

"I would appreciate your sharing anything you discover with me, in exchange for the access we allow you. And"—Este paused, then went on—"your discretion in discussing these matters. With *anyone.*"

Disavow, or derail if needed. "Part of our services includes absolute discretion within the bounds of legal obligation," Ginny said. Without a written contract, those words were meaningless, but it was the same rule she kept for her concierge business, too, and her reputation was everything. Short of the cops demanding info, warrant in hand, the details of her work were shared only with the client.

Some day, one of their off-the-books clients was going to ask for a written contract. She made a quick note to draw one up, just in case.

"You don't want Roger to know," Nora said, reading between the lines better than Ginny could. "Oh, Este . . ."

The older woman shook her head. "Don't lecture me, Nora. His health isn't good; it hasn't been for a while, you know that. The last thing I want is for this to stress him further."

"But—"

"No, Nora."

And that was that. It didn't seem as though Este and Roger were partners in the familiar sense, as well as in running the shelter, but clearly Este had a protective interest in the man.

"And you will tell us everything that you know, in order to fill out the picture?" Tonica had his bartender voice on again, slightly lower than usual, raspy and almost intimate, without being creepy. Ginny wondered if he knew he was using it, an intentional put-on, or if that just happened whenever he played bartop confessor.

"Please, Este," Nora added, already recovered from being crushed minutes before. "Whatever you know, even if it doesn't seem important, might be useful."

The director of the shelter sighed. "In for a penny, I suppose. I'm not sure how much more I can add to what Nora has already told you. I first became aware several months ago that the available cash was off what it should be, but we'd been so busy, and we were almost at the end of the year anyway, I didn't worry too much about it. I suppose I thought we'd overspent and would just have to make up the money from somewhere else." She gave a half-apologetic shrug. "I balance my personal checkbook only under duress. Finances have never been my strength. Roger worries about those. Or rather, he did."

Ginny controlled her shudder at that. Yes, she balanced her checkbook every month, and reconciled her accounts to the penny. She ran her own business, damn it. Sloppy records could put her out of work. "You said that your partner has been ill? Did the discrepancies appear before, or after that?"

Este looked thoughtful, and then pulled a manila folder forward on her desk and opened it, looking at a sheet of paper within. "After, when I noticed, but I didn't have time to go back and check if there had been any earlier losses. Certainly Roger would have mentioned it, if we came up short halfway through the year?"

"The costs are variable every month," Nora said. "Depending on how many animals we had in the shelter that needed neutering, and if there were any unusual expenses in the clinic. Sometimes we don't need all the money in the account that quarter, or we run over and have to dip into the next quarter. We don't do the actual tally until the end of the year, and yeah, I know, but we just don't have time or staff."

"Yes . . . everyone's doing three jobs, at least; that's just the nature of the beast," Este said, regretfully. "And with Roger not able to carry his usual load here, all the financial matters fell to me, and I'm afraid I've been playing catch-up ever since."

"So you think that someone here took advantage of his being sidelined, and started skimming?" Tonica asked.

Este gave that elegant half-apologetic shrug again, like she'd never really thought about it at all. "It was such a small amount of money. . . ."

Ginny tried to imagine being that nonchalant over missing money, and failed. A sideways glance at Tonica showed his usual calm expression, but she thought she saw a faint tic at the side of his mouth.

"It was a small and important amount of money, Este," Nora said, quietly reproachful. "Because it wasn't *ours*. It belonged to the foundation that gave us that grant. And we have to account for it, at year's end—which is now—or we don't get another. And if we don't get another . . ."

"Yes, I know, Nora. You've explained it all to me quite well." Este's tone was sharp, but the look she gave the younger woman was fond. "I'm an idiot when it comes to these things, which is part of why I handed this off to you."

"You think it's someone on staff?" Ginny asked, making another note on her tablet.

"It would have to be," Nora said, her expression glum. "Nobody else would have access back here, even if they knew about it. And we generally don't let outsiders back here—visitors only have access to the kennels under supervision, and if someone brought friends in without permission, they'd be fired, and everyone knows that."

Este didn't look happy, either, but she had clearly resigned herself to this being investigated, no matter her personal opinions. "You have my permission to look at anything you need: our paperwork and books—with our bookkeeper present, if you don't mind, to answer any questions you might have—and our security feed . . . whatever you ask for."

"We'll need to talk to everyone who works here," Tonica said.

Nora raised her hand hesitantly. "I thought maybe you should pretend to be prospective donors, so you have an excuse to poke around and ask questions without having to, you know, explain why, or make anyone suspicious? Asking about how we do things, stuff like that, things a donor would want to know, too."

Ginny nodded at Nora. "That's not a bad idea. We could be doing the scout work for someone with money, maybe." They'd have to tell fewer lies that way: she did research, after all. "I could have suggested this place to them, because it's where I found Georgie."

She saw Tonica roll his eyes discreetly—obviously, he thought she'd end up walking out with another animal. She considered the thought of a fluffy kitten, or a round-bellied puppy, and then steeled herself against it. She liked animals, yeah, but she wasn't a pet person: she was a *Georgie* person.

"I will also need access to your employee records, anything you can give me," she added. Tonica could talk all he wanted about reading a person, getting vibes, whatever it was he did in bartender-confessor mode, but when money was missing, the easiest way to find the culprit was to see who had access to the money, which meant job descriptions that couldn't be fudged.

And then she'd do a little tech-fishing and see who *needed* money.

Her partner coughed once, delicately, to get their attention, then spoke directly to Este. "Are you sure that you don't want to get the cops involved in this?"

Ginny glared at Tonica—this was their job; would he please stop harping about bringing in the cops, please?—but Este's reaction was far more effective.

"No. No police. Official attention is . . . no." That was definitive, confirming Nora's reaction the day before. "All I want is to find out who is responsible, so I can fire them."

"But whoever it is, they're stealing from you," he pointed out. "I know that you're concerned about how that might look to outside organizations, but simply taking steps to stop the thief isn't—"

"Any negative publicity hurts the shelter," Este said firmly, cutting him off. "We had to fight to get permits in the first place—my God, the politics because we didn't have the right background, didn't know the right people—and then we had to fight to get our funding, and even now a whisper of bad press could do real damage. This is our dream: I won't let anything damage it."

Even, clearly, if that meant letting a thief go free.

Ginny could see that Tonica thought that the older woman was an idiot, but if she could tell that logic wasn't going to change Este's mind, Tonica should certainly know that, too. The woman might be right, or not—Ginny thought that surely one bad egg couldn't ruin everything, especially if the potential scandal was handled promptly—but what mattered was what she, Este, believed.

"Everything having to do with fund-raising is perception based," Nora said, backing up Este's reaction, so she either believed it, too, or wasn't going to rock the boat. Probably both. "And we have to consider the disruption the police might cause. Would people be willing to come down here and adopt, if there was an open investigation? Would the local merchants let us use their storefronts for open house days? And what if the IRS decided that there might be other problems and brought us in for an audit? We can't afford any of that, even squeaky-clean."

The stammering girl who had approached Ginny in the bar disappeared under the smooth flow of logic. Suddenly, Ginny could see why Este had trusted Nora with such a delicate job, and why she had accepted Nora's hiring them without too much fuss.

"But if you—"

There was a low rumbling noise, vaguely familiar, although Ginny couldn't place it right away. Este looked down at her desk, and then scooped up the cell phone that had been vibrating against the wooden surface. She looked at the display and her mouth pursed in annoyance, then she made an elegant gesture with her free hand that clearly meant that they should leave so she could take this call in private.

Nora nodded and crooked her fingers at Ginny and Tonica, indicating that they should follow her back out.

As the door closed behind them, leaving them in the now-more-noisy bullpen area, the younger woman shook her head. "Probably a creditor. I wish, you know, that she would let someone else handle those calls. Este's lovely, inside, I mean, and I think the world of her, but she's a peacemaker and world-saver at heart. I mean, even for around here, she's crunchy-granola."

"Should we wait for her to finish?" Tonica asked, while Ginny looked around, realizing that the increased noise was coming from a news report coming from one of the laptops, now flipped open. There was a coffee mug next to it, and a half-eaten sandwich, but no human in sight.

"No," their client said. "Este's given her approval, however grudging. Better to get on with it before she changes her mind." Nora smiled faintly. "First thing you learn, managing this place: keep moving forward, because the moment you stop, that's when everything has the chance to go wrong."

"What happened?"

Este Snyder listened to the other voice babble for a moment, her expression still serene, but her eyes hooded. Habit, to shield what she was thinking, or feeling. Especially feeling. Too much was happening at once, and only her to juggle it.

"Again? And the security cameras didn't catch anything? Lovely. We pay them, why? No, don't do anything yet. I want to see for myself."

She ended the call and placed the phone in her pocket. Leaving her office, she headed not for the main hall but the side entrance marked EMERGENCY. No alarm sounded, and she stepped outside into a narrow paved alley, blocked on the other side by a chain-link fence easily a foot taller than she. The alley ran along the length of the building and led to a small parking lot, and the direct entrance to the clinic. The man who had called her was standing there, staring at the wall.

"Their usual games, I see," she said, and the calm tone she had used when talking to Nora was replaced with a cold edge of fury.

"Yeah." He nodded at the graffiti that was scrawled across the wall and indicated where it trailed off onto the pavement as well. "They left the cars alone, thankfully. But the paint's sticky this time."

"I wondered when they'd figure that out," she said quietly, the fury still there. "Makes it harder to clean up. Don't worry, it's not toxic, just a pain. You step in it, or touch it, and you'll carry it with you all day, and probably leave traces behind."

"Can't have that, can we?" he said, and despite her anger, Este smiled briefly.

"Why are you even in this morning?"

"I wasn't—I was driving by and saw it," he said. "Checked with the security firm to make sure there hadn't been an alarm that we missed, and then called you. I thought you'd want all the details before—"

"Yes." She managed to smile at him. "Thank you."

"Oh my God." The voice came from behind them, younger and more horrified. Este turned, and scowled at the young woman standing there.

"What happened?" Then she saw the man standing next to Este. "Doc, why're you here? Did something happen in the clinic? Oh my God—"

"No, the clinic's fine," he said. "No alarms, no broken windows this time. They just slapped paint on the outside."

The girl sagged a little in relief.

"Don't give them the satisfaction of a reaction," Este said, and the velvet and granola was back in her voice, the anger banked out of sight. "Just get it cleaned up. Block off the entrance somehow, make everyone use the main parking lot, or find somewhere else to park. Make sure all the deliveries go through the kennel entrance today, or reschedule them for tomorrow. And keep your mouth shut, both of you. No gossip, no bitching. This goes nowhere, do you understand?"

"Yes'm," the volunteer said, and the man sketched an unironic salute. "I hear and obey, my queen. We still have the tarps inside, from last time," he said to the younger woman. "Go get them. I'll get the paint remover."

"And coveralls," Este said. "I don't want any of this crap getting on anyone, or carried into the shelter itself."

The other two moved off, the young woman unlocking the clinic door and disappearing inside, while the man went back to his car to take off his jacket and change into sneakers.

Este ignored them both, staring at the graffiti and the

handbills pasted up on the door as though memorizing the sight. "Enough," she said, finally. "Enough. I will not let this shelter be brought down. Not by *anyone*."

Georgie, remembering what Penny had said about listening and remembering, tried to pay attention to what the other humans were saying, but there were too many of them all talking at once, and none of it made sense to her. When they went back into the main room, the one that smelled of so many animals and people mixed together, Georgie let out a sigh, aware that she had probably failed. Herself reached down to pet her, and then dropped the leash and gave the "at ease" command again. That meant that Georgie was free to wander, but not go too far. There wasn't anywhere to go, anyway: doors and walls surrounded them, and the doors were all closed.

There was a bulldog sleeping on the carpet. He raised his head and studied her with a wariness she half-remembered. This dog hadn't found his human yet.

The bulldog waited for Georgie to come closer. With a quick look over her shoulder at her humans, she did so.

"You the sniffing-dog? The noser? So, what's up? Do they know what's the wrongness?"

"Something about missing money," she said, not bothering to ask how he knew why they were there. Gossip went both ways, after all. "I don't know more than that yet."

The bulldog snorted and put his head back down. "Money. Money ain't what's wrong here, puppy."

"That's what the humans are worried about."

"Yeah, well, humans don't know shit. They never do."

Georgie whined a little, deep in her throat, but cut it off when Ginny looked over her shoulder at the two dogs, having caught the sound. She wagged her tail so her human would know everything was all right, and waited until they went back to talking with the woman at the desk.

"They'll figure it out. We have to let them catch the scent, is all."

When the older bulldog merely harrumphed, clearly unimpressed with human noses, Georgie added, to herself, "or Penny will find a way to tell them."

4

Teddy had expected that they would wait in the bullpen area for Este to finish her call, but instead Nora herded them through the open office and back to the front desk. Soft music was playing over speakers now, and there was a large reddish-black dog of unknown breed lying on the rug near the battered sofas. Teddy assumed, since there were no other humans around yet, that it was one of the shelter dogs given a run of the place. It certainly seemed to have made itself at home, only lifting its head enough to check out the newcomers.

"All right, before we go into the kennels, we need to do some basic paperwork," Nora said, clearly channeling her best memory of a second-grade teacher. "Can I have your driver's licenses, please?"

"Our what?" Ginny raised one blond eyebrow and cocked her head as though Nora had just asked them for a cheek swab or something.

"Your licenses. Or any other form of government-approved identification, et cetera, et cetera. We need to have them on file, before we can let you into the kennel area."

Ginny apparently decided that was reasonable, because she dropped Georgie's leash and started digging into her bag. "At ease, Georgie."

The shar-pei let out a sigh and wandered off to touch noses with the other dog, settling down next to it the way she did when tied up outside Mary's.

"Why do you need our identification?" he asked, even as he pulled out his own wallet. "I mean, we're just walking through, not actually working for you or anything." He meant it to sound casual, but it came out a little sharp.

"It's a security measure, don't worry," the receptionist said, clearly used to reassuring people about that. She took the pieces of plastic and slid them under the copier's lid, pushing a button and letting the copier do its thing. "Like Ms. Rees said, anyone who goes into the kennel area has to be officially identified. Silly, really, but there are rules. So, are you looking for another dog, or maybe a cat? We have a bunch of cats that are really good with dogs."

"They're here to scope out the place for a new donor," Nora said before he could head off any attempts to steer him toward adoption. "A potential new donor, anyway, so we want to give them every courtesy!" She made her eyes wide with excitement, and her braids danced when she nodded her head. Someone had clearly taught her the textbook mannerisms to convey enthusiasm. On her, it almost looked natural. "And yes, we're hoping to convince them to bring home a new friend while they're at it."

The hell they were, but he bit that back and just smiled at the women, promising nothing. Nora had turned on the chirpy, slightly ditzy charm to match the receptionist's, making Ginny wince noticeably before she smiled back, too, clearly remembering that they were supposed to be playing eager supporters. It was all vaguely terrifying.

Still, they had gotten at least a glimpse of the professional, responsible Nora, the one they'd seen with Ms. Snyder. He was going to trust that one, rather than the nervous Nellie who had approached them in Mary's. The girl was green, nervous in unrehearsed situations, but she wasn't dumb or ditzy. He was less convinced about the dreadlocked receptionist, who had plastic daises on her desk and dotted her blotter with little hearts and flowers. What was she, twelve? Still, she had responded smartly to Georgie's immediate distrust, and he had no reason to believe that she couldn't do her job.

Then again, as Ginny would probably remind him, they had no reason to believe she wasn't a thief, either.

The receptionist had them each sign the copy of their license, back and front, and then handed the cards back to them. "All set!"

Nora took Ginny's arm and led her off to the left, probably assuming that Teddy would follow, without thanking the receptionist or—Teddy noticed after the fact—ever introducing them. "Come on, let me show you the kennels. It's early yet, well before our normal adoption hours, so you get to see them when they're all cute and sleepy! It's okay, Georgie can stay here, she looks too comfortable to disturb, and it's not a good idea to bring other dogs into the kennel anyway, even if she's been there before."

Teddy was still putting his license back into his wallet and heard a faint sniff from behind him, as though the receptionist had her own ideas about what Nora had said but wasn't going to say them out loud. Interesting.

Georgie lifted her head slightly to see where her human was going, but when Ginny made a palm-down gesture with her hand that apparently reassured her, she went back to contemplating the carpet, her nose resting on her paws. The other dog let out a woof, and the receptionist reached into a jar on her desk and tossed them each a small biscuit, landing them a few inches away from their noses. Teddy was impressed with her accuracy.

"Tonica, come on!" Ginny was standing in the now-open doorway, looking back at him impatiently. He left Georgie to her snack and hurried to join them.

He wasn't sure what he had expected, when he passed through the door—a metal-core fire door, from the weight of it—and heard it snick shut behind him. Something like a pet shop, maybe, with cages and shelves. Instead they were in a small foyer, this one much smaller than the main lobby, with two hallways leading off in parallel, he assumed running the remaining length of the building. One had DOGS painted above the doorway in blue, the other CATS in green.

"No mingling of the species?" he asked, half joking.

"Oh, no, not every animal is comfortable with the other," Nora said, taking him seriously. "We try to keep them isolated in their sleeping areas, for maximum comfort and minimum stress. The socialization rooms give them enough time to interact, in a neutral area." It was clearly a rehearsed speech, and she presented it with the same serious mien she had used with her boss. He wondered briefly which one was real: the flustered hesitant young woman, or the professionally poised one. Both, probably.

A middle-aged woman came out from the CATS door and stopped, clearly surprised to see anyone else there.

"Beth, hi. This is Ginny, and Teddy. They're here to look at the facilities. Can you show them around? I need to get back to the paperwork." And, Teddy suspected, smooth things over with her boss.

"Um, sure." Beth didn't look all that thrilled to be handed two strangers, suddenly, but when Nora waved a chirpy "bye-bye" and left, she took them in hand with reasonable grace.

"You're early. Some of the animals aren't at their best first thing, but if you give them a little time, you also get to see them at their cutest, falling over themselves to get food and pettings." She paused. "Um, cats or dog?"

"Cats," Ginny said, decisively.

The volunteer looked at Teddy, who shrugged. "She's the boss," he said.

"Cats it is, then. We currently have eighteen cats with us, eight older, and seven kittens, all weaned and litter trained." She smiled faintly. "Well, mostly litter trained. Rather than the traditional kennels, we keep them in spaces that run vertically so they have room to climb. It uses slightly more space than a traditional cage, but we find the animals are less stressed as a result."

Teddy nodded thoughtfully. He'd thought Penny used the liquor cabinets simply because that's where her bolt-hole led to, but it made sense, if cats were natural climbers. Although he'd thought they got stuck in trees . . .

They went under the CATS sign, into a long hallway with cubbies on either side, each one with a glass front, running floor to ceiling, a normal-sized glass door set into the front. They were vertical, as advertised, and also larger than he'd expected, for cats.

"Nice digs," he said, impressed.

"As I was saying, cats need room to move around in, and having a clawing post in each kennel, as you can see, gives them a place they can scent-mark for their own," Beth said. "The kittens are bunked together by litter, with their mother if she's available, and when we have older cats who get along we sometimes bunk them together, but otherwise each cat has its own space.

"Here, just walk up and down and see if anyone responds to you. I just fed them, though, so they're going to be a little distracted."

Ginny nodded, and started browsing, looking into each cage, clearly taking her time. She cast a glance over one shoulder, looking at Teddy pointedly and raising her narrow blond eyebrows.

Right. That was his cue.

"So, you guys take care of the animals, huh?" Without a bar to lean across, the way he normally would, Teddy shoved his hands into his pockets and tilted his head, looking more at her chin than her face. Indirect but interested, and not even remotely threatening. "Feeding and cleaning and all that. Must be hard work."

"Oh, it is. But it's also the best job in the world. Okay, no, the best job in the world would pay a lot better." Beth wrinkled her nose and smiled, less at him than the thought of her job. "But this makes me feel good about the time I spend; getting the animals socialized, if they were feral or abandoned, and then finding them new homes."

Two smiles so far, neither of them as professional or perky as Nora's or the receptionist's: real smiles, not designed to sell. She seemed like an ordinary, friendly woman in her early to mid forties, maybe. But any man—or woman—could smile and smile and still be a thief, he reminded himself.

"And this is a good place to work?" he asked. "Places staffed with volunteers, sometimes you get more friction than you do at a normal workplace. . . ."

"Oh, we have our share of personalities," Beth said. "But everyone's here because we care about the animals. So that gives us something to bond over. Even the guy who mops out the kennels, he's taken home two of our puppies, litter mates, because he liked the way they kept him company at night."

"Nice. Still, it must be tough. In this economy, with budget cuts, to keep things going and still be cheerful?"

That was a little blunter than he'd wanted to be, but the woman seemed to be the say-what-you-mean sort.

"Money, ugh." She made a face. "Roger handles that side of it, or did before he got sick. Now Nora's handling all the grant requests and things like that. I don't envy her that. Oh, hey, you want to see Peaches?"

Teddy blinked, and then realized that she was talking to Ginny now. His partner had stopped in front of one cage, her fingers tangled in the mesh gate.

"I . . . yeah," Ginny said, with a single nod of her head.

"All righty then." Beth pulled the key fob at her belt and used the single small key at the end of the cord to unlock the gate, then opened it slowly. "Oh, there's a sanitizer there, just rub it into your hands first, okay?"

Ginny located the sanitizer mounted on the wall and did so, while the volunteer reached into the cage. "Hey, precious. You want to come out and meet someone?"

Apparently it did, or didn't express an opinion either way, because she reached in and pulled out a handful of orange fuzz.

"Oh my God, so cute!" Ginny said, her hands clasped almost in prayer in front of her mouth. "Can I hold him?"

"Her, and of course." Beth deposited the orange fuzz into Ginny's now-cupped hands, and the fuzz stretched, revealing four legs and a very long tail. The head lifted and swiveled, as though to ask what the hell this new location was all about.

Despite himself, Teddy grinned. Mistress Penny was such a compact and graceful thing, he had trouble imagining her as a fuzzball like this one.

"Is it—she—fixed?" The grant that had gone missing was for neutering, so he watched the volunteer to see if she reacted oddly to the question, or showed any signs of surprise or guilt.

"Peaches is too young yet," she said, her pleased smile not shifting. No nervous twitch of surprise or worry, no body language tells at all. "If she's adopted before time, we give them a certificate to have it done here, or they can go to their own vet, but we follow up on them to make sure it's done. That's one of the requirements for adopting here. Nora and Roger take population control seriously—there shouldn't be any unwanted animals."

"Pity that more people don't follow those guidelines themselves," he said.

"Hah, that's funny. Yeah."

He hadn't meant it as a joke, but just smiled, watching Ginny cuddle and coo at the kitten. She looked up and saw him watching, and held the bundle of fuzz out to him.

"What? No, I—"

She wasn't taking no for an answer, though, stepping forward and practically forcing the thing into his hands. What was he supposed to do, drop it?

"Aw, she likes you," Beth said, as Peaches stretched out in his larger hands and then reached one paw up to pat at his face. Her paws were tiny, the claws tinier still, but he felt them against his skin nonetheless. Even a tiny kitten was still armed.

"Her fur's so long," Ginny marveled.

"Yeah, she's probably got some Maine coon or Ragdoll in her, the way she's such a fuzzbutt. She's also going to be big when she grows up, based on her tail. But larger cats aren't any more trouble than small ones—in fact, they tend to be really mellow, and sleep a lot."

The volunteer had gone into sales pitch mode, although she was keeping it low-key.

"Oh, no, I'm . . ." He started to say again that he was just there for moral support, and then the fuzz patted at his nose again, and he looked down into tiny little green eyes. And the damn thing yawned, showing a pink and black gullet and tiny white teeth, and he wondered how much upkeep a kitten could actually be, after all.

Then reality slapped him and he shook his head. "Oh, no, no can do. Penny would kill me."

"Penny?" The volunteer looked puzzled; clearly she had thought the two of them were a couple.

"His cat," Ginny said.

"She's not my cat," he said, out of habit.

She was laughing at him, even though her face was serene. "Maybe not, Tonica, but you're her person."

"Older cats are sometimes tetchy about kittens," the other woman said, nodding, and for an instant he thought she'd accepted defeat. "But if you brought her home and it didn't work out, we'd always take her back. We'd rather do that than leave a pet in a bad situation."

"Another one of Este's philosophies?" he asked, handing the cat back before he did something everyone would regret.

Beth put the kitten back in her cage and closed the door carefully, making sure it locked. "She's just great that way.

Roger's a good guy and all, I mean, but Este totally understands that it's about what's good for the animals. That's why we're here."

They finally managed to escape—without a kitten, much to Ginny's disappointment—and checked out the dog kennel without being suckered into taking anyone out for a test pet. From there Beth took them out to a paved-over area where the dogs were let out to run twice a day. There was a water trough along one end and a plastic bin filled with toys clearly made for throwing and retrieving. An older man was rinsing the toys down with a hose when they came out, and he gave them a curious look. Beth gave him a friendly wave but didn't introduce them.

And then they were back in the lobby, and Beth pointed across to another door exactly the same as the one they'd come through. "That's the clinic. It's off-limits to the volunteers, though, so you'll have to be shown around either by Este or Alice. She's our vet technician."

"Off-limits?" Ginny asked, curious.

"Yeah—insurance regs, I guess. Because they've got surgical stuff in there. We sometimes help bring animals in, but never alone, and the clinic doesn't open until later."

Ginny took out her tablet and made a note, which made Beth look nervous, as though she'd said something wrong.

"Thanks," Teddy said, drawing Beth's attention back to him. "You were a huge help, and it's great to see this place through the eyes of someone who really cares about it."

"Yeah, you were a lot of help," Ginny added, giving the volunteer her best deal-closing smile, and then Georgie realized they had returned, and bounded over to welcome them back. The other dog was nowhere to be seen.

"So, what do you think?" Ginny asked as they stood in the parking lot.

"About the facility? Or the people?"

"The people." She resisted the urge to roll her eyes at him. "We've got Este, Beth, and Nora, and Stephen-the-other-volunteer who must've been the guy in the dog run, and Margaret—she's the receptionist," she said, when he gave her an odd look. "Their names were all in the file that you didn't want to see." She counted them off on the fingers of one hand. "That covers the five people who work there on a regular basis, and they've all got access."

"You're not including the guy who mops out the kennels," Tonica pointed out. "The one who adopted the dogs. He'd have access to the office, too."

"Yeah, but you didn't get a chance to observe him, so we've got nothing to go on."

Tonica stared at his car like it was going to give him an answer. Ginny waited. If anyone was watching them, they might look like they were discussing the animals they'd just met. Georgie sniffed at the ground and pulled gently at her leash, trying to get at a scent just outside her reach. Ginny pulled her back and looked at her watch: not even noon yet. There was still plenty of time to get home and do some work before she had to head out again. She was already mentally running through the things she had to do, and adding them to the list on her tablet.

And she really should call her mother again, find out how long her aunt and uncle were going to be in town, and start putting together that list. . . .

"I think they all really believe in what they're doing here," Tonica said, finally. "But that doesn't mean one of them couldn't be a thief."

"Other than Nora, who hired us to find the thief," Ginny pointed out, logically.

"Unless she did it as a cover, thinking we were incompetent, or that she could misdirect us."

"Do you really think that?" Ginny was horrified—not that Nora might do that, but that anyone might think she was incompetent.

Tonica frowned. "No. Not really. I don't think she's smart enough to plan that, honestly."

"Ouch!" But she couldn't disagree. Nora seemed sweet, and good at her job, but easily flustered and probably not plotting-things-out smart, no. "Okay, so I'm going to do a little background work on the employee files," Ginny said, and held up the too-thin folder Este had given her, "and see if anything shakes loose. If nothing else, I'll have an idea of how much they're earning. How 'bout you?"

"I have to get to work," he said. "If Patrick brings up one more change he wants to implement, or . . ." He shook his head, clearly exasperated just thinking about the possibilities. "I'll see if anyone else who comes to Mary's has adopted from here. Maybe they'll have heard something, or know one of the players."

"Oh." She was annoyed that he'd been the one to mention that. "I should have thought of that."

"Yeah, well, you're not *entirely* perfect, Ms. Mallard." He looked smug, and she couldn't blame him.

"If Claire comes in, I think she got a cat here, and oh, whatshisname, the one who owns Jezebel." She might not have thought of it, but she could do it better.

"Who?"

"The tiny dog that looks like a greyhound assaulted a mop."

"Oh, you mean Simeon."

"Yeah, him. I think Jezebel came from here, too. He mentioned something about it when I got Georgie."

Tonica shook his head again. "You realize that you know the dog's name before you know the person?"

"That happens all the time," she said, laughing a little. "It's weird, but . . . yeah. It sort of freaked me out at first, too. People know me as Georgie's mom before I'm Ginny."

"I'd noticed that. Pet owners. You're all weird."

"Yeah, well, I think that's more specific to dog owners, so you're safe."

"She's not my cat."

He raised an eyebrow, waiting for her to respond, but she just smiled smugly at him. "If you say so. I'm going to walk home—Georgie could use the exercise and honestly, so could I."

Tonica was too female-savvy to get caught by that, as expected. "Enjoy the walk. Stop by later and we can exchange notes."

"Yeah, it'll have to be tomorrow; I've got dinner plans." Tonica worked night shifts on the weekend, and there was no reason to haul him out of bed early again just because she was a morning person. "I'll call you around noon tomorrow. We can reconnoiter. Sound good?"

He grunted, checking something on his phone. "Yeah, that'll do."

She flicked Georgie's leash to get the shar-pei's attention, and got her moving before Tonica could ask what her dinner plans were.

Not that she thought he would be horribly invasive, or crack jokes at her expense—well, he might do the latter, but she could handle that. It was more the idea of him knowing about her personal life that felt weird. They worked together, but they weren't friends. Not that kind of friends, anyway. Max, she'd spill her guts to when she saw him next: her old friend was a total gossip, and could be counted on for advice or support as needed. Tonica was a more typical guy; he would probably grunt, or shrug, and change the subject.

"Not that there's much to tell Max, even," she said to Georgie, who flicked her upright ear at her mistress as though to say "But I'm interested! Tell me!" Ginny smiled at the whimsy, but complied. "See, Georgie, first dates are one thing, because you're both on your best behavior. It's like a job interview, or when you were waiting on that sidewalk for someone to come along and see what a cutie you were. Second dates are where you see a little below the surface, and third dates, that's when you find out the scary stuff. Huh. Maybe I *should* have told Tonica, so he could call me with an emergency if things get awkward. . . ."

Georgie's tail wagged, but Ginny couldn't tell if it was in approval of the plan or just because they were almost home.

When he pulled out of the shelter's parking lot, Tonica had first thought that he'd head home for a nap, since he didn't have to work until the evening shift. He quickly realized that driving all the way back to his apartment—through Friday afternoon traffic—when he was already in town didn't make much sense either. Stacy was working the afternoon shift; she wouldn't mind if he showed up early. And that would let him keep an eye on her without being obvious about it. He thought about it, and amended that to *too* obvious.

Not that he didn't think she could handle the work: if he did, he wouldn't have given her even the afternoon slot. But having backup was never a bad idea, even at Mary's.

It was barely a ten-minute drive from the shelter, even dealing with in-town traffic, so he got there before Mary's had officially opened. He pulled into the parking lot at back, slotting his car into his usual space, and got out just as Seth rode up in his beat-up old CB750. Tonica loved his coupe, but he had to admit the bike was sweet.

"You look suspiciously awake," the older man said, removing his helmet and peering at Teddy.

"I had some stuff to take care of this morning," he said, well aware that, even leaving his jacket in the car, he was better dressed than usual. Mary's dress code ran more to jeans and workboots, considering the messes that could happen, especially on weekends.

"Uh-huh." Seth looked dubious, and Teddy suddenly realized that the old man thought that he had been out on a job interview.

He started to explain, and then stopped. None of the old man's business anyway, and he shouldn't be talking about this job until it was done. It just wasn't smart, when you didn't know who might be involved, locally. And Seth was a gossip who saw no reason not to talk to everyone—and anyone.

With that in mind, all he said as he followed Seth into the bar was "shaving and showering won't kill you," getting a hrmph! in return.

Stacy was already there, shouting orders at Clive while she set up the bar. Since she was barely four years older than he was, that went over about as expected. Teddy leaned against the door and watched.

For all the chaos and petty annoyances, opening shift was actually Teddy's favorite. Most bartenders loved having people three-deep, raking in tips and keeping busy. He liked that, too—you didn't survive in this gig unless you were a people person—but there was something that soothed his soul in prep work. Getting the previous night's glassware out of the steamer, setting up the speed rail just so, even arguments with Seth over what he'd be putting on the limited menu that day . . .

All the things that Stacy was throwing herself into, with gusto. He grinned, still unnoticed in the doorway. Yeah, she'd do just fine.

Having competent people to work with was nice; it gave him time to think, rather than just reacting to crisis.

Picking a table in the back where he'd be mostly out of the way, he settled in, resting the back of his chair against the wall so that he had a view of the main room, the bar to his left. Clive and Seth disappeared into the back, and he could hear the sounds that suggested cardboard boxes were being broken down for recycling. They must have gotten a new delivery. Stacy, at the bar, raised a mug as though to ask if he wanted coffee, and when he shook his head, she simply went back to work.

Bartending was a good job, one he enjoyed. But the work with Mallard certainly gave him new and more difficult things to think about. That was half the reason she kept being able to talk him into it in the first place. She was right; he'd been bored.

And if he didn't have this, he'd be wondering what insanity Patrick was going to pull on them next, and that wasn't useful, at all. Without more information, anything he did or said there would be pointless. Focus on the things he *did* have information about.

Money, missing. Suspects and alibis and motivations, laid out on the table.

"So, oh brain trust, why do people steal?" he asked out loud when Seth came out of the back room again. Seth might be a gossip, but he also had a damn good read on people, and Stacy, well, his barback had surprised him before.

Need is usually the motive, yeah. Either that, or envy or jealousy, but they were talking cash, here. And cash shoved in a drawer somewhere could be serious temptation. If so, then their job was easy: find out who had money problems, and shake them down—discreetly. "Money problems. Right. Who doesn't have money problems, these days?"

"I got no money problems," Seth said, predictably ignoring the first question and going for the second. "I get it, I spend it, no problem."

"You probably have a mattress stuffed with hundred-dollar bills, you old faker." There was no way Seth survived on what Patrick paid him, and he didn't seem to have another job, working a full forty at Mary's already.

He didn't get paid enough himself, either, especially not for the amount of work he did, for the crap Patrick was currently handing out. But he didn't need much, and the share he got from the occasional job with Mallard made a nice little extra, if he was feeling spendy.

"I got nothing boss, sorry," Stacy said. "I mean, other than I was starving, or was a greedy ass. Or a banker. Was that redundant?"

"We need to find out if any other cash was kept in the office," he said, ignoring Stacy's usual snark and wishing for Ginny's ever-present tablet and her detailed notes. Not that he'd ever admit to that. "Stacy, toss me the notebook under the bar, willya?"

She disappeared under the bar, and then tossed him the notebook, and a pen without being asked. In the back room, Seth was now yelling something at Clive that was, mercifully, muffled.

The top sheet of the notebook had "buy more cherries" written in Stacy's slanted script. He tucked that sheet over and started on a new sheet.

"There were credit card decals at the front desk, so people probably pay that way—the adoption fees aren't pocket change." Fifty dollars for a cat, seventy-five for a dog, the sign had said, which was probably a good deal, he didn't know. The sign had said that all shelter adoptions included nail clipping and de-fleaing. Did Miss Penny have fleas? If so, she'd never shared them. And he had never even thought to clip her claws. Did cats need that?

"Hey, Stacy!" he called. "Do cats need their claws clipped?"

"You're asking me? Do I look like Dr. Doolittle?"

"Yeah, they do." Clive had overheard the question and leaned his head out to answer. Useless Boy wasn't so useless at all. "I've been doing Penny's."

"Oh. Thanks, I guess." She wasn't his cat. There was no reason why he should feel uncomfortable about Clive doing that—or annoyed that she apparently would let him do that.

"Tonica," a deep male voice called out from the front door, full of confidence that it would be heeded.

"Oh shit," he heard, and the sound of Clive decamping for the back rooms in the hope that Patrick wouldn't follow him. Stacy had frozen behind the bar and then, when Patrick didn't seem inclined to say anything to her, kept setting up. He knew that at least half of what she was doing now was busywork, designed to keep her looking busy while she eavesdropped, mainly because he'd taught her the moves himself.

"Afternoon, boss," he said, sliding the pad and pen to one side and leaning forward on his elbows in movie-perfect bartender pose, even sitting at the table. "What can I do for ya?" Patrick never showed up before open, unless the cops had shown up in response to a break-in—once, since Teddy had started working at Mary's. Then again, Patrick had never tried micromanaging before, either.

Like dealing with Mallard wasn't enough, now Patrick had to get bossy? Someone had it in for him.

"These gentlemen are going to take a look around," Patrick said, practically strutting across the bar to where Teddy was sitting. "They have my authorization to poke their noses into anything that catches their interest."

Patrick was somewhere in his fifties, bulk gone to seed and trying to hide it behind bluster and rough charm. The two men with him, trailing several steps behind, were younger, clearly more in touch with current style, and spent money on their clothing and haircuts. He would have pegged them for bankers, except for the shoes. The shoes, although expensive and polished, were designed for men who spent a lot of time on their feet, and not in an office.

He took the card one of them handed him and glanced down at it. Architects.

"Sure. What's up, boss?" He had a cold feeling in his gut that he knew exactly what was up, but it didn't pay to make assumptions.

"Just looking around, making some notes," the younger of the two visitors said, and Teddy nodded and smiled blandly in return.

"We'll be opening in about half an hour," he said. "Just try not to trip over a customer."

After showing his guests around, introducing them genially to Stacy and Clive, Patrick gave a general wave to the room and left, leaving the two men behind. Teddy had gone back to his note-taking, but everyone in the bar was intensely aware of the strangers, disrupting the previously content mood simply by being there. Finally they took their inspection outside, peering at the storefront and making notes. Seth came out of hiding then and stared out the window at them unabashedly. "Who the hell are they and what are they doing?"

"I think Patrick wants to expand," Teddy said glumly, when Stacy just shrugged. "Or at least, renovate."

"What th—why? Everything's fine the way it is. And he won't even let me use more expensive cheese, but he wants to rip the place apart? Insane, I told you, damn it, he's gone insane. Teddy, you gotta talk to him. Tell him this is foolishness."

Teddy shook his head, something he felt like he was doing a lot of lately. "He doesn't listen to me any more than he listens to you, Seth. I'm just the bartender."

The old man stomped off, muttering, and Teddy went

back to his note-making until a familiar thump-thump alerted him that Miss Penny had arrived.

"Hey, cat," Stacy said as the tabby leapt down to the bartop and stalked past the bartender, allowing a quick pet before jumping to the floor and heading toward Teddy's table.

"Hey there, lady," he said, and turned so that she could, as usual, jump to his shoulder.

But when the small tabby landed on her preferred perch, rather than curling her tail around his shoulders and kneading his arm until she was satisfied, Penny took one sniff and leapt off him, down to the floor. Once there she sat with her back to him and, pointedly, started to groom her tail.

"What's that all about?" he asked, surprised. He went to sniff his arm to see if there was something on his shirt that put her off, and then he laughed, realizing what must have happened.

"Yeah, all right. You caught me. I've been consorting with other kittens. I promise, none of them meant a thing to me."

Penny, still grooming herself, twitched an ear, but otherwise seemed unappeased.

Seth wasn't distracted by Penny's arrival. "I swear, if he starts changing things, Teddy, I'm gone. I mean it. I swear."

"He hasn't started anything yet, Seth. Relax."

But it looked like the boss was considering it enough to bring in pros to give him costs. That wasn't good. That wasn't good at all.

He looked down at the tabby. "Maybe it's time, just in case, to reconsider the short-term game." He worked hard at keeping his life uncomplicated, no obligations or undue stress, able to walk away if he needed to. If keeping that simplicity meant leaving Mary's . . .

And the thought came to him, weirdly, considering the way she had just snubbed him: Would Mistress Penny-Drops come with him, or stay at the bar? Did he even have the right to take her, without any way to know what she wanted?

She's a cat, Tonica, he could almost hear Ginny say. *She'll let you know what she wants.*

Penny purred quietly, the tip of her tail twitching ever so gently. He smelled of other cats, and dogs, and the smell of a place where too many of them lived. She had been irritated at first, then cat-sense kicked in: that was good, that he smelled of the old place, the shelter. That meant they'd gone, and looked. But had they seen? She couldn't tell, and he wasn't talking about it, with his writing and his muttering she couldn't decipher.

There were other ways to read humans, though.

She jumped back into his lap and rested her nose on the crook of his arm, lifting her lips a little to better scent him, but there were only familiar, common things. Nothing of the smells were the things the other dog had described, the smells-wrong and the sounds-wrong that so upset the rest of the kennel.

Either it was gone, or they hadn't gone to the right place. Georgie had been with them: she could smell the other's scent, fresh on the human. She needed to talk to Georgie, hear what the dog had found out.

But for now, she was content to sit in his arms, and let him pet her, while he talked to himself. A cat knew how and when to leap, and when and how to be patient, and let the mouse come within paw's reach.

At the shelter, the doors officially opened to visitors at noon, a little after Ginny and Tonica left. Only a single couple with a little girl in tow came by, leaving with an orange-striped kitten clutched carefully in the little girl's arms, and then the parking lot was quiet until around 2 p.m., when a car pulled into the lot and a man got out. The car was a Ford sedan, old enough to be nondescript but new enough to not draw attention, and still in good enough shape that it ran quietly and smoothly. The man followed a similar style: mid-thirties, hair conservatively cut, wearing jeans and a button-down Oxford, smack dab in the middle of business-casual range. Rather than going inside, he circled the building, heading for the back, and the blocked-off employee parking lot.

When he got there, though, he discovered that he wasn't alone.

"Hey, you." The man the younger woman had called "doc" earlier was standing there, now wearing a pale green lab coverall that was stained with darker blotches. He turned to look when the man came around the corner, and then stepped forward, getting into the newcomer's personal space. "This entrance is closed."

"I'm sorry, I—"

The man in the coveralls narrowed his eyes and studied the newcomer. "Hey, I know you."

"No, I'm sure . . ."

"Yeah. You're a reporter. From *In and About*. I've seen your photo on the website. Why're you sneaking around here?" The man moved forward again, his bulk just enough to force the other man back a step, or risk an actual confrontation.

"I just wanted to get some photos . . ."

"No press here without permission. We don't like getting the animals upset—or people, either. You have permission?" The tone said, quite clearly, that he knew the reporter didn't.

"It's not that big a deal, I just . . . you're the vet for the clinic, right? What're you doing—is that blood?" and the reporter pointed to the dark red stains, his voice quivering with manufactured excitement, trying to get a rise out of the other man.

"It's paint," the veterinarian said, not biting. "And the only thing you 'just' want to do is go 'round front and talk to our receptionist. Give her your bona fides, and she'll set you up with a formal interview and all the photos you want." The vet kept moving forward as he spoke, forcing the other man into a backstepping dance until they were back around the corner of the building, well out of sight of what was left of the graffiti.

"Hey! The press has a right to know about events that affect them, and this shelter, and what's going on—"

"The press has no rights on private property. This? Is private property. You want to come in, you come in during our regular hours. But you don't snoop around and you don't take photos that aren't approved. That simple enough for you, Simon?"

"My name's—" The reporter recognized the reference and shook his head. "All right, fine. But there's going to come a day when you want my help, and boom, guess what?"

"We'll take that risk."

He watched as the reporter got back into his car—not, as expected, going inside to ask for an official interview—and waited until the car drove away.

"Damn it." The fact that a reporter—even from a small-town freebie rag like that—was snooping around meant that someone had let something slip. LifeHouse wasn't newsworthy, any other way. He looked at his hands, and then he went back inside through the front entrance, ignoring the looks that two young girls waiting in the lobby gave him, and told Margaret to call Este. They had a problem.

5

Once the two architects were gone and the first of the afternoon crowd wandered in, Teddy started to relax. The familiar noises of drinks and conversation formed a backdrop to his work, soothing without being distracting. He was trying to put together a list of reasons why people would steal cash, and matching it against what he'd seen in the staff members he'd interacted with, but it was hard. You could play with theory and psychology all you wanted, but the truth was that most people, if presented with available, theoretically untraceable cash, probably *wouldn't* steal it. He wasn't sure if they were naturally honest, or naturally afraid of being caught, or if the two were somehow actually the same thing, but the results were the same: most people, unless in dire need, or utter personal shits, wouldn't take someone else's money.

He hadn't gotten the "personal shit" vibe from anyone he'd met at the shelter. Admittedly, he hadn't met everyone yet, and some folks could keep their stink hidden, but . . .

"If it were easy, they wouldn't hire you guys to do it," he said, and flagged Stacy down for that coffee. While he waited, he took his phone out of his jacket pocket and entered a contact number. Nobody answered—he hadn't expected them to—so he left a message. "Hi, it's Tonica. I was wondering if you know anything about Lightspeed Security? Give me a call. It's not life-or-death, but it's kind of time-sensitive. Thanks."

Ginny might have contacts in local government and with credit card companies; he knew bouncers and bartenders. And bouncers, as a general rule, knew about security companies. Especially, they'd know if the company hired part-timers and college students rather than trained professionals. Not that he suspected the night watchman of being their thief—most of them knew better—but better to rule that out now rather than regret it later.

Despite the growing crowd, as the after-work rush built, nobody came over and bothered him while he worked, for which Teddy was thankful. The beer at his elbow was refilled without a fuss, a platter of cheese and coarse toasted bread showing up at one point, although the kitchen wasn't open yet. He ate and drank methodically, and at six o'clock switched over to water, before the start of his own shift.

When his phone rang just as he was closing the notebook, dissatisfied with his results but unable to think of anything else, he stared at it in surprise, as though not sure what it was at first, then accepted the call.

"Hello? Oh, hey, I didn't expect to hear . . . huh. Really?"

He'd hit the jackpot: his contact not only knew Lightspeed, but had done some work for them.

"Good to work for? They pay on time? Hire decent people? I mean, other than you."

His parenthood got roundly insulted, and then his contact gave him the skinny on the company. Teddy opened the notebook again and jotted down whatever he thought was relevant, and asked a few more questions before thanking the other man and hanging up the phone.

"Hrm." He poked his notes with the pen, thinking through what was written there. Nothing that needed to be acted on—or even could be, considering it was after business hours on a Friday night. There were ways to reach people, especially security service people, after hours, but if it wasn't urgent, that only pissed them off, and rightfully so. It could wait.

Besides, he was on shift, and Stacy looked like she could use the relief.

Friday nights were usually pretty quiet at Mary's. It wasn't the kind of place where people got out-of-control drunk, more like politely shitfaced, and normally the only time Teddy had to break out the bouncer moves was when a guy creeped a little too much over the line—and most of those times, the patrons shut it down before he had to go under the bar and get involved. That was another reason that he really liked working at Mary's.

Tonight, though, a little after nine o'clock there was a tension in the air that was making him scan the crowd more alertly than usual. It wasn't terribly crowded, but the noise level was high. Clive had gone home, Seth was in the kitchen, and Stacy was back to working the tables, taking orders and clearing away tables as people left. Everything looked normal.

If Ginny were here, she'd—but she wasn't. Dinner plans, she'd said. Jesus, when had he gotten so used to her being around all the time?

He finally spotted the trouble when Stacy let out a yelp that carried, even through the noise. Three guys, college students or recent grads, well dressed and well into their third round, and they might've been drinking before they got here, too. One of them seemed to think that Stacy—petite and young-looking—was fair game, and his buddies weren't dissuading him.

"Damn it." Normally he'd send Seth over—it took a seriously drunk idiot to hit an old man who looked as tough as Seth still did—but it would take too long to get his attention in the kitchen. And leaving the bar unattended was a massive Don't.

"Hey!" His voice cut through the crowd, conversations falling silent in its wake. The three drunks looked up, same as everyone else, wondering who he was shouting at.

"Hands off the staff!" Teddy said, still not shouting, but clearly audible. He'd done time onstage in high school, and some lessons you remembered, even two decades later. "Yes, you three," he added, even as Stacy was removing herself from Grabby's hands, giving him a glare worthy of Mistress Penny at her most offended.

There was a moment when everything could have stayed

calm, where the three would either slink out, embarrassed, or shake it off as harmless fun, or—

Teddy saw the sea change in Grabby's face, the hint of anger that too often led to violence, and he was heading under the bar before anyone else got involved. He didn't bother grabbing for any of the implements of drunk-correction stashed within reach. With luck, nobody would try to play hero, because he really didn't want the cops coming back here anytime soon.

"You sleazy little prick," he heard Stacy say, while he was still half under the passway, and came up again in time to see her swing at Grabby's face, her fist connecting perfectly with his chin.

Seth, the ex-boxer, had been teaching her some moves. Grabby didn't go down completely, but he did let go of her, falling backward into his chair like someone had cut his strings.

Teddy halted his forward momentum and watched as she took a handful of the guy's collar and leaned in to say something in his face. She'd taken down their would-be assailant last time, too, although she'd used a tackle to do it. Maybe he'd let her handle all the drunks from now on?

Grabby's buddies had apparently decided to treat this as hysterical rather than threatening, and were laughing their asses off. In the corner, someone hooted in derision, and there was a scattering of applause for Stacy before everyone went back to their drinks and conversations.

That was Mary's. Patrick was insane if he thought fiddling with it was going to improve things. Teddy shook his head and wondered, briefly, if Ginny was enjoying her evening as much as he was.

At that moment, an older man walked in, and Teddy raised a hand in greeting. “Hey, Simeon!” Ginny had said he owned a dog who came from the shelter. Maybe he’d gotten to know some of the staff there.

Ginny woke up a few minutes after 6 a.m., still bleary-eyed from getting in too late—alone, but not entirely sober—and utterly unwilling to do the responsible dog owner thing, even with Georgie’s big brown eyes staring hopefully at her from the side of the bed.

“No.” Her voice was too thick, and she coughed to clear it. “Go back to sleep, baby. ’Nother hour?”

Georgie whined a little, deep in her throat, and Ginny relented.

“All right,” she said, reaching out to tousle Georgie’s flopped-over ears. “All right, give me a minute. Go get your leash.”

The sound of clawed paws on the hardwood floor receded into the living room, and Ginny slipped into sweatpants and a long-sleeved cotton T-shirt, shoved her bare feet into sneakers, and went out into the living room, where Georgie sat patiently waiting, leash in her mouth. She took the leash—no longer wincing at the inevitable drool on it—and hooked it to Georgie’s collar, and then the two of them took the elevator down to the street.

Saturday morning walks were more social than the weekday ones—fewer people rushing through before heading off to work. Ginny spoke with the owners of a pair of Pomeranians named Max and Valerie, a Labradoodle she only knew as "Pookie," and Chester, a black-and-tan mutt of dubious but friendly origins, passing the time while their four-legged companions did their thing.

It was a good day for shmoozing: the leaves on the trees were turning pale red and gold, and the morning wind rustled them lightly, making people even more inclined to take it slow. They talked briefly about the weather, the latest local zoning scandal, and the chances of the Seahawks making a decent pick in next year's draft. Ginny didn't actually care about football, but she'd done some work with a player's wife back when she started her business, and had discovered that being able to half-ass some interest was a good networking tool.

Ginny knew that she should have been trying to work the dog owners for information while they chatted, see if any of them had heard any rumors or gossip about the shelter, but couldn't think of any way to bring it up, short of "and is your dog a rescue," and then what? "Oh, have you heard anything about them maybe having financial trouble?"

It was a relief, after that, to be alone again on the street, just her and Georgie. Ginny's head ached despite the fresh air, and her ankles ached from wearing heels all night, and all she wanted to do was crawl back into bed and have a lazy weekend watching movies, or catching up on her reading.

Freelancers didn't get weekends, though. And freelance investigators certainly didn't get weekends, not once they were on the job. Once they said yes, the clock started ticking. Problem was, unless Tonica had found something out last night, they had no idea where to start.

She'd totally blown chances this morning, probably. Tonica could have done gotten information from the other dog owners without blinking, and made them believe that they were the ones who'd asked originally. She was good at telling people what needed to be done, or asking them what they needed and making it happen, not getting them to share something without making it seem important.

She did have one undeniable skill that Tonica lacked, though. And she could do it while Tonica was still asleep. Ginny had learned from experience that after a closing shift, he wouldn't wake up until ten at the earliest, and more likely noon.

So as soon as Georgie finished her social and scatological rounds, and had been rewarded with breakfast, Ginny went into her office, flipped open the slender file she had tossed there the night before, and went to work.

"This," she told the dog, who had curled up and settled in for a nap under her feet, "this I can do better than anyone else. Well, better than most, anyway."

Georgie merely burped in response.

The employee records she had gotten from the shelter were bare-bones, just their resumes, start dates, job descriptions, and salaries where applicable, but it was enough to start digging through the public records, at least.

"First things first. Nobody has any immediately obvious outstanding debt, but how do they look under the surface?" She tapped her fingers on the desk, frowning. "And how do I look under the surface, without access to a Social Security number or authorizations?" Usually a client gave her the information she needed to do her job. Here . . . the client didn't have access to that, and Este was too savvy to leave a detail like Social Security numbers in the files she handed over.

Usually Ginny appreciated competence, but here it was making her job more difficult, not easier.

When in doubt, ask someone sneakier. Or someone who has that access legally, and owes her a favor they really want to pay off.

She picked up the phone again and checked a number against her database before dialing it.

"Darren. Buddy. Old pal."

Her IT guy grunted a response, already suspicious.

"How would you like to dump that poker game debt you've been carrying for the past few years?"

"I've already worked it off twice over, fixing your computer, woman," he said. "Just tell me what you want and I'll tell you if I can do it."

And Tonica said she had no people skills.

* * *

Several hours later, feeling rather pleased with herself despite now owing Darren a large, unspecified favor, Ginny called her partner and told him to meet her "at the office" in an hour.

She got to Mary's a little later than that. After pausing to say hello to the regulars, already set up for the afternoon, she saw Tonica, looking rumpled despite his brush-cut and freshly pressed shirt. He was behind the bar even though he wasn't working that afternoon. He'd probably chased Jon, the new guy, off for not wiping a glass right, or something. Not that she had any right to nitpick someone else's perfectionism tendencies . . . "Hey," she said.

"Hey yourself," Tonica said, half of his attention on the drink he was mixing. She slung herself onto a bar stool, placing her bag on the stool beside her and pulling out her tablet and a folder.

He finished what he was doing, took a sip, and made a face, dumping the rest of the drink into the sink behind the counter. "Okay, whoever requested that drink last night is insane, or a masochist."

His voice had the usual tone of cranky bullshit he'd perfected, but there was something off. "What's wrong?"

She was getting better at reading people. Or maybe she just knew him well enough now to see that the usual easy snark was strained today.

He made a face. "Busy night last night, and Patrick came by earlier. He brought people in to look over the place. They were making notes and drawings and basically annoying the hell out of everyone."

"Drawings?" She knew he'd been giving them crap about costs, and hanging over their shoulders rather than letting them get work done, but this sounded like something new.

Tonica lifted his hands in a "who knows" sort of gesture. "Architects, their card said. I think he wants to do renovations. Maybe, I don't know, turn the parking lot into an open-air patio? They spent a lot of time out there."

"Well. It would be nice, in the dryer weather," she said, doubt coloring her voice. It wasn't as though all that many people drove to Mary's except on trivia night, so parking wasn't an issue, but she wasn't entirely sold on the need for a patio, either.

"This place is exactly the way it should be," he said. "It's got the right vibe, we have enough room, and shutting down even for a while, or trying to make a go of it during renovations, could be a disaster. He's an idiot. But he's the idiot who owns this place. It just made last night somewhat stressful." He shrugged, and gave the bar back to the new guy, then came out to join her on a stool on the customer side. "So, how was your night?"

She felt herself blush, and hoped against hope that he didn't notice. Yeah, no luck there.

"Why Gin Mallard, did you have a date last night?" He leaned forward, his expression moving smoothly from annoyed to intrigued. "A good date, from the way your ears just turned red. Do tell."

"A pretty good date, and no, you don't get any details." So much for her theory that he wouldn't be nosy. She should have known better—if he thought he could get under her skin somehow, he'd never let up. Teddy Tonica was like the king of annoying, if he thought it might be useful later—or amusing, now.

The truth was, it hadn't been so good that there were any details to share, anyway—unless he really wanted to know how her veal had been, or how many glasses of wine it took her to consider and then discard the idea of inviting her date up for a nightcap.

At least one more than she'd had, it seemed.

"Waiting for Max to show up before you spill, huh?"

"I don't tell Max *everything*," she retorted. Not now, anyway. When she and Max worked together, he'd had more chance to dig the details out. Of course, there had been more details to dig then. And Max had shared all of his, too. In intimate and occasionally gory detail.

"But I, at least, did not let play interfere with work," she said, changing the subject. "Spent the morning working my mojo, which, despite what you may think, is just as useful as poking people until they squeal." She put the folder down on the countertop with a solid thwap. She preferred to copy everything from her desktop onto her tablet for convenience, but Tonica liked paper. And since she didn't trust him not to drop her tablet, or spill something on it, she was perfectly happy to give him printouts.

"I have never doubted your ability to make the Internet sit up and beg," he said. "Or anything else, for that matter."

"Flattery gets you nothing not already agreed to," she said tartly, and he grinned back at her. Whatever had been bothering him when she came in, it seemed like work was the cure. She totally understood that.

"There are a total of eight people working at the shelter, plus occasional volunteers who only come in every now and then, or when they hold one of their sidewalk paws-and-greets, like where I saw Georgie. I'm discounting them for now, because it's unlikely they'd have access to the inner office, and certainly not unsupervised."

"Okay," he nodded, listening. "So who do we have?"

"Starting with the bosses? Este Snyder and Roger Arvantis founded the place when they retired. Not married, have never filed any partnership papers, but they've been living together for the past twenty years, although it looks like Este owns the condo, at least on paper. She worked PR, was really hot stuff for a while, and he was office manager for the firm, so I'm guessing that's where they met. He's younger than she is, by the way."

She looked up to see how he took that, but he just raised his eyebrows and waited for her to continue.

"Since they started the shelter, she's been the public face, such as there is one, doing all the daily hands-on stuff, while he's more behind-the-scenes. Once an office manager, always an office manager, I guess. And, as we learned, he handled the grant-writing. At least until he had heart problems about six months ago, at which point we know what happened."

"What kind of heart problems?"

"I don't know." She hated having to admit that, and she knew he knew it. "Digging into hospital or insurance records is harder than it looks, without access to, well, anything personal." Her agreement with Darren definitely did not go that far, even if he had the knowhow to hack hospital records.

"Not to mention all that's probably illegal." Tonica worried more about that than she did, which wasn't to say she didn't worry at all. Just . . . not as much. Especially if she had plausible deniability.

"They're private people, once they retired. Not much in the public eye, which supports my thought that Este, at least, got burned-out on the corporate whirligig. She's got the shelter, and that's about it. No other charities, no board work, no volunteering at the local playground, et cetera, et cetera.

"Arvantis, though, keeps his hand in a couple of other concerns," she added, "none of which seems to have anything to do with animals, or money. He's low-key about it, too—a volunteer, not on any boards or holding an official position."

Tonica finally looked at the top sheet. "Huh. 'Younger' is an understatement; she's almost a decade older."

Ginny could practically feel her shoulders go back. "Would you comment if it was the other way around?"

"Probably not, because that's more of a societal norm. Quit trying to push my buttons, Mallard."

She stared at him, silently calling him on the fact that he'd just been trying to do exactly the same thing to her. He just smirked at her, and she made a face, annoyed at being caught out.

"Anyway, any discrepancy from the norm is something to make note of," he said. "It can trigger people in weird ways."

"So noted. Then there's Margaret, the woman who was at the front desk. She's their only full-time paid employee. Even Roger and Este don't take salaries."

"The girl with the middle-class dreadlocks? I talked with Simeon and the one thing he did say was that he thought Margaret was the boss there, the way she ordered everyone around and made decisions. How much does she make?"

"Twenty-four K, no health care or retirement fund."

"Pays the bills, keeps her in granola, but not much else. So a few extra thousand could be a serious temptation for her."

"I suppose, yeah. Unless mom and dad are kicking in. She lives alone, so no roommates covering the rent. But her resume is solid—she has a degree in psychology and a minor in business from Seattle University. If she wanted to make more money, she could. I think she just really loves working there. You saw how she was with Georgie."

"She was a little scary-happy with Georgie, actually," Tonica said, and Ginny couldn't argue with it. "And loving animals doesn't make you a saint. You need to remember that, Gin."

"I know that." She did. She just . . . she didn't want to believe that anyone who willingly took a lower salary to work with animals would then steal from them. But he was right. She chewed at her lip, and then continued reading off her tablet display.

"There are three part-timers who keep the shelter clean and functioning on a regular basis, other than their nighttime janitor. That's Stephen Maund, Beth Owens, whom we met, and Nora Fletcher Rees, our client. None of them has any debt that I could find on record, although off-the-book gambling debts or some terrible blackmail scandal are always possible."

"You need to stop watching those old detective movies, Mallard," he said.

"You have your hobbies, I have mine," she shot back. "And anyway, my point is we don't know what's off the books, so you're going to have to check on them. Or we sneak in and toss their apartments."

"*Definitely* need to stop watching those movies," he muttered. "Anyway, we've met Beth, and she really doesn't seem to be the type to be carrying any deep dark secrets. Unless it's that she flunked out of cheerleader squad."

Ginny suppressed a grin. He probably wasn't wrong.

"I talked to a friend who does some sideline security work," he went on. "Lightspeed Security supplies the overnight security. They mostly hire college students and retirees, and my friend said they don't pay top dollar. I bet every single person who works for them is carrying debt that they'd love to get rid of. And a security guard would not only have access, but continued access, if they got the building code. It wouldn't take even a nongenius long to figure out where the money is, and how much he could possibly skim."

"So, whoever has a regular detail there would be a serious contender?"

"I'd say so, yeah. Plus, they wouldn't have any emotional connection to the shelter, or the animals, so stealing from them would have one less barrier."

"So . . . we interview whoever that might be?"

"On what pretext? We can't ask to see their records, or even who was working any particular night. Not without misrepresenting ourselves significantly—and, must I add, illegally."

"No, not us, but Este could, right? Ask for the information, I mean, as their client-of-record? And we could go in as her authorized proxy . . ."

"And by 'we' you mean me," Tonica grumbled.

"Unless you'd rather I did it?"

"No, that's quite all right," he said immediately, and then shook his head ruefully. "All right, all right, button pushed, point to you."

"But we can't not look at the rest of the in-house staff, too. There's Alice Lind, who is the vet tech. The serious stuff—surgeries and any prescriptions needed—is done by one of their pro bono volunteers, one Dr. Scott Williams, who had no resume in the folder but I presume his degree is in veterinary medicine."

"Ya think?"

"Hey, never assume, Tonica. Never assume."

"Their vet tech checks out? What's a vet tech?"

"Not-quite-a-vet, near as I can tell. Like a nurse practitioner, I think. Alice is a part-timer, she makes ten dollars an hour, comes in for about five hours five days a week."

"They're keeping her just below full-time. Classy."

"Yeah, well, it's not like they have any kind of benefits she could qualify for," Ginny retorted. "So I wouldn't bother reporting them just yet."

Tonica hrmmed thoughtfully. "I wonder if she's paid out of that grant, too?"

"No, that's strictly for the vet and specific to neutering." Ginny tapped the screen of her tablet and checked something. "Yeah, Este, or maybe Nora, gave me a copy of the grant. It's really clear about what the money *can* be used for, which would be travel expenses for the vet performing the neuterings, and any related supplies specifically for it. Williams doesn't take an actual salary for this."

"Can he afford to work for gas money? Probably. What about Alice, maybe she thought she should be earning more? That would give us a good clean motive, case solved. Until we know, though, they're all possibles."

She had just been thinking all of that, in more or less that order. For all that they had very different processes and preferences, the two of them tended to end up in the same place, conclusion-wise. That was probably why they could do this, and not kill each other. Yet, anyway.

"So," Tonica went on, "out of all of them, who has unsupervised access to the back office, where the money's kept?"

"Williams and Lind wouldn't, I don't think—they do all their work in the other wing, and I can't imagine they have much reason to wander over, unless they make them come fetch their paychecks, doggie reference totally intended. But everyone else? It looks like they'd all have access, and often when there aren't many other people around. We should check out what kind of internal security they have." She dropped her gaze down the display and added, "Speaking of security, there was a note in the file that *valerian* is their safeword. I know we're supposed to be accepting of all lifestyles, but do I want to know why an animal shelter needs a safeword?"

Tonica made a "don't ask me" gesture, and she went on. "According to the duty roster, the volunteers have a rotating schedule during the day, covering the hours the clinic's officially open. Stephen's a retiree, Beth has kids, so she works during school hours, and Nora has a floating schedule depending on what she's working on—I guess the switch to grant-wrangling changed things up, same as Roger's illness."

"But they didn't take on anyone new?"

"Not according to their records. I guess they thought he'd be back soon?"

"Or they didn't want to bring anyone new into the mix, which could be indicative, or totally innocent. When was the last person hired?"

As usual, even though he had his hand on the paperwork, he wanted her to look up the details. Ginny rolled her eyes and then tapped the screen, skimming the information. "Stephen was the last one to come on board, and that was, yeah, seven months ago. Just before Roger got sick."

"So Nora and Margaret have known each other for a while?"

She had to check the data again. "Two years since Nora started volunteering there, when she was still in college. Margaret's been there for a while before then, um, about a year. Why?"

"They don't like each other."

Ginny didn't like to doubt him when it came to things like that, but . . . "You got that from a few minutes' exchange?"

He raised his eyebrows high. "That's why you bring me along, isn't it?"

It was. Ginny knew she was a whiz with ferreting out information, and putting together pieces of data to reveal patterns. She also, without modesty, excelled at solving problems that made other people throw up their hands and take to their bed. But when it came to reading people, to taking one look at a situation and understanding where everyone stood, Teddy Tonica blew her out of the water. Well, he was a professional bartender; people-reading skills were probably more important than actually mixing drinks.

It pissed her off, sometimes, that he was so much better at that than she was; she didn't like coming in second to him in anything. But there it was, and she'd be an idiot if she didn't take advantage of it.

"So is that an issue here, or just interoffice politics?" This was going to need more than a spreadsheet. She wondered if her tablet had the ability to double as a whiteboard. Was there an app for that?

"Don't know. For now, it's just a factoid of no particular

relevance, I suppose. The vet doesn't have access to the office, you said?" Tonica took a box of coasters from where Jon had put them on the counter and then apparently forgotten them, and started sorting them into the usual pile-of-five that lined the bar in the evenings, keeping his hands busy while he thought.

"Far as I can tell from what Este gave me," Ginny said, "Williams comes in on a regular set schedule to do the neutering, or is called in when an animal gets sick. But since he works on the clinic side, there wouldn't be any reason for him to be in the main office. The kennels, maybe, but I'd guess that any animals that he sees come to him, not the other way around?"

"Once in the kennel, though, people would be used to seeing both of them around, right? So they're on the list, but lower than the others. Especially if they're only there during the day, when there are a lot of other people around?" He made it into a question, tilting his head and scrunching his forehead at her until he looked enough like a shar-pei himself that Ginny almost laughed. He really needed to never do that again, ever.

"Yeah," she said. "And then there's the night janitor, the one Nora mentioned. He's got access, but . . ."

"But?" Tonica finished lining up the piles of coasters to his satisfaction, then pushed them to the side for later, and finally flipped open the file. It didn't take him long to skim down to the relevant information. "Oh. Yeah."

Guy was a former Marine.

"That doesn't make him a hero," Tonica said.

"No, I know. But . . . I can't see a guy who volunteers to muck out cages, who adopted not one but two animals, as stealing from the shelter. Can you?"

"Keep him on the list," Tonica said. "You know anyone can get sticky-fingered. Even a Marine."

"And people say I'm cynical? And then there are the socializers," Ginny added.

"The what?"

She tilted her head and pulled at the curls at the nape of her neck, resisting the urge to bop him one on the nose the way she would Georgie. "You know, this would be easier if you actually read—never mind. The volunteers. Socializers are volunteers who come in on a regular basis and play with the animals."

"Play." He sounded dubious.

"Yeah. To get the animals used to people, and to see if there are any quirks or stuff that might require them to be put into a specific home. But the paperwork Este gave me says they don't have a regular cast for that—a bunch of people who got vetted to work there, but aren't actually on a schedule. People come in for a while, then stop, then come back. . . ."

"Do any of them have access to the back offices?" Tonica asked.

"Not officially, no. The way the website describes the process, the animals are brought to them in the socialization room, which I guess are those glass-fronted rooms off the main lobby, and the work's done there."

"So, unofficially, any of them could have access.

Wonderful. We need to find out how decent their security is. Assuming they have any at all, that is."

Ginny thought about that, then thought about how many people might just walk into the clinic under the guise of looking at pets, and slip into the back room if Margaret weren't paying attention. "Great. I think I need that gimlet, now."

She scowled at her tablet, and then let it go to sleep, unable to think of anything else she should call up.

"Right. One gimlet for the frustrated lady researchtigator," Tonica said, going back under the bar and reaching for a glass, waving off the new guy when he would have come over to take care of it.

That was what she'd dubbed them, when Tonica had balked at signing on, originally, because they weren't licensed, and therefore weren't legally PIs. Researchtigators. They researched people's problems, the same way she did as a concierge, and solved them, that was all. No official paperwork needed. It limited what they could do, sure, but she'd looked into the requirements for getting licensed here, and yeah, no. Way too much trouble for what they were actually doing. Maybe next year. Or not. Did she really want two full-time jobs?

That thought led to others and, lacking anything else she could do just then about any of them, Ginny put down her tablet and studied Tonica while he was mixing her drink. Her earlier thoughts during Georgie's walk, about her skills versus his, resurfaced. How did he get people to confide in him? At first glance, he didn't seem like the kind of guy you'd rush to confess anything to. For all that he could pass for a bouncer, he wasn't particularly menacing. Average height, with shoulders that were broader than average, a face that wasn't particularly good-looking but gave you a sense of recognition, as though you'd always known and liked him, even though you'd never seen him before that day. The brush-cut hair gave him a vaguely military look, although she knew, now, that it was just because he didn't have the patience to deal with styling his hair in the morning—gel-and-go, and he didn't have to think about it again.

She touched her own hair, pulling at a strand again, thoughtfully. Guys had it easier—they could get away with jeans and a T-shirt, and gel-and-go short hair, and nobody thought that worthy of comment. Then again, she didn't have the body for a T-shirt and jeans. Or she did, but it would be even harder to make people look at her face, instead of her breasts. That was one of the things she'd liked about Tonica from the first: if his gaze dropped from her eyes to her chest, he did it discreetly.

And he made the best gimlets she'd ever had.

"You're going to have to go back and talk to people again," she said, accepting the glass he passed across to her. "All I've got is flat data, but you're right, everyone who is on the list could have had access to the back office either honestly or by stealing a key, or sneaking in under another pretext. So you need to—"

"Go see who sounds guilty?"

"Actually, I was thinking you could see who rats out on whom."

She took a hasty sip of her drink, trying not to look at him, in case he had that Disapproving Tonica look on his face.

"You know we can't actually question anyone. Not legally. We don't have—"

"An investigator's license, yes, I know, you remind me enough." No need to tell him she'd looked into it, and decided against it—for now. "But people are people. This may be an all-volunteer organization but it's still an office. There are going to be slights and crankies and feelings of favoritism, and somebody's going to say something because they *want* to say something."

She was speaking from experience. Her last office job had been for a start-up company that she loved, and she had enjoyed working with most of her coworkers, but there hadn't been a larger bunch of misunderstood primadonas and cheerfully nonmalicious troublemakers in the world, and that totally included Max, much as she loved him.

"So I should go in there and start asking who's the one they think most likely to steal petty cash out of the cookie jar?"

She studied the flow of liquid inside her glass, and then risked looking up at him. "Yes?"

"Yeah. I think you're right."

She blinked, but held back her surprise. Usually he made her argue a bit harder before he agreed.

"Stir the pot a little, see what floats. I'll go back and say I'm considering the kitten." He frowned. "Or maybe not.

Penny gave me the cold shoulder yesterday. Literally. She landed on my shoulder, took one sniff, and then disappeared. I haven't seen her since."

Ginny held back a smile at his slightly put-out tone. "I thought she wasn't your cat?"

"She's not." He scowled at her. "Drink your gimlet, Mallard. Maybe it will inspire you to some kind of insane breakthrough."

She raised her glass in salute. "In Gin, Inspiration. At least, once the gin's in Gin."

She laughed at the expression on his face, and drank.

6

Saturday night was usually Teddy's main shift, with Stacy running the tables. After yesterday's incident—specifically, after he saw how well she'd handled herself—Teddy made an executive decision to switch that around, giving Stacy her first go at being primary bartender on a Saturday night. He decided to do it then, rather than waiting a week or two, so she didn't have time to think too much about it. Saturday was as close to crazy as it got: if she could handle that, she'd be ready to fly solo anytime.

"You playin' Momma Duck to your duckling?" one of the regulars asked, a little unkindly, when he came out from behind the bar with a tray.

"You lot are a tough crowd," he said in response, depositing their drinks on the table in front of them, sliding each pint in front of the correct person with the ease of many years of practice. "If I wasn't here, who'd help her out with the foofy drinks y'all try to order—Seth?"

That, as expected, got laughs from some of the regulars. Seth was a good man, and handy to have around, but he had no interest in the front room, and would be about as useful as Mistress Penny-Drops when it came to serving drinks.

And speaking of the long-tail, Teddy thought, where was she? Penny occasionally came by in the afternoons, but she was always there at night, particularly when he was working the night shift, but there hadn't been ears or tails of her all day. Maybe she'd holed up somewhere, sleeping off a hard day of mousing or . . . whatever it was she did all day.

He wanted to take a nap, too. His normal schedule had him sleeping until noon, but he'd been up by 10 a.m., and even though he'd gotten a quick run in before meeting up with Ginny, his body had never quite gotten into gear.

Ginny had gone back to the office soon after her single martini, leaving him the printout of reports of everything that she'd found out, annotated with her comments. He knew that he should have been studying them; he'd even taken them with him when he had dinner pre-shift, bolting down a chicken club and a bottle of seltzer, but never actually opened the folder. He'd figured he'd have a better chance to look them over in the morning, when he was less distracted, but the fact that he was obviously avoiding it bothered him.

He was her partner, however he'd backed into it. He was supposed to have her back. And having her back meant staying current with the case.

The guilt was half expected, and entirely unwanted. He hadn't planned on any of this—not the partners, not the responsibility, and sure as hell not the guilt—when he agreed to help her out on one job. One job, no more. He already had a full-time job, and he wasn't *that* bored. But he had no idea how to get off now. He'd committed. He was, as Ginny herself had gleefully pointed out, hooked.

He didn't have much time to think tonight, though; the tables were hopping. He spent most of the night collecting drink orders and delivering them, busing tables when needed to make sure there wasn't too bad a buildup at the close. The one night they'd gotten behind on that, it had taken until nearly 3 a.m. to get all the glassware washed and sorted. You made that kind of mistake once, and the lesson took.

"Hey, Tonica, what's tonight's menu?" someone called out as he passed.

He stopped and noted that their table was covered in empties. "If you're too drunk to read the chalkboard, Henry, you're too drunk to be trusted to order anything. Do I need to take your keys?"

Henry, who "drove" a motorized wheelchair, gave Teddy two fingers, and then saluted him with it, while his companion deposited their empties on Tonica's tray. "Flash us some leg, maybe we'll leave you a tip," the other man suggested.

"Down, boys," he said, hoisting the tray, shaking his head and laughing. These guys were pussycats compared to some of the idiots he used to have to deal with, before he landed here. Even yesterday's Grabby Hands was, all things considered, mild.

So what was it, that drove someone to misbehave? That was the question they needed to figure out.

Teddy scanned the bar again, gauging where he'd be

needed, and what groups were reaching the end of their stay, when he caught a glimpse of familiar blond curls. She had come back in and settled at the far end of the bar in what had become her usual spot, where she could look out the front window and make sure that Georgie was all right.

It had been pissing down rain earlier tonight, so he hoped to hell that she'd left the dog at home.

Seeing her brought on another moment of guilt about the unread file, and then he shook it off. This was his job, keeping Mary's running like a well-oiled or at least reasonably well-maintained machine. Playing researchtigator was his job, too, but at the same time it was . . . something else. He'd get to the file in the morning, and to hell with her if she said anything about it tonight, guilt be damned.

There was a burst of laughter from the group she was part of, and he identified Ginny's friend Max, and a tall, lean black woman with a buzzed haircut and strongly muscled arms sitting on either side of her named . . . Lillian, he remembered finally. The three of them together looked like an upscale liquor ad, glossy and cheerful.

"Hey, Mallard," he said, moving behind the bar and depositing the tray of empty glasses in the sink, sliding out of Stacy's way with the ease of experience. "Couldn't stay away, huh?"

"They came to see me off on my maiden voyage," Stacy said, slapping his arm with the bar towel she'd slung over her shoulder, and then giving the bar a quick sweep, as though to emphasize her ownership of that bar, at least for tonight. "Because *some* people are civilized."

From that, he was guessing that Jon, the other full-time bartender, hadn't been happy about her taking on more bartending duties, and he'd been vocal about it that afternoon, never mind that he'd just worked a full shift himself. Tonica could see trouble coming, but Stacy shouldn't be catching the flak from it. They needed three qualified bartenders, just to keep from burning out. Three, and another barmaid—or barboy. Teddy wasn't going to squabble over gender so long as they were competent, and . . .

If Patrick was serious about whatever plans he had for Mary's, maybe he could talk the owner into hiring more staff, too. You couldn't expand without, well, expanding, right?

"Tonica!"

He realized that he'd been staring at the glassware for longer than they really deserved, utterly tuning out the conversation flowing around him. Christ, what the hell was wrong with him tonight? "Yeah, sorry," he said to Stacy. "I need two pints of Epic, and a Floater. Want me to make it?"

"Nah, I got it," she said, and went into motion, setting up the two beers and pulling a highball down for the mixed drink, each movement smooth and precise.

"You trained her well, Obi Wan," Ginny said, watching him watch her.

"I did. But there was natural talent there, too. Also natural stupidity," he said, raising his voice a little. He still hadn't forgiven her for the flying tackle she'd made when they'd been threatened in the bar during the Jacobs job, no matter how impressed he had been, or how well she'd proven she could handle herself now. That idiot'd had a gun.

"Well, like calls to like, I suppose," Ginny said with a smirk, and he sighed.

"I walked right into that door, didn't I?"

"Yeah, you did." She raised her cocktail glass at him and took a sip. "But she doesn't make martinis as well as you do. Yet."

"Hah!" Max said, making everyone turn to look at him. "I just got it!"

Lillian, clearly used to playing the straight man in the group, sighed. "Got what?"

"Ginny! And Tonica! Gin and Tonic! Aw, so cute!"

The groans were heartfelt, and Lillian rewarded Max with a wallop across the back of his shoulders that sounded like it hurt.

"I get top billing, you note," Ginny said smugly.

"Drinks up," Stacy called, cutting off whatever response Teddy might have made, and he nodded, building the tray and carrying it back to the table.

Neither of them had mentioned word one about the shelter, or the missing money, but he was pretty sure they were both thinking about it. He was pretty sure neither of them could stop, no matter his earlier thoughts.

"Next time she bats those eyes and plays on your ego," he told himself as he delivered the order, "just say *no*."

* * *

The humans weren't working. Penny's tail twitched back and forth irritably, watching them. Finally, she'd had enough: sliding through unwary legs, she left the building. She trusted Georgie, she trusted their humans, but she needed to see for herself. Her own nose and whiskers would tell her what to do.

It was damp outside, the pavement unpleasant against the pads of her feet, but she would not let that deter her. Moving down the street, she kept to the shadows as much out of habit as caution: there weren't many humans walking down here, and those who were didn't notice her moving past their ankles. The rain had stopped, but the air and ground were both wet, and her fur was soon unpleasantly damp. She shook herself briskly and sneezed once, to get the moisture out of her head, and kept moving on to her destination.

Once there, though, she hesitated, staring at the building. There were two lights in the front, illuminating the empty parking lot, and another over the door, and a few dimmer ones around the edges of the building. Compared to the rest of the neighborhood, the building was well lit, and yet . . .

This was the place the other animals were talking about, the one the humans had gone to visit, the one Georgie had come from. She'd been able to find it easily enough, but now that she was here, her paws seemed stuck on the pavement. Her first impression was that it stank. In the damp night air she could smell antiseptic, and piss, sweat, and fear. But there were happier smells, too: of grooming and petting and playing, and if there were too many animals in too small a space, it was clean and warm inside. And Georgie had come from there. So it couldn't be too bad.

Right?

Her tail, upright, twitched just slightly at the tip.

Bad enough that the animals there were unhappy. Were scared. Bad enough that their humans had come here to sniff around, and then talked in the low voices they used when they were serious. But they weren't doing anything; they were in the Busy Place, talking not in the low voices of serious, important things, but the higher voices of not-serious.

As she stepped around the building, avoiding puddles and looking for a space in the fence she could slip through, something else caught Penny's attention. A confusion of smells: fresh paint, and gasoline, and another scent, different. Harsher, thicker . . . dangerous.

Her whiskers twitched, and her tail involuntarily lowered and lashed back and forth, a whiplike movement. This was what the other animals had been talking about. This was why they were afraid.

Penny hadn't survived on the streets by being stupid, or overly arrogant. She didn't recognize this smell, couldn't say where it came from or what left it, but that alone was cause for caution. Not everything was a threat, but the wise cat looked both ways and then looked again.

She stepped past that opening in the fence, and kept looking for another, farther away from the source of that smell.

Pssssst.

The growl came from farther down, almost at the end of the fence. A flat face with an upturned nose stuck out through the slats. Dog, but not unfriendly.

"You the noser?" the dog asked

"I am. One of them, anyway." But Georgie wasn't with her. Suddenly, she missed that larger bulk standing over her.

"C'mere." And the nose withdrew, pulling the slat with it. That left enough room for a small-boned tabby cat to slip through.

On the other side, there were half a dozen dogs of various sizes, and Penny had to fight the urge to arch her back and hiss. None of the dogs seemed aggressive, huddling together at one end of the cement run. Unlike the rest of the building, the yard was well lit, with no shadows for a cat to hide in. A human was at the far end, spraying water around from a hose, keeping an eye on them but not really paying attention.

The dogs were restless, uneasy, their ears saying one thing and their tails another, and all the while their noses twitched, as though trying to smell something they didn't want to find. When they saw her, there was a small start of surprise, like they were resisting the urge to give chase, and waited while she moved cautiously toward them, the bulldog trotting at her side.

"This is the noser," the bulldog announced, as though he'd gone out and found her himself. Since she'd still be on the other side of the fence if he hadn't stuck his nose in, Penny was willing to admit that he had, sort of.

That seemed to throw them into a mild frenzy. "Have you found out what it is yet? Do you know how to make it go away?"

Having only just then smelled what they were talking about, Penny had no answer for them. But she'd give up her whiskers rather than admit that. Instead she merely twitched one ear in a superior manner, and let them yammer around her, casting looks over their shoulders at the human every now and again as though looking for a signal. If she listened well enough, they'd tell her where she should look, and what for.

"All right, kids," the human called, turning off the water and

coiling up the hose. "Last call. Everyone inside, so I can get my ass home, too!"

The dogs turned, with varying degrees of speed and grace, and raced to the other side of the enclosure, leaving Penny with the bulldog and one old greyhound.

"We can't do anything," the greyhound said. "We go here, and we go into the kennel, but we can't go There."

"We daren't go There," the bulldog corrected. "We'd die. You be careful, noser."

"Always careful," Penny told them, and then touched noses briefly, before he trotted off to join the others being herded back into the building through a narrow door.

The human paused as the last tail went inside, and looked back over the courtyard as though thinking there was one animal left uncounted, but Penny had already disappeared by then.

Time to go hunting.

7

In the end, Teddy did open the file in the morning, but only in the sense that it was after 2 a.m. Normally, when he got home after a night shift, all he wanted to do was fall facedown into bed and sleep for about ten hours straight. He stared at his bed, and then at the folder in his hand, and sighed. Part of it was the desire to do right by their client, to find out who took the money, and keep them from losing the grant next year. And part of it . . .

Part of it was the desire to get the drop on Ginny, to find something that would solve the case before she did. They weren't keeping score, not like on trivia night, but . . . they were still keeping score. A little. Maybe. And it would feel so good to find something that she had missed. Teddy wasn't proud of that fact, but he wasn't going to deny it, either.

"And there's only one way to win."

With a painful flashback to college, and the all-nighters he'd sworn he would never ever pull again, he sat down at the kitchen table in his apartment, the empty silence echoing around him, and set a mug of coffee and the folder down in front of him.

"Rock on, old man," he said, and flipped the file open.

Two more cups of coffee and ninety minutes later, he couldn't keep his eyes open any longer, but he felt better about the case.

There wasn't all that much information on either the players or the shelter itself beyond what Ginny had already told him, but seeing it in print gave his brain something to chew on, matching what he had already seen to what was on the page. After rereading the same paragraph twice and not being able to remember what it said, though, he gave in. Giving up sleep to get things done became counterproductive after a while, and those all-nighters were for younger idiots.

Putting the file aside, Teddy rinsed his mug out and left it in the sink, then headed for bed. Maybe, if he was lucky, his unconscious mind might be able to sort through possible connections and loose threads better than his sleep-deprived conscious brain.

Before he made it to the mattress, though, his attention was caught by a book shoved into the bookcase, not shelved neatly like the other titles but resting sideways on top of them. The bright-colored cover, against the more sober spines of textbooks and hardcover novels, was like a yowl for attention. He pulled it out and held it, thinking.

He had bought *Investigation for Morons* months ago, half as a joke, half as a way to keep Ginny from making a mistake that could get them both arrested. Instead of giving it to her the way he'd originally planned, though, tied up in a bow like the most ironic present ever, he'd made the mistake of flipping it open randomly and starting to read.

An hour later, he had started dog-earing pages, and had highlighted at least three passages, and if he was going to give her a copy, he would have to buy another one, because this was his.

It wasn't that he had any great desire to be an investigator. In fact, reading the book had taught him that he had no desire at all to be an official, licensed private eye. But he was also fascinated by it, the way you could uncover things, even without official channels or authorization, how far it was possible to snoop without actually crossing the line. Everyone was so worried about the government snooping, they forgot to worry about their neighbor.

"What do you say about this gig, huh?" he wondered, and flipped to the index to see if "theft, petty and grand" was listed.

Petty theft, he learned, was the taking of anything under a set sum, usually around five hundred dollars, while grand theft was anything worth more than that amount. Petty theft was a misdemeanor, while grand theft was a felony. That much he'd known, more or less. It also convinced him that they were once again poking their noses into things better left to the cops. But, short of getting her nose chopped off, Ginny wasn't going to back down, and . . .

"And they're not going to go to the cops, so saying they should be handling it is a nonstarter. Go to damned sleep, before you get stupid."

* * *

The alarm on his phone went off at 8 a.m., jolting Teddy unpleasantly from his pillow, his heart racing.

"Hell. Right. Oh hell." He reached over and managed to fumble the alarm off, falling back against the pillow. Normally on a Sunday, he'd sleep in a few more hours to recover before picking up the evening shift. No such luck today. Too much to do.

"I hate you, Mallard," he said out loud, and then reached his hand out and picked up his phone, typing those words in with laborious care. "I. Hate. You. Mallard." He hit SEND and closed his eyes again.

Less than a minute later, his phone buzzed with the response.

"I have to deal with my mother today. You're getting off lightly."

Hard to argue with that.

He got going, thanks to an energy drink and a painfully cold finish to his shower, dressed, and was out the door by 9 a.m. The air was cool and damp, and he had pulled his battered North Face jacket out of the closet for the first time since last spring, his watch cap still shoved into the pocket. No need for that, yet. But winter was definitely on its way.

The first stop was Lightspeed Security. They had an office in downtown Seattle, and another in Kirkland, but Teddy wasn't going to try the corporate office. On a Sunday morning that would be pointless anyway, since the only people he'd find there would be cleaners and midlevel grunts.

He wanted to talk to a low-level grunt.

The local office wasn't all that impressive to look at: a storefront in a strip mall, with frosted windows and a small sign that didn't say much about who they were or what they did. But the windows were well maintained, and when he pushed open the door, Teddy was greeted by a professional-looking office, with a receptionist who was alert and professional-looking as well.

"May I help you?" the young man asked, looking Teddy straight in the eye while still managing to assess his age, weight, probable income, and social status without offense. Teddy was impressed.

"I was wondering if you could answer a few questions,"

"About Lightspeed? Let me get someone who can help you." He tapped a button on his console, and spoke into the headpiece set against his ear and chin.

Expecting that this would end in a polite runaround, Teddy prepared for a long wait, but almost immediately a door in the back opened and another man came out. He was wearing shirtsleeves and dress slacks, and had the look of a man who had been in the office for a while already.

"Hi. My name's Jerry Cavanaugh. I'm security coordinator for this office. What can I help you with?"

Teddy hadn't really had questions in mind; he was more of a read-the-person-and-wing it guy. In the noir movies Ginny liked, the PI would swagger in and demand answers, or sweet-talk it out of the secretary. Somehow he didn't think the young man at the desk would be amenable to sweet-talking, and he was all out of swagger.

"I'm doing some work for the LifeHouse Animal Shelter, out in Ballard," he said. "And your company's name came up in discussion."

"I'm afraid we cannot comment on any clients," Cavanaugh said, and Teddy held up a hand to stop him.

"Of course not, wouldn't think of it. And there's no doubt being cast on your work, I assure you. No, I merely wanted to ask about your retention rate. I know firsthand that a lot of these jobs are temporary—college students and part-timers—but Ms. Snyder, the woman who runs LifeHouse, said that they had regular guards on duty, the same people every night?" He smiled, one former security guard to another. "That must be reassuring to the clients, to know the same person's on the job."

"I can't speak to the specifics of that assignment," Cavanaugh said, his shoulders easing, "but yes, we make a point, whenever possible, to keep people in a regular loop. We find that it builds a level of reliability, when a guard feels particularly responsible for one site. Plus, they are able to learn what is normal for that area and what is not, and therefore react more swiftly when something is wrong."

Or, possibly, get too familiar with the assignment and start slacking off. Or poking around offices they shouldn't be in. But Teddy could see how you could argue both points of view.

"Of course, all of our employees are also regularly screened and reevaluated, and occasionally rotated as seems appropriate."

"Of course," Teddy echoed, even as he translated the corporate-speak in his head: *if someone screwed up, they were shifted to junkyard duty.*

"Now, I'm afraid that if you have any further questions, you will have to direct them to our corporate headquarters." Polite, still friendly, but a clear line was being drawn.

"Of course. Thank you so much for your time. You've been most helpful." Teddy suspected that he was supposed to ask for the guy's card in case he needed to reference the conversation, or do a follow-up, but he didn't want Cavanaugh asking for one of his, in return. Especially since he didn't have any.

Back out into the parking lot, Teddy half expected one of the two men to come out and call after him, asking what exactly he was looking into and why he hadn't simply asked the guard himself. But that was why he'd come in person to a branch, rather than calling the main office: the odds were better that nobody working here was all that invested in making more work—or possibly bringing up trouble—for themselves by thinking too much.

He sat in the Volvo and pulled out his cell phone.

"Ginny, hi. Yes, I'm awake, give me a break, okay?" He would have rolled his eyes if she could see it, but it wasn't worth the effort without a possible reaction. "I talked to someone at the security company. Looks well run, reasonably organized, and the moment I started to prod they shut up and directed me toward corporate."

Her voice came through clearly, despite background noise, and with more than a touch of exasperation. "So you think we should strike a suspect from the list because a midlevel manager fielded questions well?"

He just waited, silent.

"Right. Right. I know, a well-run organization is a sign of a well-run organization, fear of losing a semi-secure job will keep people on the straight and narrow, blah blah blah, and I should trust your people skills."

He grinned at that, not bothering with his usual poker face since she couldn't see him.

"Also, I think we should strike them from the list because the troops know damn well what happens to them if there's a complaint—even to a starving college student, a few thousand dollars in cash set against being fired without a reference probably isn't worth it. Especially not if it requires them to break protocol and go inside a building when they're only supposed to be patrolling the outside."

"Laziness is the surest road to law-abiding behavior? You're probably not wrong. Besides, apparently Nora, bless her perky eyes, spent some time flirting with both security guards and was willing to hand over their names. They both have student debt up to their eyeballs, but it's nothing out of the usual, and neither of them has ever missed a payment. Gates has never missed paying either his rent or his tuition, far as the school was willing to admit. The other one, Ford, his landlord said he's, and I quote, 'an utter doll, pays two or three days late every month but in full.'"

"For someone who hates interacting with actual people, you are somewhat terrifying on the phone."

"I don't mind interacting with people," she objected. "I just can't shmooze them the way you do."

"You're getting better," he admitted. Then, quickly, he added "I mean, starting from tone-deaf the way you did."

"Go talk to the animals, Tonica," she said, and hung up, but he was pretty sure she was laughing.

He put the Volvo in gear and headed toward Ballard, and the shelter. Traffic was picking up, even on Sunday, and by the time he pulled into the parking lot, his mood had soured slightly, and the lack of sleep was starting to catch up with him. He eyed the front of the shelter, then rearranged his features into something more socially acceptable, bit back a massive yawn, and pushed open the front door.

As he'd expected, despite it being before opening hours, the external door was unlocked. The nighttime security company might be competent, but the shelter itself seemed to have the same approach to daytime security as his coworkers at Mary's, which was to say: none at all. The receptionist looked up when he came into the small foyer, surprised but not particularly alarmed. She was still wearing her coat, keys in her hand: she had clearly just arrived, too.

"Hi! I'm afraid we're not open yet, but—"

Teddy matched the receptionist's cautious cheerfulness with a more low-key warmth, as though he had every right to be there. "Hi . . . Margaret, right?"

Remembering someone's name did amazing things—both to their own self-esteem, and to what they thought of you. Even knowing that, Teddy wasn't quite prepared for the smile she gave him. It wasn't a come-on, either; it was a purely joyful, happy-to-be-alive smile that brightened the entire room on an overcast day like today.

He felt like an utter shit for even suspecting a woman like this could be a thief.

"I know it's too early," he said. "I was here yesterday, to meet with Nora? And she said I could come back again this morning, because I was thinking I might actually want to adopt a cat after all, and I've got to be at work when your visiting hours start."

Hopefully she hadn't spoken to the volunteer, Beth, who'd shown them around, to know that Ginny had been the one interested in cats, or remember that they were supposed to be here on behalf of someone else.

Thankfully, she didn't ask. Most people, he'd discovered over the years, took the last thing you told them and ran with it, rather than back-checking it with previously known facts.

He liked people, he really did, but that didn't stop him from thinking, sometimes, that many of them were idiots.

"Well, Nora's not here . . ." Margaret paused, looking down at the keys in her hand as though expecting the office manager to appear there.

"I know. She said I should tell you," and he paused as though trying to remember what the other woman had said. "Oh, right: Valerian?"

He was taking an utter flyer with that, and Teddy held his breath, waiting for it to backfire. According to Ginny, *valerian* was some kind of password—no, a safeword. He was hoping that having a strange man walk in outside of regular business hours was exactly the sort of thing a safeword was used for. . . .

Margaret smiled again, and Teddy exhaled in relief. "You're okay, then. Come on." She unlocked the interior door and pushed it open, a faint beeping noise greeting them.

He'd guessed right. "What does that mean, anyway?" he asked, following her inside, careful not to get too close and spook her.

She stopped just inside the door to enter a security code into the pad on the wall, and the beeping stopped. "Valerian? Oh, it's an herb, one that's supposed to calm cats down, make them mellow. So when someone uses it here, it means everything's okay, be calm."

"You need a code system, in the shelter?"

She flicked on the lights in the main lobby, and the shadowy interior brightened. In the distance, a single dog howled, low but not mournful.

Margaret laughed. "That's Bob. He's saying good morning. I don't know how he knows I'm here, but he always does."

Teddy let himself be diverted. "He's been here a long time?"

"Almost a year. We're a no-kill: he's with us until he finds a home. But he's not . . . he's a bluedot, he's not good with kids, and that's a strike against him."

Teddy had a thought that he should meet Bob, and then crushed the thought with extreme prejudice. Looking at the animals was just a cover; he wasn't here to adopt a housemate. Although that did explain the color coding system on the photo board he'd noticed. Pity you couldn't do that with people . . .

"So: a code system?" That could be relevant to the job, if they'd had break-ins or troubles before. None of that had been in the file—was her boss trying to hide something? Or was Este still not taking this seriously?

Margaret had gone behind the front desk, and was flicking switches there, too. Monitors came to life: apparently she had control over the security system from there, as well. Made sense, considering their limited staffing. He wandered over, casually, and counted four camera feeds, one each on the kennel rows, one out front of the building, and another in what looked like an exam room—the clinic itself, he guessed. That also made sense, since that would be where any drugs or medical supplies would be stored. No feed from the inner office, though. Interesting.

"Oh, that," Margaret was saying. "About six–seven years ago, in Portland, a guy came in to one of the local shelters. He was high, crazy, and he wanted all their drugs. I guess he figured a shelter's clinic would be less guarded than an ER, or a real vet's, or I don't know."

"What happened?"

"They had a security buzzer under the front desk, and they called the cops, but he managed to cut up one of the workers there before the cops arrived. So when Este started this clinic, in addition to making sure that none of us had access to the clinic storeroom, she insisted that we have code words so that we'd know immediately if someone was in trouble or not."

All right, maybe they weren't so slack with their security, after all. "And have you had to use it?"

She laughed. "Please. Here? The only trouble we ever have is—"

She cut off her words as though she'd had them yanked back down her throat, and he could almost hear her teeth click as she shut her mouth.

He didn't push, just waited. He let his head tilt slightly, his mouth set in neutral, not smiling or frowning, eyes soft, his body language as inviting as he could make it. To all intents and purposes, he was the perfect confidant, ready to take all your woes and make them his own.

But Margaret had swallowed whatever she was going to say, and was looking up at him with a less brilliant smile on her face, as though sitting behind the desk had reminded her of the required behavior of a professional receptionist.

"I'm afraid you're going to have to wait until one of the volunteers gets here, before you can go back into the kennel area," she said. "I'm sure you understand; even though you're already on record, it's for liability insurance and all that."

"Of course." He started to sit down, prepared to wait, when the door to the right of him, the side away from the offices and kennels, swung open and a man came storming out. "Margaret, there you are, can you—oh."

Teddy turned. "Hi."

Unlike Margaret, this man didn't respond to his greeting. He was tall, mid-fiftyish from the silver in his hair and the wrinkles around his eyes, but in good shape, the kind that came from physical activity rather than time in the gym. He was also, clearly, agitated.

"Margaret, I'm pressed for time this morning, I have a surgery this afternoon I can't reschedule. Can we get started early? I know, I know, but—"

"Oh, oh dear. I can't leave the desk, you know that, and we already have someone—"

The man looked at Teddy again, this time actually seeing him.

"You a new volunteer?" His voice was still stressed, but hopeful, as though Teddy had the potential to answer all his problems.

"No," Teddy said. "I'm a . . . Nora suggested I come in early. I was here to—"

"Damn. Of all the days for people to not be in early. Usually this place is full by now."

"By full," Margaret said in a mock-confidential aside, "he means that usually there's someone else he can bully into helping him."

"Very funny. Oh, I'm sorry." The older man recollected himself, and offered his hand to Teddy. "I'm Scott Williams. I'm the on-call vet. I do a once-over of the animals every Sunday, and handle any surgery or serious illness."

Another face and voice to slot to a name. "Oh, so you were the one who worked on Georgie."

"I'm sorry?" Williams's expression was briefly puzzled, as though he thought he should understand the words, but didn't.

"Geo— Ah, she had another name when she was here. A shar-pei? Mostly shar-pei, anyway. You did her neutering."

"Oh, yes, of course, I remember the bitch. Sweet-tempered, and yeah, mostly shar-pei. I could never understand how she ended up here, that's an expensive breed. You adopted her?"

"No, a friend did. I'm more of a cat person, myself."

"Ah. And here to find a companion? Excellent." Williams was clearly distracted by his own issues, although still polite, giving Teddy a nod to indicate that the conversation was over before turning back to his coworker. "Margaret, I'm going to start anyway. The day I can't fetch an animal out of its cage without help, I'm going to retire."

Margaret looked dubious at that. "You know you're not supposed to be there alone. . . ."

Teddy saw his opening. "If opening cages and standing by is all that's needed, maybe I can help?"

Both receptionist and vet looked doubtful.

"There are liability issues. . . ." Margaret started to object, again, obviously aware that she was in a losing battle, but giving it a valiant effort.

"I'm bonded," Teddy said. "My regular job's as a bartender, so . . . I know it's not the same, but it proves I've a history of being trustworthy, right?"

It actually proved no such thing, but he was betting that Williams wanted the help badly enough to overlook it, and

Margaret wouldn't gainsay the older man, especially if it made her day go more smoothly, too.

"None of the animals are allowed into the kennels until they finish their quarantine period in the clinic," Williams explained, once they were both outfitted with gray paper smocks and thin latex gloves. "But some of them are cleared while still being treated for minor items that need to be monitored, and some, sadly, are malnourished enough that we need to weigh them on a regular basis, to make sure there is no backsliding. And, of course, I look over all of them, to make sure that nothing has come up that needs attention."

"Only once a week?"

"The shelter has a vet technician who comes in more often. If an animal gets cut up or bitten, she can handle that, likewise the inevitable fleas that will get in, no matter how careful we are."

Teddy knew all of that from the file, but he wanted to keep the man talking, see what fell out.

"And, of course, the volunteers who are in daily contact with the animals are trained to spot signs of discomfort or distress. But there are things that take a trained eye, and an actual exam, to identify. Here, we'll start with Sweetums."

Sweetums was a hound of some mix, the size and shape of a small hippo, but with a trusting expression. When Teddy opened the cage, her tail wagged so hard, he thought her ass was going to come off.

"She's well named," he said, coaxing her out onto the wheeled table they'd brought with them. It had a cotton pad on top of the metal surface, and an assortment of brushes, combs, and other tools on the shelf underneath. Sweetums acted as though this was all terribly routine, letting him drop her onto the cotton pad without a wiggle.

"Yes, she is," Williams agreed. "As soon as we get her down to fighting weight, she'll be adopted quickly, I think. Won't you, girl?"

He had reached out to touch her head, and then had to jerk his fingers back as the overweight dog growled at him.

"Whoa," Teddy said, surprised.

"Easy, Sweetums," Williams said softly, his surprise not translating into any harsh sound or movement. "Easy. What's wrong, girl? Are you okay?"

She didn't growl at him again, but the tail stilled, and her head lowered slightly as though embarrassed by her behavior.

"All right, girl. If you're not up for being handled, that's okay. Teddy, if you could mark her chart that she's NFH, and my initials, please?"

"NFH?" he asked, adding the notation to the chart with the pencil tied to the clipboard.

"Not for handling. It gives her a day off to recover. The last thing you want is a dog growling at someone who might want to adopt them."

"I know a lot of people who could use that warning on their charts."

That got a smile out of the older man.

"So you do this on a volunteer basis? That's a hell of a commitment."

Williams was studying Sweetums, clearly doing as much of a visual exam as he could. "The shelter covers the basic costs, the surgical supplies, and a small fee for my time, which, I will admit, barely covers the cost of my gas to get here. It keeps me humble, filling out the invoice every week." Scott kept talking as he offered his hand again to Sweetums, who had apparently exhausted her annoyance and now submitted calmly to being examined. Teddy had watched Ginny handle Georgie enough to know that most dogs weren't thrilled with having their gums pulled back or their ears lifted and cleaned: the vet made it look easy. So the guy was competent, and not easily spooked.

"So, for the love?" he asked, to keep the man talking.

"Most of these animals, they're good, sweet-tempered beasts. They deserve homes with people who will love them, not to be euthanized simply because someone didn't give them a little time and effort. So, yeah." He smiled a little, giving Sweetums a scratch behind her ears. "For the love."

They finished with Sweetums and moved on, only to discover that almost every dog they handled had the same reaction—pleasure that their cage was being opened, but the moment they went on the cart, their entire demeanor changed. A small terrier, faster than the others, even managed to nip Williams, although not hard enough to break the latex of his gloves.

"That's odd," Williams said, frowning at the terrier less in anger than puzzlement.

"They don't seem to like you this morning," Teddy said. Most of the dogs had squirmed a little when he reached in for them, but none of them had reacted that badly to his touch.

"Something must have disturbed them overnight," Williams said. "Hopefully, once the regular crew gets here and can bring them out into the run for breakfast and playtime, they will calm down."

"Yeah, that should do it," Teddy agreed, but he was dubious. One dog, or maybe two, you could see having an off night. All of them? And the reaction seemed specific to the vet, or they'd be snapping at him, too, right?

He didn't know enough about dogs. He'd have to toss this one to Mallard.

"Hey, doc. Oh." The voice came from a man standing at the far end of the kennel corridor. A much older man, with a hairless scalp and a protruding chin, he was definitely the guy they'd seen in the dog run, their last visit. Now he stared accusingly at Tonica. "Who's this?"

"A volunteer, who helped out while you were catching your beauty sleep," Williams replied. "But now that you've deigned to roll in . . ."

"Bite me entirely," the other man said, but without any heat: clearly, the two of them had a good relationship. Stephen, the other volunteer. "You're just about done with the puppies, then? I'll go prep the kittens."

"Good. And thanks for your help, ah—"

"Teddy," he supplied.

"Right, Teddy. You can dump the gloves and smock in the bin over there, and there's a washroom off to the side where you can clean up. And tell Margaret that you earned access to the coffee machine in the back—that's where they hide the good stuff."

He hadn't managed to get the man to open up as much as he'd wanted—although he now knew enough about ear mites and signs of ringworm infestation to put him off breakfast and possibly lunch as well, but Teddy didn't mind. He'd learned something unexpected: the dogs, for whatever reason, didn't like their otherwise competent vet.

The coffee *was* damned good. Having an actual mug to pour it into rather than a Styrofoam cup didn't hurt, either. Teddy doctored it to his satisfaction and took another sip.

"Oh. Hello."

The man who had come up to the coffeemaker looked at Teddy quizzically, as though he assumed he should remember his name, if he just wrinkled his forehead enough. Teddy sized him up quickly: anywhere from late fifties to early sixties, a narrow frame hunched in on itself slightly, an intelligent, open face with once-dark hair now more salt than pepper, and a carefully trimmed beard and soul patch that didn't disguise the pallor of his skin underneath.

"You must be Roger," he said, taking a calculated guess. "My name's Teddy. I'm a friend of Nora's, helping out this morning."

He wasn't comfortable as Mallard, bending truth, but it was close enough. He *had* helped out that morning.

"Ah. I'm afraid I don't know all the new volunteers as well as I should." Roger smiled, briefly. "I've been sick, as I'm sure you've heard."

Teddy allowed as how he had, yes.

"So welcome aboard, and I see that you've already been directed to the stash. Este keeps trying to talk me into retiring a hundred percent, but when the employee discounts are this good . . ."

Roger noted Teddy's puzzlement, and smiled with a hint of embarrassment. "I retired from the desk job when we started the shelter—I always hated that job, honestly—but I work part-time as a roaster for Bean There, over in Fremont. So we're always stocked with the best caffeine in town."

"If you put this out in the front lobby," Teddy agreed, "you'd probably adopt out every animal in twenty-four hours." He'd never heard of that coffee place, but this was Seattle, it was hard to keep track.

"That's a thought," Roger agreed, then his attention was distracted by the sound of voices from one of the interior offices. "Now, if you'll excuse me, I have been informed that there is a massive pile of paperwork that I need to sign off on, or risk Este's not-insignificant wrath."

Teddy raised his mug in farewell, just as Nora walked in from the lobby.

"Oh, hi," she said, clearly surprised to see him there.

"I seem to get that a lot around here," Teddy said, mock-ruefully. "I'm sorry, I know I was early, but—"

"No, I heard, I just hadn't thought . . . Well, anyway. Um. Thank you for helping out. Scott's a great guy, and he does so much work here for free, we feel guilty. So I'm glad we were able to keep him on schedule. And you found the coffee! Isn't it great?"

The coffee was very good, even for local standards. But it wasn't that great, that everyone kept mentioning it. She seemed distracted, more the ditz she'd seemed on their first meeting than the professional whose face she'd put on when showing them the kittens the day before.

Focusing on small, probably insignificant but easily identified items was a popular evasion technique, he'd discovered over the years. Normally he'd let it ride, allow the person to unload at his or her own pace. But he didn't have that luxury now. At any moment, someone would remember that he really shouldn't be back here, and ask him—politely, no doubt—to leave.

"Is everything okay, Nora?"

"What? Yeah, of course. I mean . . . other than, you know, that thing. Everything's fine. We're just a little crazed here on the weekend, what with the clinic work and full hours, and—" She shrugged, a little half smile pasted onto her face. "Is there anything you need, anything I can do?"

"Nope. Just point me toward the kittens, and let me shmooze," he said, rinsing out his mug and placing it in the sink.

He might not have found out what he came here for, but something even more interesting was going on: between Margaret's false start and immediate shutdown this morning, and the reaction of the other volunteers to his being there, something was definitely not-okay. Something that seemed to have happened overnight, something the vet seemed oblivious to. And then there was the matter of the dogs being so upset. . . .

It might be worthwhile having Gin make a closer run at Scott Williams's background.

8

Mom, no."

"But—" Her mother had That Voice going. Ginny had to be ruthless, or she'd be talked into something that would give her an ulcer.

"No. Seriously. And especially not with Aunt Dee and Uncle Alex coming, okay? If we're still together next year, then yes, I will ask him if he wants to come." Hopefully, that would hold her mother off.

"All right. But—"

"I love you, Mom. Gotta go."

Ginny ended the call, and put her head down on her hands. She shouldn't have mentioned her date, should have known better. Normally Ginny wouldn't even let her mother know she was seeing someone until they'd been together for six months, certainly not after only two dates. She'd been trying to distract her mother from worrying about Thanksgiving, and it had slipped out, and God, when would she *learn*?

"Georgie, your human is an idiot. Fetch me some more coffee, will you?"

Under her bare feet, the shar-pei shifted and muttered something, showing no inclination whatsoever to head into the kitchen and refill Ginny's mug.

"As a housegirl, you're an utter failure, dog," she said, digging her toes into the soft brindle pelt.

Georgie rolled over on her back, presenting her belly for toe-scritches.

"Forget about it," Ginny said. "You didn't get me coffee, so I have to go get my own."

Feet removed, Georgie rolled back over on her side, barely waking up long enough to notice her human was leaving the room, secure in the knowledge that Ginny would be back.

"Huh. Was a time, dog, when you followed me everywhere."

Even to the bathroom, waiting anxiously as though she were afraid the human might disappear behind that door forever. Ginny had to admit that she was glad that particular habit had been broken. It was weirdly difficult to pee, knowing that a dog was staring at you on the other side of the door.

She refilled her cup from the carafe, and added milk and sugar, thinking about the work she'd been doing before her mother called. She had been hired, originally, to arrange the baby shower for a young couple who were about to have their first baby, and who'd utterly flipped at trying to maintain their jobs plus all the baby-related essentials that needed to be done. That had gone so well they'd also asked her to work with their contractor and designer in putting together the nursery, and arranging for house cleaning and food delivery and all the things that they knew they'd forget or be too tired and stressed to manage once the baby was born. They were lovely people, perfectly willing to spend money to get things done right the first time, but they kept trying to get involved in the things they'd asked her to handle. She was ready to give them both a time-out until the baby was born.

If she didn't like them so much, and if they didn't pay so well, she'd probably kill them.

"Dogs are much easier to bring home than babies," she said to Georgie as she went back into the office. "All you needed was a bed, a leash and collar, and a couple of raw-hide chews, and you were happy. Why can't humans learn that?"

Georgie woofed, but it was probably in response to whatever dream-squirrel she was chasing.

Thankfully, the shelter job was more of a challenge. She had been in the process of doing more in-depth searches on the staff when Tonica called—luckily she'd just talked to Nora and done a quick search on the names, so she wasn't caught out by his information. Teddy was smart, and keeping a step ahead of him was a goal more than a guaranteed achievement. But then, that was part of why she liked him, and most of why they worked together so well. She never had any hesitation that he was doing his share, and she assumed he felt the same.

Her office took up what would have been the second, larger bedroom of her apartment. An L-shaped desk was split between the computer on one side, and on the other piles of paperwork, to-file baskets, an empty bowl that had held oatmeal a few hours ago, and a pile of micro-USB chargers that she needed to untangle and sort and hadn't had a chance to yet. Once she would have been uber-organized; she really needed to get back to that. The past week, things had just gotten . . . disorganized somehow.

"That's the downside of working with someone else; you're having to wait for them to bring their part of the puzzle in, before you can put everything together, and that starts to run over into the rest of your life, too. Fine. Whatever. I am still a capable and competent person, and I bet I can still kick his ass on trivia night, if I ever get back to it."

Maybe that was the answer: help her team kick his team's ass, and reassert the proper pecking order. If they got this wrapped up by Tuesday . . .

Sitting back down at the desk, she opened her email program and sent off a quick email to the painters, confirming that they would be there on Monday morning to finish the trim in the nursery, and then clicked open the spreadsheet she'd put together for the shelter case.

Tonica could go do his thing, and she'd do hers, which in this case was chasing the money. Or the lack thereof. She was used to dealing with people who could throw money at problems—or rather, throw money at her to make problems go away, current clients a case in point. But everyone involved with the shelter seemed to be in that gray area of "decent income." That meant, in her experience, that they were conscious enough about money that they wouldn't take from someone who needed it. Only the wealthy and the desperate did that.

"This would be much easier if they'd kept the damn money in a bank account, and paid people by check. Who does everything on a cash basis, anyhow?

"People who don't want to have to report income," she answered herself. "Not so good-looking for the home team. I wonder how much they're actually paying the vet to do these surgeries? Is it just enough to cover the costs, the way the terms of the grant specified, or is he getting an extra payoff . . . or maybe less? I wonder how much they fudged the expected costs, to get more money in . . . or maybe they screwed up and underestimated?" She needed to see an invoice.

The sound of a buzzer startled her: she looked up, and Georgie scrambled to her feet, alerted by the noise. The phone she could ignore. Visitors were more rare.

The buzzer sounded again. Ginny got up and went to the front door, touching the intercom pad. "Yes?"

"It's me."

Tonica. Georgie let out a little whine, recognizing the voice even through the static.

Ginny hit the building's door buzzer, giving him access, and looked around the apartment to make sure the place wasn't too much of a disaster. Then again, the last—and first—time he'd been here had been after the break-in, when someone had literally tossed the place, so it had to look good now, in comparison. She spent most of her day in the office, so the main room wasn't too bad: the sofa only had pillows tossed on it, the rug only had a scattering of dog toys, and there wasn't any indiscreet clothing tossed around.

Hell, she couldn't remember the last time she'd *worn* indiscreet clothing, much less left a trail of them. Ginny made a mental note to change that during her next date, for her own good if not his quite yet, and then opened the apartment door when Tonica knocked.

"What are you doing here?" she asked.

"I brought lunch," he said, holding up a white paper sack.

Her stomach rumbled at the smell of warm food, and she realized that it was well past lunchtime. She'd been running on fumes and coffee since 7 a.m.

"In that case," she said, "come on in."

"Hope this isn't a bad time," he said, following her into the apartment. "I just finished at the shelter, and figured we should catch each other up on notes."

"Yeah. Good idea." She hoped that he'd gotten further along than she had.

"Sorry, Georgie," he said, bending down to tousle the dog's ears in an affectionate noogie when the shar-pei sniffed at the bag hopefully. "You're stuck with whatever Gin feeds you."

"She eats more expensive food than I do," Ginny groused, and went into the kitchen, gathering plates and napkins together and handing it all to Tonica. "Put this on the coffee table, will you?"

She grabbed a container of green salad out of the fridge and followed him out to where he was pulling things out of the sack: a cheeseburger for him, and a chicken club for her. He'd seen her eat often enough to know what she liked, apparently.

She placed the salad container on the table. "At least put some lettuce on that thing, pretend it's not trying to kill you."

"Hey, I went running this morning. What've you done, health-wise?"

"Took Georgie for her walk, and drank a lot of coffee," she said, sitting down and placing the sandwich and some salad on her plate.

"And stared into your magic machine. Find out anything more interesting about our list of suspects?"

"Not a damn thing. They're so boring and ordinary, it's enough to make me suspicious of them, just based on that. Nice people, doing a nice thing to make the world a nicer place." She sounded as disgusted as she felt.

"Most people are nice," he said. "Petty and judgmental, sometimes, but nice. You're nice."

"I know." She bit into her sandwich, gloomily. "It's so depressing."

She hadn't said it to make him laugh, but he did anyway.

"Well, I spent the morning at the shelter," he said, "and it was . . . interesting."

Good. Interesting was good. Well, it had possibilities, anyway.

"Too much to hope for that someone confessed?"

"Yeah, sorry. But I did get to talk to Roger Arvantis, who showed up unexpectedly, and the vet, whose schedule includes Sunday morning visits to the kennel itself, not just the clinic. So that theory's confirmed. But he didn't appear to go anywhere near the main office, even for coffee. The vet, I mean."

"And Roger?" She took a bite of her sandwich and waited. Tonica took his time, putting his thoughts together. She'd learned that rushing him got her nowhere.

"Roger seems like a nice guy, somewhat vague. Part of that might have been his being sick, and maybe out of touch with the daily routine, but I think he's just like that, you know?"

"Like what?"

Tonica made a face. "Hippy-dippy vague."

Oh. She knew what he meant then.

"So is he on the suspect list, or off?"

"Off, I think. Or at least, way down. Nora and Este both said that the grants had been his bailiwick before; they noticed money missing after Nora took over."

"All that meant was that he might have been hiding it before. Easy enough to do, if you handle all the money and your partner doesn't seem to have a clue—or care. Absolute trust can drive people to stupid things."

"Okay, yeah. But he just doesn't feel right for a petty thief."

She'd gotten Tonica on board because he could read people better than she could, so she wasn't going to discount that; but she wasn't ready to take the cofounder off the list just yet, either. Hell, she wasn't ready to take Este off, even though the likelihood of either of them stealing from their baby seemed improbable as hell.

"So a cautionary no to the founders, and our client, and a probable no to our security guard?" She waited, and then asked, "Anything else?"

"Oh yeah." His smile was less amusement, and more "wait until you hear this." "I don't know if it's directly related, it could be utter coincidence, but we seem to have a bit of 'don't ask, don't tell' going on in the office."

Ginny raised her eyebrows. "Oh?"

"Not that kind," he said. "At least, I don't think so. Nora started to say something about another problem they'd had, I presume recently, and then changed direction and kept it changed. And Margaret, the receptionist? Earlier, she'd started to say something about stuff that's been going on that had everyone jumpy, and then clamped her mouth shut so fast and hard I thought she'd bite her tongue in half."

"Huh." Ginny frowned. "So something's going on under the happy-lovey-puppies-and-kittens exterior? That's . . . interesting. And yeah, potentially relevant to our interests, because secret dirt and missing money are like peanut butter and jelly. But does that make Margaret a suspect, or a possible informant?"

Tonica considered the question, his face doing that thing where he was obviously digging through his recall. For a guy who normally had an awesome poker face, his remembering face looked like he was chewing a lemon. "She wanted to gossip. Rather badly, I think."

"But she'd been warned off?" Ginny put her sandwich down. "You think Este warned people not to talk to us?"

"She and Nora are the only ones who know why we're actually there, and not only would Nora not have the authority to say anything, if she did, I think Margaret would start talking just to spite her."

"So maybe Nora said she should talk freely?"

Tonica raised an eyebrow at her the way he did when he thought she'd overthought something.

"All right, okay, fine," Ginny said. "So she was told to shut up. Both of them were, probably. Which means probably Este, yeah, because nobody else would have the authority to do it."

"Except Roger. Who happened to be in the office . . . but no, he came in well after I talked to Margaret. And he sounded like he hadn't been in for a while; he thought I was a new volunteer."

"I think we can agree that whatever is or isn't going on, Roger's out of touch with everything, and Este wants to keep him that way." When Tonica nodded, Ginny went on. "Nora would be hard to pump for info if she's already determined not to say anything, even to us. I think she's too loyal to Este: she was so relieved that her boss wasn't pissed at her, above and beyond not losing her job, she wouldn't rock the boat anymore. Any way you could sweet-talk Margaret into spilling whatever it is she wasn't supposed to say?"

"Not without actually adopting a cat," he said, and there was something in his voice that made her look twice.

"Hah. You thought about it, didn't you?"

"No."

"You did!"

"All right, I did. But it's not gonna happen. Oh, and that's the other thing. When I got there, I told you, I talked to the vet, Williams."

"Right. He can go into the kennels?"

"Yeah, but not alone—none of them can, something about liability issues. I guess in case someone gets bitten, or something goes horribly horribly wrong and the ASPCA and PETA and the local news team van all show up at their door."

"But he doesn't seem to have any interest or inclination in going to the main office, you said?"

"No, I suspect he comes in, does his thing, and leaves—seemed like a busy guy. I also don't see him as the sort to be filching money. He was wearing good-quality clothing—worn, but not worn-out, if you know what I mean. And he wasn't getting his hair cut at the local barber's, either. So he's not hurting. I'm going to believe that he's volunteering in good faith."

"Yeah." Ginny pulled out her own records, not going to be outdone. "He's partner at a clinic in Washington Park, so he's not hurting for money. High-end pooches out there. And he drives a nice little Audi A6, not brand-new but still shiny, to go with his nice clothing. Usually someone in debt either has a flashier car or something more run-down."

"All that said, something weird did happen," Tonica said, cutting into her confirmation, and one-upping her neatly. "Something you'll be able to explain better than me, maybe."

Either one of them admitting that to the other, out loud, was unusual, so Ginny shut up and listened.

"When I got there, he showed up, wanting to start his rounds early, but there wasn't anyone to help him. So I volunteered."

"Clever of you."

He inclined his head, accepting the praise. "I thought so. Anyway, we started with the dogs, and every single one of them reacted badly to him. They were okay until we got them on the cart and then they snarled at him, or drew back, like they were afraid."

"Oh, that's not good," Ginny said automatically, more in dog-owner mode than investigator. "What was his reaction to their reaction?"

Tonica closed his eyes, trying to remember the man's exact reaction. "He seemed surprised by it, too. Surprised and a little worried, I think."

"You're thinking . . . what? That this is a clue?" She drummed her fingers, trying to place that into the puzzle. "A clue to what?"

"I don't know, but considering the man works with animals, and seemed to be familiar with all of them, even if he wasn't handling them every day, it's odd enough to pay attention."

"True. So I'll add it to the Giant Spreadsheets of Doom." His term for her databases, not hers, but she had to admit that the name was probably warranted. Between that, her tablet's calendar function, and Post-its, she could keep her life organized. Mostly.

"It's worth noting, yeah, but seriously, Tonica, that reaction might just have been coincidence. Animals are iffy sometimes, and they can act weird for reasons that have nothing to do with what the person handling them did. Ask any professional animal trainer who's ever gotten bitten. And, seriously, there's no way to connect that reaction to missing money."

"Yeah, I know. It just stuck out, when everything else was so normal. I liked the guy, he seems like a nice guy—they all seemed like nice people—but this is the first off note we've found, and without it, we're nowhere."

"We're eliminating people from probable suspicion," Ginny pointed out. "That's not nowhere."

Tonica plowed on, so stuck on his theory he couldn't drop it. "I mean, he's a vet, he knows how to handle animals, and they know him, so why would they react badly? Maybe they know something?"

Ginny sighed, the sound less annoyance than amusement. "Tonica, you know I'm all in the 'dogs are smarter than most people think' camp, but contrary to whatever you're thinking, dogs can't smell guilt. Or cash. Can you, girl?"

Georgie, who had settled under the table in hopes of some scrap of food falling to the floor, lifted her head at Ginny's voice and then, seeing there were no treats being offered, went back to ignoring them both. Her stumpy tail wagged once, though, as if to reassure them that she was in fact there, and content.

"So what, that they just didn't like his aftershave?"

"Maybe. Or even his body chemistry that day. Like I said, animals are weird. Or"—Ginny raised a finger as she thought of something—"if he came from the clinic, maybe he smelled like antiseptic. . . . A lot of animals really, really don't like the vet's office."

"All of them? The entire kennel?"

She made a face. "All right, point made. But I don't know what we can do about it, short of interrogating the dogs, which even you'd have trouble doing."

"Yeah. People are no problem, but getting dogs to spill their guts, that I'm not so good at." He looked under the table. "Georgie, can you do that? If we took you to the shelter, could you find out who took the money?"

Georgie's tail thumped again, and she looked hopeful, one ear perked up, as though she thought they were offering her treats.

"Tonica. Focus, please?" Ginny shook her head, and wondered if she was the only adult in the room.

Ginny was looking at him like she thought he'd lost his mind, asking the dog for help, and never mind that she'd just asked the dog a similar question minutes before. Double standards going on there, just a bit. He wasn't dumb enough to say that out loud, though.

Teddy leaned back, stretching his legs out under the coffee table, the sole of his left foot poking Georgie, who didn't even lift her head this time. Apparently he'd been judged nonthreatening enough that she could sleep while he was in the apartment. He wasn't sure, but he thought that was a doggy compliment.

"So what else do we have?" she asked. "I mean, we've knocked off half the people who work there, so . . ."

"Their security people," he said. "You said they hired an external company to do sweeps, right? We need to talk to them, too. And see if there's any video footage. I did a quick recon of the space when I was there, and there are only two entrances: the front door, and a side door into the clinic. There was another door in the back office, which I suspect leads to the back alley, but it's a fire door, so I doubt anyone's getting in that way, unless someone left it open. I am presuming, although I don't know for certain, that the clinic door is locked."

"Easy enough to check," Ginny said. "And we should have done that already. Make note of it, Tonica: next time we get a theft case, we check security, first."

"How about next time we don't take a theft case? Or any case, for that matter?"

"Aw, come on. You're not having fun?"

"I want about seven hours of sleep, a solid lead, and another cup of coffee. Then I'll be having fun."

Ginny's mouth twitched in an almost-smile, and she looked away, but not before her expression betrayed her amusement. "All I can offer is the coffee." When he nodded, she went into the kitchen, then returned with two mugs. He took one from her, tested the temperature, then took a sip. Slightly bitter—it had been on the burner a while, but the caffeine would do the job.

"Thanks. So we can assume that nobody gets into the actual building without either having a key or going past Margaret. They have a display at the front desk that covers closed-circuit TVs in some of the shelter, but not all—and once you get past Margaret, the lack of any kind of security is somewhat terrifying. I've been in their back office twice now, once with you and Nora, and once by myself, and nobody stopped to question me the second time—even people who didn't know me from John Doe assumed that I had the right to be there because I *was* there. Margaret's their only line of defense. The password may reassure them everything's okay up front, but it's not exactly a secure space."

"We're still thinking an employee or insider though, right? I mean, wouldn't whoever went there need to know already that the money was there?" Ginny was doing the tap-tap-tap thing with her fingers that meant her brain was working overtime. Once he would have been hesitant to interrupt her: now he knew that she could listen just fine while she was thinking.

"Yeah. It's not like a store, where you assume they're going to have cash somewhere. And anyone who went in just looking for something to grab would have grabbed other stuff, too." Nora had said that only money was missing, and only in small amounts at a time. That marked against the idea of a break-in, unless it was the most patient penny-ante burglar ever.

"So, we're back to the original list of suspects." Ginny sounded depressed, which was unlike her.

"Hey. What's wrong?"

She looked at him, her internal through process broken. "What?"

"Usually you're chomping at the bit, ready to solve all the world's problems, first girl in with the solution. So what's wrong?"

For a minute he thought she wasn't going to tell him. "It's not the job. Just . . . stuff. Thanksgiving. Dating."

"Oh." He remembered her saying something about a new guy, second or third date-ish, and put the three words together. "Let me guess, your mom wants you to bring him over for a look-see?"

Her entire face twitched, and he snorted in amusement. His mother would have done exactly the same thing, if he'd let it slip he was dating someone, and he was within reach.

"And . . . no, or hell no?"

Ginny shrugged. "No. He's a nice guy. I like him. It's just way too soon, and way too much." She made a face. "I don't want to talk about it, okay?"

They worked together occasionally. That didn't make them friends, though, and she'd already warned him away from her private life. Teddy let it drop.

"All right, let's start again from the top. We clear Nora off the list?" she asked, sliding her tablet into position in front of her and bringing up a file.

"Yeah. I mean, we could go on the assumption that she was stealing it, and brought us in rather than the cops because she thought that we were incapable of actually nailing her for it, so she could say she'd done her best, but I think that's paranoia and tricksy behavior above and beyond."

"Agreed." Ginny tapped the screen, he presumed checking Nora off the list. "So what about Este and/or Roger? We agree that they've got the access and the knowledge . . . and it might have been going on for longer than Nora was aware, since she only noticed it when she took over the grant paperwork. One of them could have tried using the money as their personal petty cash fund, thinking that, Hey, they're the boss, so why not?"

"Not really in character," Teddy said. "Not impossible, just . . ."

"People tend not to act wildly out of character unless they're pushed to it, yeah," Ginny said, agreeing. "Maybe his illness? I mean, financially they're doing all right, but medical stuff stresses people wildly. A little impromptu kleptomania on her part, maybe?"

She looked disconcertingly hopeful at the idea of kleptomania.

"Este could have shut us down without raising any suspicion, and she didn't," he pointed out. "So that probably drops her down on the list. And kleptomania usually manifests itself in the need to steal everything, not just cash. Nora would have mentioned if other things had gone missing."

"True. Maybe that's what Nora and Margaret didn't want to talk about? The fear that the boss has gone nuts?"

He raised his eyebrows at her. "You're a little too excited about that idea, Mallard. It's possible. Probable, even. Not sure how I'll raise that particular topic in discussion, but I'll try."

Ginny made another series of notes, her fingers moving on the screen with a speed he was starting to seriously envy. "And Roger? You met him, I haven't. Too hippy-dippy?"

The term, in her voice, sounded almost clinical.

"Too hippy-dippy," he agreed. "But hippy-dippy doesn't always mean honest." He'd met a few light-fingered New Age types before. "You should take a look at the shelter's financial records anyway, make sure that money wasn't being siphoned off earlier, and Nora just didn't look closely enough."

"Oh, joy." She didn't look joyous, despite her usual love of digging into actual facts. "You want me to talk Este into handing over their ledger? I'm going to have to go at least a year back, and I'm not even sure what I'd be looking for. Seriously, they get the check and then just pay it out. . . . That's an incredibly stupid way of handling money, especially for a nonprofit. And I bet their cash-out records are crap. Or done on the back of napkins."

"So you'll teach 'em how it's done, and feel better," he said, ignoring her grumbling. If Ginny had her way, everyone would keep perfect records, annotated and properly filed. "Would you rather have me do it? Really?"

He could see her consider that, and shudder.

"Fine," she said, grumbling, but they both knew it was for show. "I'll ask for the ledgers, and I think I know someone who could help out, faster than I could do the job. You know, if I'd wanted to be an accountant, I would have become an accountant. . . ."

"Bitch, bitch," Teddy said without sympathy. "Eat your sandwich."

Normally Roger Arvantis wouldn't set foot in a bar in midday, or even often at all—he was more the glass of wine at home with dinner sort, when he did drink. Normal had gone out of the window months ago. This was the new normal, he supposed. The more you tried to keep things together, the faster they tried to fly apart. He couldn't do anything about the state of his heart, but he could at least keep the shelter safe. His mouth firmed, and he felt every one of his years in a way he never had before he fell ill. Keeping the shelter safe meant he needed to know what was going on, no matter how much the others tried to protect him.

"Hey." The bartender, a young man with orange-dyed hair styled in an oddly old-fashioned-looking cut, paused in front of him and raised a not-orange eyebrow. "What can I get ya?"

Roger looked around, then looked up at the bottle display behind the bartender, and then back to the beer taps. "Hot Tiger." It was more of a question than he'd wanted, showing his unfamiliarity with beer, and bars, and this entire scenario.

"Nice choice." The bartender pulled the pint and passed him the glass. "Five dollars."

"You the usual bartender?" Roger asked, trying to be casual. "I thought there was another guy . . . ?"

Orange-hair nodded. "That'd be Teddy. He's working tonight's shift."

"Ah. Interesting guy, Teddy."

"I guess so, yeah. He's a good guy." The bartender shrugged then, like Teddy's being good or bad didn't make much difference, and moved down the bar to serve someone else.

Roger let him go, preferring to study things without someone watching him.

Interesting guy, indeed. Good guy . . . maybe. And maybe not.

When Roger had asked Margaret about their visitor earlier this morning, she'd said that he was a bartender at one of the local places, that the place he worked, Mary's, was considered the "quiet" bar in town. She had said it with a hint of distaste—clearly she'd been here and not been impressed—but Roger liked quiet. He liked discretion, and style, too, and Mary's seemed to move that way: no music blasting, the tables placed far enough away that people could have conversations, but not bolted to the ground, so they could be moved around to accommodate larger groups.

He had also noted the watering station set up outside for dogs: too close to the bike rack for his preference, but there was a bowl of water, clean and fresh, and a rubber mat, similar to the ones he saw women carrying to and from the gym, set down on the concrete to provide a small comfort zone. It spoke of people who thought of their four-legged companions, and welcomed them here.

All well and good, but why was their bartender poking around the shelter? What was he hoping to find? Margaret and Nora might buy the "possible donor" bullshit they were passing around, but he didn't. That wasn't how donors worked. They came in themselves, looking to get their egos patted in exchange for emptying their wallets. They certainly didn't send bartenders in to do the job for them. Este knew that better than anyone. So what was really going on?

Roger might not have his finger in the day-to-day running of the office anymore, but being out of the office didn't mean he was out of the picture, damn it. This was his baby, too, and he had things to protect as well.

He sipped his beer, thoughtful, and then, leaving a fiver and a single on the counter, headed back to the office. He'd been away too long already, and there was clearly a lot to do.

9

The insistent buzz that woke Ginny up the next morning wasn't her alarm, nor was it the equally insistent, if much quieter, sensation of being stared at by a dog who rather desperately wanted to go for her morning walk.

"'Lo?" Her voice was scratchy, and her brain not quite functional, but when the phone rang at five in the morning, you answered it, and assumed the worst.

But it wasn't her mother or stepfather, or anyone identifying themselves as the police, so Ginny exhaled in relief. That relief was short-lived, though.

"Nora, slow down. Wait a minute." She sat up, trying to untangle what the girl was saying. "What happened? Who died?"

The name meant nothing to her—it hadn't been on the list of volunteers Este had given them—but clearly it was someone connected to the shelter, since they had apparently been killed there and Nora was clearly upset. Although having someone not to do with the shelter killed there could be upsetting, too.

"All right, just hang on." She sat up in bed and tried to get her brain working. "Are you at the shelter?"

Nora was; as de facto office manager she was the official contact person in case of emergencies or disasters, and so the police had called her first. She'd gone down immediately, taken one look, and, apparently, called Ginny.

Ginny was quite sure that this hadn't been in the job description. But what was she going to do, hang up on the poor girl and go back to sleep? Not possible.

"The police are there? All right, just stay calm, and we'll meet you in an hour. It's okay, Nora. Let the cops handle it. All you have to do is be there if they have any questions. Yes, yes, you should answer the questions."

If she'd told Nora to do anything else, Tonica would've had her head, and justifiably so. Avoiding official notice did not include lying to the cops, even by the sin of omission. "If anything else happens, call me."

She hung up the phone and, after hauling herself out of bed, texted Tonica on her way to the kitchen. There was urgency, but no rush: whoever it was was already dead, the cops were going to do their thing, which would probably take a while—and she thought better after caffeine got in her system.

What Ginny really wanted was another hour of sleep, and then a hot shower, but that clearly wasn't going to happen. A cup of strong black Kona was going to have to suffice.

In the living room, Georgie raised her head as though to ask why her human was up so early, and did that mean it was time for a walk?

"Go back to sleep, baby," she told the dog. "Back to sleep."

With a low whine, Georgie lowered her head back to her paws, but rather than going back to sleep, she watched her human with unblinking eyes.

After starting the coffee and throwing an English muffin into the toaster, Ginny went back into the bedroom to get dressed. She stared into her closet and ran her hand through her hair. "And here's a question for the ages. What the hell do you wear to a dead body?"

The answer ended up being a pair of black jeans, a gray cotton sweater, and a pinstripe gray jacket from her officewear days, over a pair of black walking shoes. Professional, somber, but not trying too hard to look either. She hoped.

By the time she'd buttered the English muffin and poured her coffee, her phone had beeped with a response from Tonica. Unlike previous visits, he would meet her there. Fair enough. She'd be there, even walking, by the time he got himself into his car.

Ginny cleaned up the breakfast debris, deciding against another cup of coffee. She needed to be awake, not jittery with caffeine and lack of sleep. She washed her face, brushed her teeth, and put on enough makeup that the black and gray of her outfit didn't make her look like a blond corpse, and went back out into the main room to find Georgie sitting there, tattered pink leash in her mouth, eyes expectant, as though to say "don't you even *think* about going anywhere without me."

"Oh, baby, I don't think that's a good idea. . . ."

But neither was leaving Georgie here without her morning walk. That was bad dog ownership, and Ginny had spent the past year learning how to be a good dog owner. Big brown eyes stared at her, and Ginny relented.

"Oh hell, it's not like the shelter blinked when we brought you with us last time, right? And God knows when I'll get back, and you do need to be walked." The shar-pei thumped her tail once as though in agreement.

"Okay, girl, let's go." She shoved a few treats and a poo-bag in her pocket, slipped her tablet and wallet into a bag, and snapped the leash to Georgie's collar.

It was cool outside, predawn, but not actively cold. By the time they made it all the way downtown, Ginny had warmed up and woken up, while Georgie was practically prancing in excitement at walking somewhere other than their usual route.

Now that her brain was less sleep-fuzzed, Ginny was wondering why the hell she had agreed to come down. Yes, Nora was in a panic, and Ginny knew that panic brought out her not-so-deep-seated need to fix all things. But they had been hired to investigate missing money, not dead bodies. Unless the guy had died with his hand in the till . . .

The neighborhood the shelter was in was usually quiet, especially at this hour. But today there was a crowd outside the shelter, mostly people who had been out jogging or walking their dogs, or coming off shift and having breakfast-for-dinner at the local diner, and who couldn't resist the siren call of a cop car and ambulance. Ginny assumed the ambulance, anyway: by the time she got there, it was long gone. But the uniformed cops remained, as did yellow tape strung up in the parking lot. She'd always thought was just a TV cop show conceit, but apparently not.

"Ginny!" Nora, on the other side of the official line, wrapped in a long coat, her unbraided hair a tousled mess, waved her hand. The man who had been talking to her, not a uniform, but clearly Official in some capacity, didn't look thrilled at the interruption. Ginny waved back but stayed where she was, indicating via hand gestures that she'd be there when the cops were done with their questions.

As Tonica often reminded her, they had no official status, and they'd learned the hard way that once a dead body showed up, you were either a cop, a suspect, or a problem.

Problems had a way of becoming suspects. Better to wait.

In the meantime, Georgie was straining at the leash, as though she had scented old friends inside the building. Or maybe she just wanted to be where all the excitement was happening. Ginny pulled her away, distracting her with the presence of a friendly poodle-mix who wanted to exchange sniffs.

"What happened? Who died?" Tonica came up along the sidewalk, with a takeout coffee in his hand. He scanned the front of the clinic, and she could see his brain ticking away the number of cop cars—two—and cops—three uniforms visible plus the guy who was probably a detective, still talking with Nora. There was also a single news crew; a woman holding the camera and an Asian man in front of it, talking earnestly.

"Nothing high-profile," he said, making a quick assessment. "So we've got a dead body, but not anyone important, or otherwise bludgeoned to death with a stray cat."

"Teddy. That's sick."

"What, the dead body, or death by cat? Okay, both, I get it. Hey, Georgie." He bent down to scratch behind her ears. "So who died?" he asked Ginny. "Your text was short on detail."

He was wound up this morning, bouncing on his feet, and taking almost furtive sips of his coffee, exactly the state she'd tried to avoid. He looked like an oddly healthy junkie, sneaking his fix.

"How much sleep did you get last night?" she asked him.

"Considering I got woken up at five-fucking-ayem by a text telling me we had a dead body?" he asked, still petting Georgie, and not looking at her. "Nowhere near enough. Who died?"

Ginny shook her head, deciding to let him deal with his own caffeine jitters. "The bookkeeper."

"The who?"

"Yeah, that's what I'm wondering. I didn't even know they had a bookkeeper. He wasn't on any of the employee or volunteer lists we got, and Nora sure as hell didn't mention another person. I guess I would have found out when I asked for the ledgers, huh? Oh, sorry about that, there's someone *else* who has access to the inner office, and oh yeah, *all* of our money, whoops!"

★ ★ ★

Teddy heard that tone come into Ginny's voice, and despite the hour and the news, his mood brightened. There was the acerbic diva he'd first gotten to know, not the thoughtful, softer version he'd been seeing recently. He was way more comfortable with Mallard in this mood. "I think Este mentioned a bookkeeper, when we first met her, but no mention of him on the employee lists, so I just . . ." He shrugged. "So, what are we doing here, anyway? If this has anything to do with the event we were looking into, the cops are going to be all over it—and they're going to want us *out* of it."

She was too smart not to have thought of it herself, but she bristled anyway, her cool exterior cracking a little with indignation. "You want us to just hand over our information to them and walk away?"

"Yep." He didn't think they were going to, though. Just a hunch.

"You know people, Tonica," she said. "What do you think the odds are that anyone in there has mentioned the missing money to the cops?"

He thought about what he'd seen, what he'd heard, and what he'd managed to suss out. "Slim to none," he told her.

"That's what I thought, too. They're going to try to keep it some little thing, ignore it as much as they can, even now, thinking that somehow they're protecting the shelter. And hey, I can see the logic. Far more likely this was an actual break-in gone wrong, and whoops, there's this guy there in the middle of the night, and a robber becomes a murderer-by-accident . . . and not our problem."

"You know, though, a bookkeeper?" Teddy said thoughtfully. "When we're looking into missing funds? The odds of it not being related are—"

"Slim to none," she repeated. "Yeah. And that makes it our problem. Damn it."

"So what do we do?"

Ginny stared at the small circus in front of them, watching as the news crew finished up and rolled out, and the rubberneckers slowly drifted away. "Damned if I know. Play it by ear? Maybe we're wrong, and they're spilling their guts to the cops right now, telling them everything."

"Yeah. Maybe." He was about as convinced of that as she was, which was to say, not at all.

Eventually, bored with watching the front door, they wandered over to the local café and grabbed some coffee, coming back in time to see the last squad car pull away. There were still people wandering round looking official, but the bulk of the investigation seemed to have followed the body off-site.

The moment she saw them, Nora rushed over to where Ginny and Teddy were standing. Georgie had settled comfortably at Ginny's feet, apparently no longer interested in the shelter or the crowds.

"Oh, I'm sorry," Nora said, "I didn't think, they kept asking us questions, and I didn't know what to tell them. Come on, Este's inside; they insisted we all be kept separate while we were talking, although I don't know why, none of us were even here!"

She kept talking, gesturing madly, as the three of them

followed her through the double doors and into the shelter's lobby. Este was there, still talking to an older man in uniform, although he didn't seem to be interrogating her. Este looked her age, having obviously thrown on her sweatshirt and jeans in even more of a rush than Ginny, and not bothering with makeup. Her silvered hair showed definite signs of bedhead, and her face was lined, but she managed to smile when she saw them come in.

The cop turned, just enough to see who she was looking at, and his face deepened its scowl. "And who the hell is this?"

Este stood, graceful even then, and patted the cop on the shoulder as though he were an old friend. "Concerned members of the shelter family," she said. "Thank you both for coming down. I assume Nora called you?"

Teddy heard the faint note of disapproval in that question, even if Nora—and, thankfully, the cop—didn't. Or maybe he was projecting.

"Yes. Terrible . . ." Ginny's voice was professionally smooth, like she'd been a funeral home worker in another life. For all he knew, she had. "For all the good the shelter does, for something like this to happen . . . We just wanted to come and offer our aid, if there was anything you needed."

"If we're done, here?" Este said to the cop, who made a noise like Georgie muttering and got up.

"Yeah, we're done. You all stay in town, until we tell you that you can go anywhere. And don't touch anything in the office."

He left, and Este turned to them, her eyes wide. "I didn't know they really said that."

Her voice was a little too close to hysteria for Teddy's comfort. "They do. And they mean it. But you'd be here anyway, right?"

She focused on that, nodded. "They said it was all right to keep the shelter running; they've moved the . . . the body, and taken photographs and so much else, but . . . oh, poor Jimmy, what a terrible way to die."

"What happened?" Ginny demanded. "And—" Teddy gave her a quick glare; he wasn't sure if she caught it, but she did stop herself from demanding to know why Jimmy hadn't been on the list she'd been given, to check out backgrounds and alibis. "What happened?"

"The police say that he must have had a heart attack, or maybe a stoke. He just fell over. He was working in the office, and he was leaning back and the chair collapsed under him. . . ."

"So not murder?"

"Oh, no, nothing like that!" Este looked somewhere between horrified, as though she'd never thought of murder, and relieved that she could quash that idea immediately. Teddy couldn't blame her for either reaction.

Nora shook her head, looking slightly embarrassed now. "No, oh God no. I overreacted when the police called me. I was just so flustered, and I thought, well, you two are investigators, so . . . But no, of course it's not murder. But how horrible, to think that he might have been there for God knows how long, maybe needing help, and—"

Nora had a ghoulish streak in her, Teddy decided.

"Este? I think—oh." Roger came out through the office door, and stopped at seeing the small crowd there. His gaze flickered over Nora and Teddy, stopped to linger on Ginny, a slightly puzzled expression on his face, and then down to Georgie before returning to Teddy.

Teddy knew he was busted even before the man opened his mouth.

"You're not here for any would-be patron," Roger said. "What's your game, and why are you harassing my staff?"

Maybe the man wasn't quite so hippy-dippy after all.

"Roger. It's all right. They're . . ." Este dropped her gaze, and her voice faltered under his glare. Interesting.

"They're investigators," Nora said, falling on that particular grenade. "I hired them."

"Investigators." The way he said it made Teddy think that wasn't a surprise to the other man. "Because of Jimmy?" Now Roger looked befuddled. "But that just happened . . . and the police said that was a terrible accident."

"No. Because . . ." Nora faltered, too, then went on. "Because money's been going missing, Roger. From the grant fund. I didn't want to tell you. We didn't want to worry you while you were still recovering."

"You hired investigators to look into our finances?" He turned from Nora to glare at this partner. "Este, you approved this?"

"Don't use that voice, Roger," she warned, her voice cold. "You weren't here, and I was. Nora was impulsive, but what would you rather we do, report it to the police?

Bad enough they had to come in now—we can play Jimmy's death for sympathy, a terrible loss to the community, if need be. But someone stealing from within? There's no way to spin that—and we couldn't just keep ignoring it!"

Roger, Teddy noted, seemed more horrified that someone was looking into the missing money than he was about someone he knew dying a few hours before. Not hippy-dippy at all, once the surface was scratched. The timing might be wrong, but he really wanted to have Ginny look into this guy's alibis and finances, now.

The guy was still talking. "Nora . . . it's wonderful that you care so much about the shelter—God knows, Este and I appreciate your dedication. But hiring investigators? I hardly think that's necessary. Especially without checking with us first. Anyway, now that the police have been called in, and with Jimmy's death, it's no longer necessary."

"You think Jimmy was taking the money?" Este sounded horrified. "He took over the books—for free—when you got sick. He's saved us so much money, volunteering—why would he steal?"

"Excuse me," Ginny said, stepping into the conversation. "This Jimmy, he wasn't with you very long?"

"No, only about six months, since Roger had to step back. He's a CPA, works for a local firm. A friend of a friend, you know how it goes? He came in after hours to go over our books and make sure everything was going smoothly, so nothing got tangled come quarter-close."

"So he knew about the money, and the vet's payouts."

"I suppose so, yes. The payments are all on the ledger.

But there's no way he would . . ." Este's voice trailed off as she realized that any objection she might raise was the same they'd already raised—and rejected—to exclude the rest of the volunteers, too.

Everyone had to be considered. And someone who had opportunity to know exactly what money was there had to be considered first, even without motive.

"Maybe whoever stole it came back, and Jimmy caught them, and they killed him, hit him over the head or poisoned him or something." Nora's face had a vaguely disquieting glow to it, as though the thought that someone she knew might have been murdered was an exciting development. Their client definitely had a ghoulish streak. It went badly with her crunchy-granola exterior.

Teddy looked sideways at his partner. Gin had a look on her face that he couldn't quite read: not so much thoughtful as . . . processing. She was thinking something, but she hadn't quite *thought* it yet.

"The police said it was an accident," Roger said.

"The police said it *probably* was an accident." Este corrected him. At some point, one of them had taken the other's hand, they weren't exactly standing side by side, but the clasped hands told Teddy that the founders of the shelter were, in fact, a couple, no matter what the official paperwork didn't say. They were closing ranks even as they disagreed, with the unspoken smoothness of a long-term relationship, working out how they were going to play all of this for the public. "They weren't ruling out foul play yet, that's what Officer Reynolds said."

"But there's no sign that it was anything other than a terrible tragedy," Roger said. "Surely—"

"They're not going to rule anything out until the autopsy's done," Ginny said. "They can't. But was there any sign of a disturbance? Locks broken, things missing?"

"Nothing." Nora shook her head. "The door was open, but there was no sign of anything being *wrong*."

"Were any of the animals upset?" Teddy asked, thinking of the way the dogs had behaved the day before.

"The animals?" All three of the shelter people looked at him, but Nora was the one who answered. "No; I checked on them as soon as I came down. Most of them were still asleep, and the ones who woke up when I turned on the light just thought breakfast had come early. The new dog in quarantine yowled at me, but I'd yowl, too, if I was stuck in there overnight."

"So anyone who might have been here last night had access—keys, and the security passcode—and knew enough not to upset the animals."

"Wait . . . you think that someone *here* stole the grant money? Someone who works here?" The thought distracted Roger entirely from the dead man just taken from the office behind them.

"Of course we do," Este said, acerbic. "If you'd been paying attention at all, you'd know that." She didn't let go of his hand, but the tone in her voice was that of someone who had just used up the last of her patience.

Couples squabbling. Teddy wanted no part of that, and from the way Nora moved ever so slightly away, neither did she. Known trouble in paradise? And if so, did that change anything?

"I think that assuming the two—the missing money and the death—are related is as bad an idea as assuming they're not," Ginny said, addressing Nora's comment. "Anyway, today's death, however tragic, isn't our concern. Teddy's and mine, I mean. That's for the police to investigate. We're here to find answers about the money."

"And that's not the same," Nora said. Her earlier fascination with murder seemed to have faded, faced with the practical demands of the shelter.

"No," Ginny said. "It's not. We're working for you, for the shelter. That's our only concern."

Something inside Teddy twitched at that—it sounded too much like Gin was promising them that they'd withhold anything that might make the shelter look bad, or . . . he didn't know what, but it was on a line he'd rather avoid. Money was one thing; dead bodies made him nervous.

Whatever she meant, it seemed to shut both Este and Roger down, and now they merely looked concerned. But there was something about them, the way they were frowning, clearly trying to think one step ahead of the situation, that bothered him. Something was off there. And it was more than a "being hauled out of bed to find out that a volunteer had died in your office" off.

Letting Ginny handle the ongoing discussion, Teddy stepped back mentally, and watched their body language.

"I'm still not sure that your continuing to work is a good

idea. The police will not want amateurs messing around," Roger said, preparing a brush-off, and Ginny nodded.

"Of course," she said, every inch the peacemaking professional. "And if this were an official murder investigation, we would not dream of muddying the waters with our own inquiry, if it seemed as though paths might cross. But you said that the police have indicated no reason to believe that it was anything other than a tragic accident, and have in fact said that you can reopen the shelter, and conduct business as usual?"

"Yes," Este said. "They don't want us using that office, but I don't think any of us could, right now. When they give the go-ahead, I'll have the office professionally cleaned and . . . painted maybe."

"And smudged," Nora suggested, and both of the founders nodded.

Nora had removed herself almost entirely from Teddy's field of vision; she was still there but on the outskirts. She might have hired them, but she'd given over all authority to Este, which made sense. Este was the one she had gone to, admitting what she had done. Este was the one still dealing with the day-to-day events, not Roger.

Este herself looked tired but firm, determined . . . but not pushing to have them continue the investigation the way Teddy would have expected, if this was a dominance fight.

"So there is no reason why we cannot continue our research into your problem," Ginny said, still trying to keep them on the job.

"I really don't think this is such a good idea," Roger countered. "No offense, Miss . . ."

"Mallard. Virginia Mallard."

That got Teddy's attention. He couldn't remember her ever using her legal name to introduce herself, not to anyone. Change in routine meant something. Usually it meant that Ginny had decided that she didn't like someone. What was going on?

"Miss Mallard. I'm not sure that's such a good idea."

"Let it go, Roger," Este said, although the tone of her voice said she wasn't happy, either. "I've already given them permission; if we stop them now it looks like we don't *want* the person taking the money to be found. And it's quite clear to me, at least, that we can't handle it internally. Discretion—people we hired, rather than complete outsiders—is the next-best thing. Especially, in light of . . . recent events."

Roger clamped down on whatever he was going to say, and looked mulish, but then nodded. "You're right, of course. As usual." He half turned his head and smiled at her, a grudging but affectionate expression. "I should just leave the shelter to you, entirely."

"Not a chance," she replied.

Teddy caught Ginny's eye and she nodded slightly. Time to go, before they were asked to leave.

"I hate to ask this, in the aftermath," Ginny said, "but we didn't have anything on Jimmy in the paperwork you gave us. Would it be possible—"

"He wasn't an employee, he wasn't even, technically,

a volunteer," Este said quickly. "He was just helping us out for a little while. . . . There really isn't any paperwork, other than the agreement he had us sign, to authorize him to"—her hand waved vaguely—"do what he did."

"His full name, at least, then, and the hours he regularly worked, and if you could show us where he worked?"

"Why?" Roger was still being prickly.

"Routine," Ginny said. "It helps us narrow our search if we can say for certain that everyone has been accounted for."

"They teach that in detective school, I guess," Este said, but her smile was tense. "James McAdams. Nora, if you could handle the rest of what they need? And if you'll excuse us, we need to talk to the rest of the staff when they get here, let them know what's happened."

The reminder of how early it was set off the urge to yawn again, and Teddy stifled it long enough to say goodbye, then gave in, enough that his jaw cracked, audibly.

"Sorry," he said, not at all apologetic, when Nora and Ginny both looked at him.

"Come on," Nora said. "I can show you . . . God. He died in the office he worked in. I don't think we're supposed to go in there, Este said?"

"It's okay," Ginny said. "We've seen dead bodies before. The spot where one fell isn't going to be much worse, and we won't touch anything."

Technically, they'd seen a dead body wheeled out of a hotel room on a gurney, after the paramedics were finished, which wasn't the same thing at all. But it sounded more hard-boiled the way Ginny said it.

As they left the lobby, the sound of an argument, low and bitter, started up again between the two founders. Teddy tried to hear what was being said, but then the sliding door shut behind them, and he couldn't hear anything more.

10

The dead man had, apparently, worked in Roger's office while the other man was on medical leave. There was yellow crime scene tape still dangling across the doorway, and Nora gave it a dubious look, but Ginny reached up and untied it, letting the end drop on the floor and stepping over it, Tonica on her heels and Nora a distant third.

It took all of three seconds for Nora to excuse herself and back out, looking distressed. The other two, not having known the dead man, felt no such hesitation.

The office was slightly smaller than Este's, and dustier around the edges from being abandoned for several months now, but otherwise similar in layout. One wall was filing cabinets, chest-high, and topped with banker boxes, while the other two walls were filled with framed certificates. Ginny stepped closer to examine them without touching: some were academic, some were job-related, some had to do with the sideline Tonica had told her about, the coffee-roasting place. He seemed very proud of the certificates they got from various food-rating organizations.

There were two photographs hung on the wall, mixed in with the certificates: one of the two founders, together, looking younger and grinning widely, and one of the entire staff standing in front of what she presumed was the newly opened shelter, a handful of dogs at their feet and several of the staffers holding cats.

"Who's that?" she asked, pointing to one of the men in the photo.

"Williams," Tonica said, coming around to look over her shoulder. "Scott Williams, the vet."

"Huh."

"What?"

"Oh, I'm just surprised that he's in a staff photograph. I guess he's been with them since the beginning, though, just like the others. And unlike the dead man. Last in, first out."

"Nice," Tonica said. He was looking at the desk; there was no chair, although there was a plastic chair mat that had seen hard use.

"They said the chair broke when he fell over. I guess they took it out as evidence."

"We're not here to investigate his death, Tonica," Ginny reminded him, even as she moved to stand behind him, trying to see what he was seeing.

"There's enough room for someone to stand behind him, pull him backward."

"Or to lean over the desk and push him backward, if they were big enough."

"If he hit his head hard enough, and then was left there

with a hemorrhage in his brain . . . This might not have been an accident, or a random tragedy."

"It's not our place to investigate. As you're fond of reminding me, we're not cops; we're not even licensed investigators. Dead bodies are for professionals."

"Right." But Tonica kept staring at the space where the chair had been.

"Teddy." She rarely called him by his name, so he looked up with a start. She pushed a wayward curl off her forehead and tried to tuck it back into the barrette it had escaped from. "Do you think he stole the money, and got killed for it?"

Tonica shrugged, and then ran a hand over his own brush-cut hair, as though it had somehow gotten mussed, too. "I don't know. Maybe. If the timing's wrong for Roger to be our thief, the timing's perfect for him. He came in late at night, when nobody else was around, he knew the money was here, because he was working the books, and there wasn't anyone to bother him. And he came into the picture at the right time, after Roger was out on sick leave, assuming Nora didn't miss earlier errors."

"I'm hearing a *but* in your voice."

"But. Yeah. If this guy was going to come in and skim, don't you think he'd do more damage? I mean, why only take a little at a time, when he could hide the entire thing going missing?"

Ginny considered that. "Maybe he stole for fun? Because the cash was there and he couldn't resist it? I know the statistics say that most people are honest, if only for fear of getting caught, but some people, they'd never think of robbing a bank or taking money out of someone's wallet, but when they see something they want, unguarded. . . ."

"Maybe."

Neither of them seemed to believe the dead man had been their thief, but there wasn't anything that conclusively said he wasn't.

"It's too easy," Tonica said, finally. "I'm not a believer in too easy."

"People are pretty simple," she said. "Sometimes, it's not so much easy as lazy. We take the quickest way to what we want. My father . . ." She stopped. "Okay, bad example, moving on. But it's entirely possible that this guy came in, saw that there was cash on hand, and figured he'd be in and out before anyone noticed. . . ."

"Except," she went on, seeing the flaw in her own theory immediately, "if he was a half-decent bookkeeper he'd know that someone would see that the money was missing, more or less immediately, because it had to be paid out on a regular basis, and there's no way to hide that it's missing. So a once-and-out would make more sense than a slow skim. Damn."

"This is why it's best to pay everyone in bank funds," Tonica said. "Under the table just always ends in headaches. Okay, first thing we need to find out was, was he a half-decent bookkeeper?"

"Let's go find out."

* * *

"Jimmy?" Margaret scrunched up her face as she thought, her usual overhappy personality subdued in light of the news. "I didn't know him well, only met him a time or two, but he seemed like a good guy."

Stephen, the older volunteer Teddy had met earlier, had been standing by the front desk, poking at the box of Danish someone had brought in and left there. When Tonica turned to him and asked the same question, he could only shrug and offer, "He was polite, the one time I met him, when he came on board. Quiet. I got the feeling he wasn't big on the socializing, so he'd mostly come when everyone was gone. I can't believe he's dead, poor man."

Ginny, with Georgie at her side, left Teddy to his interrogation and went in search of the vet tech, who had reportedly arrived while they were in the office. She found the other woman out back, watching some of the dogs roughhousing in the dog run. It was the shelter equivalent of a playground: a narrow concrete-floored courtyard with a dog-washing setup at one end, and a pile of old tires and well-chewed ropes at the other.

"Nope, I never met him," Alice, the vet tech, said. She had been called in to make sure none of the animals had been upset, and clearly wanted to deal with that, not answer questions. But she had been amenable to letting Georgie go play with the other dogs, so Ginny was inclined to like her. "But he had a good rep, and Este said we were lucky that he volunteered. Otherwise we'd have to hire someone, and decent accountants aren't cheap."

* * *

They needed somewhere to talk, away from the chaos of the shelter. Tonica had suggested Callie's Shack, the diner down the street.

"So the one thing we can say for certain," Tonica said, once they were settled in their booth, and his hands were wrapped around a mug of coffee like it was his lifeline, "is that James McAdams hadn't taken this job to expand his social network. He worked at Latham and Ford, previously. I suspect he considered most of the shelter workers, including Este, to be several steps down the ladder from the sort of company he was accustomed to."

Most of the time Ginny didn't think about it, but every now and then something Tonica did or said reminded her that his family, apparently, came from East Coast Money. Or at least East Coast Society. This was one of those moments: he not only recognized the name of the accountant's firm, but knew it well enough to extrapolate what sort of clients they had.

"And he didn't do it for the money," she said, tapping the rim of her tablet, placed well away from her coffee. "All I can find is the public record stuff, but he was well-paid, didn't have any obvious debt, and was living well within his means. Unless he had a secret blackmailer hidden somewhere, or a relative bleeding him dry . . ."

"Likelihood of that?"

"Anything's possible. But usually, after a while, rumors

float. He wasn't shiny-shiny—there was a newspaper article that quoted him as being part of a fracas at the local development meeting. Apparently he took objection to a restaurant in his neighborhood wanting to get a café permit."

"A fracas?"

"He shoved someone, who shoved back. I swear, grown men."

She moved her foot, half expecting to feel Georgie's bulk under the table, and then remembered that the shar-pei was back at the shelter, hanging out with the other dogs in the courtyard while they had a late breakfast. She really should try to find a playgroup for Georgie.

"I've seen worse over less," Tonica said, bringing her attention back to the discussion at hand. "But usually there's booze involved. Any charges filed?"

"None that show up on search." Ginny had no false modesty about her abilities in that regard: even if the charges had been dropped, she would have found a mention.

"Excuse me?"

A man stood next to them: older, white, and grizzled. He was wearing faded jeans and an equally faded blue denim shirt, but they were clean, and his remaining hair was neatly trimmed.

"You the two working for the animal shelter?"

Ginny had a moment of inner panic, and beat it down with a thick mental stick. "Depends on what you mean by 'working for,'" she said, pleased that her voice sounded cool and steady. "And who's asking."

She half expected the man to flash a badge, some kind of undercover cop who'd put them on the top of his list of suspects. Instead he just nodded and looked around as though afraid someone else was paying attention to them. Nobody was.

"My name's Paul. Paul Kelley. I work there, nights. Cleaning the cages."

"You're the one who adopted the two dogs," Tonica said.

Kelley looked surprised, then pleased. "Yeah, AJ and Max. Trouble with feet and fur, those two, but I never regretted it, not for a moment. But that ain't why I tracked you two down."

"Please, sit down," Ginny said, glancing at Tonica, who shoved over on the bench, giving the other man room to join them. The waitress came over, sensing another tip, and offered to refill their coffee.

"No, thank you, ma'am," Kelley said, and waited until she retreated back to her corner to go on. "I work nights. Late nights, early morning, really. Been doing it since they opened, three–four years now. Seen staff come and go, seen things . . . heard things."

"Things you should maybe go to the police about?" Tonica asked.

"Maybe. Maybe not. I didn't see anything, and they mostly want to know about *seen*."

"But you heard something?" Ginny sneaked a look to see what Tonica was doing, what his body language said. He'd told her once, after a few drinks, that she got too intense, scared people away from talking, so she wanted to copy what he was doing. But no, he was sitting forward, too, intent on the man's next words.

"Heard . . . Yes, ma'am. I heard things. The past couple–three months, there've been noises when it shoulda been quiet. I know Jimmy was in some nights, he'd come by to let me know he was there, so I wouldn't get spooked." That seemed to amuse Kelley. "Good man, he was. Damned shame."

"But you heard these noises over a period of months?" The same time period, according to Nora, that the money had gone missing.

"I did. And . . . there were nights, the animals were all twitchy. Like they could smell something wrong on the road up ahead. I listen to it when dogs get upset, but ma'am, sir, I listen real hard when cats are upset."

"What sort of noises," Ginny asked, even as Tonica said, "Where did the noises come from?"

He had the better question, she admitted.

"There's the thing," Kelley said. "Different noises, from different places. None of it from the areas I've got access to; otherwise I'd have gone and checked 'em out. Nothing messes with the four-foots while I'm there, and if there'd been something wrong and I didn't see what's what, I'm not doing my job."

His job, Ginny recalled, involved disinfecting the floors and emptying cages, and sorting out the trash and recycling. Not patrolling the building. That was what they had a security guard for, technically.

"One of the noises, I figured was never-my-mind, if you know what I mean." His grizzled face lit in what Ginny could only call a reminiscent smile. "From the main office that was, couple–three times."

Never-his . . . Ginny blanked, and then his expression tipped her off. Oh. Tonica still looked puzzled, though, so she filled in the blanks.

"Someone was using their access to avoid paying for a hotel room?"

"Two someones, ma'am, and I would not venture to accuse anyone but . . . they didn't sound like they needed a third interfering."

"But that wasn't what had the animals upset."

"No, sir. That was the nights the noises came from the clinic wing, the office itself. I don't have the keys to go in there, on account of there being drugs and whatnot stored there. I don't want any part of that, but a few times I'd walk by, after, to see if there was anything I saw out of place, worth writing up to Ms. Este about."

"Was there?"

He shook his head. "Once, I ran into a couple kids, hightailing it out of the parking lot, the one the volunteers and delivery trucks use. But kids, they're always hightailing it out of somewhere. No broken windows, no damage I could see. Bunch of papers scattered, like somebody's upended the recycling bin, so I dumped them in the trash and went home.

"There was one night, though . . . there was a light on

in the clinic. At three in the morning, there shouldn't be any lights on save the security lights, and those're red, not white. I may be getting old but I know the difference."

He might be getting old, but Ginny would have hired him in a minute, if she had actual staff. This one conversation had given them more information than talking to the entire daytime staff, Este and Roger included.

"And that's all I have. You two have a good day."

"Wait, is there somewhere we can reach you, if we need more information, or . . . anything else?"

Kelley stared at her a long minute, then, apparently deciding that she was worthy of such information, fished a pen out of his shirt pocket and scratched something down on the clean napkin in front of her.

"You can reach me there," he said, and turned and walked away.

She glanced at the phone number, then turned to look back at him, but he had already left the small café.

"Well. That was interesting," Tonica said. "Especially in light of what I saw the other day with the vet."

"What?"

"The way the animals reacted to the vet? Maybe it wasn't him. If there was something happening in the building, enough to make them twitchy, then they could still be upset come the morning."

"Oh, right. Yeah." She shook her head, annoyed at herself for having forgotten that. "But if something was happening in the clinic, Teddy, then it has nothing to do with our investigation of money gone missing from the office. Or what happened to the bookkeeper." She frowned, and stared down at the napkin. "Does it?"

Tonica toyed with the remains of his eggs, then finally put his fork down, no longer hungry. "You noticing that the more we look under the surface, the more stuff floats up?"

"I'm trying not to," Ginny said. "I'm trying really hard not to."

Back at the shelter, it seemed almost like a normal day: Margaret, behind the front desk, was slightly subdued, but there were cats sleeping and playing in the socialization room, an unfamiliar older woman in there with them, while a small, short-legged dog with a black and white coat was keeping Georgie company in the lobby. Stephen came out to greet a young woman waiting in the lobby, and Teddy was pretty sure he blanched when he saw the two of them waiting there.

"Just here to collect Georgie," Ginny was saying to Margaret, even as the shar-pei abandoned the other dog and came to stand by her legs, leaning against her so heavily she almost fell over. "Georgie, sweetie, I wasn't gone that long. Relax."

"And we'd like to have a word with Roger and Este," Teddy said. "If they're still here?"

They were. They didn't look particularly happy to be interrupted, either; apparently the argument hadn't been settled. Or it had and neither of them had won.

"I had a question about—"

Este interrupted him. "I think maybe it's best if you simply ended the investigation."

"What?"

"Let it go. There's been so much . . . in light of this recent tragedy, it's best if we simply move on."

"The money is still missing," Ginny said sharply.

Este swallowed. "We know. We'll find a way to replace it. Take out a loan, if need be. If anyone asks . . . we'll say that Jimmy took it."

Teddy had heard a lot of justifications in his life, but that one staggered him. "You'd libel a dead man, throw his reputation in the trash, to avoid a little bad publicity?"

"Jimmy would be okay with that. He believed in the shelter. That's why he volunteered here."

"We could hold a fund-raiser in Jimmy's name," Roger said, and it was clear that they'd already discussed this. "Bill it as a way to remember him, raise the money that way. We could raise more than a few thousand dollars, I bet."

"You know that whoever took the money won't just disappear," Ginny said. "In fact, you'll be encouraging him to take more, by covering it up."

"We won't keep cash in the building anymore," Este said. "Roger and I have agreed on that. Scott will have to be paid by check, same as everyone else."

Too little, too late, Teddy thought.

"So thank you, but we won't be needing your help any longer," Roger said, giving them the smoothest bum's rush Teddy had ever seen or experienced, escorting them out of the office, through the lobby, and out to the parking lot without giving them a chance to protest or any of them looking rude to observers.

The door closed behind him, and Ginny and Teddy were left blinking at each other.

"Well," Teddy said, at a loss.

"We don't work for him," Ginny pointed out, ever practical. "Or Este."

Teddy had to, reluctantly, give her that. And neither of them was good at giving up, not once the puzzle had started.

"It seems wrong not to find out what happened. I mean, they're being naïve, thinking that if they just replace the money, no harm, no foul. Anyone who gets away with it will just feel emboldened, right? So more things could go wrong, and hurt the shelter."

At their feet, Georgie looked back at the kennel wing, and let out a low woof, as though agreeing with her mistress.

"What if Nora agrees with him, and tells us to stop investigating?"

Ginny looked at him with wide, utterly innocent hazel eyes, a look that made knowledgeable men step back. "We don't ask her."

Penny had come down to the shelter, hoping to sniff around a little more, when she saw them standing on the sidewalk in front of the building, Georgie with them. She folded herself around the corner of the building and hissed lightly, pitching it for a dog's ears, not humans. Georgie looked up and saw her, and let out a low woof of greeting, mixed with the suggestion of something new learned, something new to tell.

Something had happened. Not bad, or the humans would be reacting differently, and Georgie would be upset. But something enough to get them here . . . but in the wrong place.

Penny hissed again, and stepped forward, her tail erect and her head held high, just enough for Georgie to see her, and then faded out of sight.

Another low woof told her that the message had been received, and then there were the sounds of humans talking, Herself trying to scold Georgie as the dog tugged at the leash, pulling her toward the corner of the building where Penny had just left her scent.

"Georgie, sweetie, where are you going?"

And then Theodore, his voice a comforting rumble next to the woman's higher voice: "That's the clinic wing. I wouldn't have thought she'd be so eager to head back there."

"Hush." The woman was laughing: good. Humans were easier when they were happy. "She probably scented something. A squirrel, maybe. She's just discovered squirrels. Or—"

They came around the corner, and Penny waited, confident that neither human would see her in the underbrush.

"What is it, Georgie? Suddenly you think this parking lot would be better to do your business in? Or—"

"Gin." Theodore's voice, solemn. "Look."

Penny preened her whiskers, satisfied in her choice of humans. You had to lead them to it, sometimes, but they picked up the scent reasonably well after that.

* * *

"At what?" Ginny tugged at Georgie's leash again, then realized that Tonica was staring at the same wall Georgie seemed fascinated by. "What?"

"Does that look like someone tried to wash off graffiti, to you?"

She looked, then shrugged. "Yeah." Then she looked again. "Yes. And recently, too. Funny that nobody mentioned graffiti."

"Well, no reason to, really," Tonica said. "We get a smattering of it on the back wall at Mary's, sometimes the front window. Mostly kids leaving tags, trying to be gangster, or someone being a wiseass after a few too many drinks."

Ginny stepped closer to the wall, tracing her fingers along the faded lettering. Pale pink, which meant that it had probably been red at first. Georgie pressed against her legs, as though trying to get her to move, but Ginny flicked the leash gently, and the dog sat down with a muffled sigh.

"Let not the innocent be . . . replaced? Reduced? Renounced?" She scowled at it as though daring the words to make sense. "That's not the usual kind of slogan of a drunk."

"No." Tonica stood next to her, studying it, too. "And the writing's too even—usually by that point they can't paint a straight line. And it's not a gang tag, either."

She didn't ask how he knew about gang tags. "But the shelter folk were determined to erase it totally, even back here where most folk wouldn't see. So what is it, and who put it there?"

"You think it's relevant to what we're investigating? C'mon, Ginny. Kelley said he chased kids away from here, remember? This could just be more of that."

Georgie whined again, but didn't move from her spot on the ground.

"I don't know," Ginny said. "But right now, we can't afford to ignore anything. And if it isn't part of our case . . ." She paused, then added, "We can mention it to the cops. As concerned citizens."

"Este and Roger won't like that," Tonica said.

"Right now, I'm not finding myself overly concerned with what Este and Roger want. You?"

He shook his head slowly. He was all for making lemonade out of lemons, but there were limits, and the way Roger and Este had been willing to use the dead man didn't sit right with him. He was glad that he and Ginny were in agreement on that.

11

They stood in the back parking lot, contemplating the graffiti and their own thoughts until a truck rumbled by, the noise breaking the moment.

Teddy looked at his watch, then at his partner. "You going home?"

Ginny nodded, and then shrugged. "Probably. Easier to work on the desktop, for some of this stuff." But she didn't sound enthusiastic about it.

"Look, let's swing by your place and pick up your laptop, and go to Mary's. It's delivery day, so Seth will be there, and Stacy's working this afternoon. You can work there. It only makes sense, so we can discuss the job in person, rather than trying to text or email."

He waited while she considered the options. He could tell when she'd decided to give in.

"Yeah, all right. You're right." She didn't sound too grudging about it, either. She must be as tired as she looked, her curls falling out of her clip, the somber clothes making her look oddly washed-out.

Leaving a message for Nora to get in touch with them when she got off shift, the three of them—Teddy, Ginny, and Georgie—piled into Teddy's coupe. By now the shar-pei seemed to accept the small backseat as her due, settling on the upholstery like it was her dog bed back home. She stayed there while Ginny ran inside at her apartment to collect her laptop, and Teddy found himself reaching backward between the front seats to rub at the wrinkled skin of her head.

"What do you think, pup?" he asked. "Did the dead guy take the money? Did our client? Or do you think it just slipped behind a credenza, and the cleaning lady found it?"

A blue-black tongue swiped at his hand, and he pulled it back, grimacing. "Thanks, dog," he said, rubbing it dry against his jeans. "Score one for cats." Penny occasionally groomed him, but her tongue was raspy and dry, not sloppy-wet.

The passenger-side door opened and Ginny slid back in, her computer bag on her lap and a dark purple bag in her hand that Teddy recognized as holding Georgie's assorted bowls and toys. "Right. Let's go."

Mary's wasn't officially open yet, but there were lights on behind the blinds covering the plate glass front, and the red-painted door was unlocked.

"You realize, of course," Ginny was saying as they walked in, "that people are going to start thinking I work here, I'm in place so often when you guys open. Hi, Stacy."

"Hey, Georgie!" Stacy cried out a welcome from behind

the bar, only adding, almost as an afterthought, "Hi, Ginny!"

"And I don't even get a hello?" Teddy groused, bring up the rear.

"Hey, boss. Sorry, boss." Stacy didn't sound sorry.

She was here way too early, and from the way she was looking over the clipboard in front of her, she'd come in to get a jump on the afternoon's shift. If Teddy actually was the boss, he'd be thinking about promoting her to nights, and icing their current off-nights bartender to afternoons.

But that wasn't his decision. Anyway, Jon wasn't going to last long—his behavior last Friday night had been a serious warning sign of someone who thought too highly of himself for teamwork—and then maybe they'd be able to promote her. Or maybe she'd quit, too. If Patrick kept giving them shit . . .

"You do work here," he said to Ginny. "In fact, we're thinking of putting your name on one of the stools. 'Here rests the second-most-winning cheeks of trivia night.'"

"Excuse me?" Her eyes widened, even as she slid onto one of those stools. "Whose team beat the pants off yours last time?"

"Only because I missed that night. We'll see who's smirking tomorrow night."

She let that drop, and pulled her tech out of her bag—phone, netbook, charger—and started setting up on the bartop.

Georgie, allowed into the bar rather than left in her usual spot outside, had immediately headed for the wooden banquette against the far wall, settling underneath it with a tired sigh. Teddy guessed getting up at 5 a.m. wasn't her idea of fun, either.

"I need to set up," Ginny was saying. "Password still the same?"

"If we ever changed it, we'd all be screwed because nobody would remember the new one," Stacy said cheerfully. "You want your usual?"

"Please."

Ginny's usual, before sundown, was a ginger ale with lime, in a highball glass. She'd told Teddy once that if she drank soda in a soda glass in a bar, people gave her shit. If they thought it was booze, they left her alone.

"Where's Seth?" he asked Stacy, looking around the bar. The deliveries were due soon; he'd have thought the old man would be fussing in back by now.

"Called in sick," she said, her voice muffled as she bent below the bar, checking on supplies.

"What?" Seth hadn't been sick a day since Teddy had started working at Mary's. Seth didn't *get* sick. He would take it as a personal affront if a cold germ dared land on him, much less take up residence.

"That's what he said." She popped up again, placing a box of swivel sticks on the counter and opening it up. "Sick."

Teddy scratched at his shoulder, frowning. "He sound sick?"

"Not really, no. If it were anyone else I'd say he was slacking off. But, y'know, Seth. So I'm covering for him, since you said Useless wasn't supposed to sign for anything. But hey, now that you're here. . . ."

"Right. You need anything hauled up from the back?" Normally he wouldn't dare imply a woman couldn't handle a job—he had too many sisters and female cousins to be that dumb—but he had at least forty pounds and five inches on the younger woman, and a case of booze was heavy.

"Nope, I'm good. I don't know what we're going to do about the kitchen, though."

"Mondays tend to be slow," he said. "We just tell 'em the kitchen's closed, or even more limited than usual. I can whip up something later." So much for his day off. He really should know better than to show up when he wasn't on the schedule. "Meanwhile, I'm starving. Think Jilly's is open yet?"

"It's not even noon," Stacy said. "Maybe, I don't know. Don't you ever eat breakfast?"

He decided against telling her that he had been hauled out of bed at 5 a.m. on his day off. "Nope, just coffee this morning." Callie's Shack was known for three things: her coffee, her history, and breakfast platters meant to feed the fishermen and lumberjacks who used to work this section of Seattle. They were filling, but greasy as hell, and he wanted his arteries to see forty unimpaired.

"Jilly's opens at one," Ginny said. "But there's usually someone in there early. If you go and make piteous faces at them, maybe they'll have sympathy and throw you a burger." She looked up from her tablet and saw their expressions. "What? I've lived here longer than either of you. There are some things I know that you don't."

Tonica chose not to debate that fact, just took their orders and slipped back out the front door, making sure to close it carefully behind him.

Ginny heard the click and looked up, then exchanged a glance with Stacy, who shrugged a shoulder as though to say that she wasn't responsible for anything the boss did, and went back to counting glassware.

Not too long ago, Mary's front door would have been wedged open with a chair when someone was setting up but the bar wasn't open yet, letting fresh air in—and, Ginny suspected, giving Penny the resident feline an easier entrance than whatever cat-sized route she normally took. But then, a few months ago, during their first case, two well-dressed thugs had taken advantage of that open-door policy to attack her, Tonica, and Stacy. Georgie had saved them—Georgie, and Stacy's surprising skills at wrestling takedowns—but Ginny hadn't seen the chair since then, no matter how nice the day. The door was still unlocked, though, when they had come in. Anyone could have come in.

Tonica had locked it when he went out, just then.

Ginny thought about getting annoyed at him for being overprotective, then remembered how terrified they'd all been when the two goons showed up with guns. She decided she didn't mind the extra caution, at all.

"That door, you really shouldn't," she said, and stopped, not sure if she had the right to lecture Stacy at all.

Stacy sighed. "Yeah, I know. Especially without Seth here. I just . . . yeah. Okay. Promise, next shift, even if Seth *is* here. The door stays locked until we open."

"Maybe you can get Patrick to get windows that open," Ginny suggested, logging into the bar's network. "Instead of a patio, or whatever, just give us some air flow inside, if the door's going to be closed?"

"Patrick? Spend money?"

"Tonica said he had architects in . . ." Ginny said, but Stacy shook her head.

"Boss was yanking someone's chain," the other woman said. "He's about making money, not spending it."

Ginny couldn't argue with that, so she let the topic drop and went back to what she had been doing. Pulling up a browser, she entered "Let not the innocent" into her search engines, and waited, sipping at her drink while the machine worked.

Most of being a good researcher was getting a sense for what "information clutter" you could ignore. A broad search returned too much: you had to winnow it down. She looked at the first batch of returns. Religious quotes, maybe. Historical quotes. . . . Roman? Probably not, but couldn't be ignored. Fan fiction? Ginny checked the source, and then shook her head. Highly unlikely. But that still left too many options to check easily, and none of them seemed to scream out as relevant to an animal shelter.

Maybe it wasn't relevant. Maybe they had someone channeling Cicero, or the Old Testament. Seattle was definitely not immune to either classicists or religious nuts. Or, for that matter, fan fiction. She needed to check anything that looked viable, to remove the possibility.

"Let not the innocent be re," she typed in this time, giving the search the option to fill in the last word, which had been cleaned up on the wall beyond legibility.

She barely had time to take a sip of her drink before a new batch of returns appeared on her screen. She scanned them, and her eye stopped, four lines down.

"Let not the innocent be reduced," she read out loud.

"What?" Stacy looked up, but Ginny flapped a hand at her, indicating it was nothing. With her other hand, she tapped on that link.

"Let not the innocent be reduced!" the banner screamed, over a picture of the sweetest, most appealing puppies and kittens Hallmark could ever have concocted, all fluff, tails, and oversized, pleading eyes. She forced her gaze off the banner, and started to read the text.

"Oh, lovely," she muttered, wishing she'd gone for something alcoholic. "I just got crazy-bingo."

Nora got off work at 4 p.m., officially. She showed up at Mary's at 4:40. She was wearing different clothes than that morning, so Teddy suspected she'd gone home and taken a shower first. He didn't blame her.

Ginny had taken Georgie for a walk around the block, so Teddy saw their client come in and look around, clearly searching for Ginny's blond curls and not finding them. It was before the postwork rush, such as it was on Monday, so there weren't many people—he had been prepping the kitchen to cover for Seth while Stacy handled the bar. He'd called Clive's cell phone and left him a message to come in to cover the back after 7 p.m., when things got busier. The kid would welcome the extra money, probably, and he could plate up prepared food without too much trauma. Hopefully.

For now, everything was under control, so he wiped his hands down on the bar rag and flipped it back over his shoulder, then waved Nora over. She seemed relieved to see him; he figured at this point, any familiar face was a friendly one.

"It was insane today," she said, sitting down on the stool and planting her elbows on the bartop. Her usual perk had faded considerably, and her gaze skipped over the taps and went straight to the bottles behind him.

"Rough day," he said sympathetically.

"Yeah. And whatever you said to Roger and Este didn't help. They were yelling at each other all morning, and then not talking to each other at all, all afternoon. I would not want to be living in that house right now. Give me a vodka sour."

Teddy could tell a great deal about someone by what they drank, but he tried not to judge.

"What were they yelling about?"

"I don't know," she said, shrugging, watching him mix her drink. "When they get that mad, they start yelling in Swedish."

"Swedish?"

"I think so. Maybe Danish?" She shrugged. "Lots of folk around here come from there, and Este's family's been here since forever. It's not German."

"They both speak it?

"Roger not so fluently, but yeah. I think they use it like my folks used to use pig Latin, when I was a kid: so people can't understand private conversations."

His parents had done that, too, until his middle sister accidentally let them know that all the kids had learned it in self-defense, years ago. Interesting, though. There had definitely been trouble on that front, but the shouting was an escalation.

"How is everyone else holding up?" He put her drink down in front of her and waited.

"Once the shock wore off, everyone was okay. I mean, it's not like anyone really knew Jimmy, except in passing, maybe."

"Because he worked at night."

Ginny came in, sans Georgie, and saw them immediately. She came up behind Nora and slipped onto the empty stool next to her, without saying anything.

"Yeah." Nora didn't seem to notice Ginny's arrival. "I

guess Paul, that's our janitor, might've actually said more than 'hi' and 'bye' to him. But Paul's working in the kennels, the outside area, and the dog run. He wouldn't go into the office, except when he had to report—"

She stopped, and he heard the same automatic jaw-clamp that Margaret had done a few days before. This time he didn't let it go.

"When what?"

"Nothing."

"Nora." He pitched his voice low, commiserating but stern, and she made an unhappy face, but shook her head, not saying anything.

"Nora. Does it have anything to do with the graffiti on the clinic wall?" Ginny asked. "Has the shelter been targeted?"

"I . . ."

There were times you waited for someone to spill their guts, and times you had to hook it out of them. "Este told everyone not to talk about it, didn't she?" Teddy said. "That's why everyone got so skittish. It wasn't the money that had her stressed, it was the graffiti? The clinic's being targeted by protesters?"

Nora nodded, still looking miserable.

"Antineutering." Teddy was still having trouble getting around that idea, despite Ginny's having shown him the website. "Like it's some kind of noble thing, to let your pets breed endlessly?"

"They're a little crazy," Nora said, her misery sliding into indignation. "They think it's cruel or inhumane or something to interfere with the natural breeding cycle. Like animals are still in the wild and need to have a litter of ten just to make sure two or three survive, or . . ."

"Yeah, their website was pretty clear on their philosophy," Ginny said dryly. "'Free the Womb' was a catchy slogan; I'm surprised the anti-choice protesters haven't picked it up."

Nora continued the litany of offenses, clearly glad of the chance to vent. "They've hit us a few times before, but usually it's pamphlets, sometimes a 'no spay' sign sprayed on the wall, once a window got broken and they left their brochures in the waiting room, but this one, last week, was worse. Doc Williams found the graffiti there, it was all over the wall, and some kind of sticky paint, gross. He saw it and called Este . . . the same morning you met her."

"So they tried to wash it off, and pretend it didn't happen . . . why?" Ginny tapped her fingers on the counter, a restless move that meant she was thinking hard. She pulled her tablet out of her bag and pulled up a screen—Teddy couldn't see if it was the Spreadsheet of Doom, or something else.

"Roger said, first time they came around, that we should ignore them. The cops said they couldn't do anything, they had the right to be there, so long as they didn't bother anyone. I guess Este figured that went for the graffiti, too."

"Not a bad theory, normally," Teddy said. "But you guys have been having a run of serious bad luck, and if this all started with the protesters . . . maybe it's time to do more than ignore them. It did start with protesters?"

"Three or four of them, yeah. Handing out pamphlets in front of the shelter, first, trying to convince people coming in to refuse the low-cost neutering. It didn't work, mostly, but it was . . . annoying. And then they started papering the clinic with their flyers, and then with the graffiti."

"And the cops knew?" Ginny was making notes on her tablet—at least he assumed that was what she was doing; her fingers were moving faster than he could ever have managed.

"Yes. That's why they came out so fast, when Jimmy died. Because it might have been something, but it wasn't. There wasn't any sign of break-in or struggle, so they're ruling it an accident, or maybe natural—you were right, they have to wait for the autopsy report before they'll tell us anything officially, but they pretty much said it was just bad luck he died there, and not at home." She made a face, as though aware of how callous that sounded.

"There were never any actual problems with these loons, I mean, other than the annoyance factor?" Teddy asked, while Ginny kept tapping at her tablet.

Nora shook her head. "No. They're crazy, I mean stupid-crazy, and annoying, but harmless. Even though Este wants to kick them all into tomorrow for the cost of cleaning up after."

"Harmless—you mean they're not physically threatening anyone, or making them feel threatened?" Ginny asked, not looking up from her tablet. "But crazy-dedicated to their cause?"

By now Nora had finished her drink and was seriously

looking like she was considering another. Teddy pulled a glass of water and set it next to her instead.

She looked at it and made a face, but took a sip anyway. "Yeah . . . pretty much."

"Dedicated enough to break into the shelter and steal the money expressly earmarked to pay for neutering, and leave everything else alone?" Ginny pressed.

"Oh. Oh . . . dear." Nora clearly hadn't thought of that. She took another sip of water. "How would they know, though? And how would they get into the inner office? We lock that."

An insider told them. Teddy figured Ginny was thinking the same thing.

"We did have a set of keys go missing, about six–seven months ago. But in the chaos after Roger got sick, we just thought that they'd gotten misplaced."

Ginny and Teddy exchanged glances over her head, and he shook his head. If people would just *tell* them things, this wouldn't be so hard.

As though sensing their annoyance, Nora paid for her drink and left, not even asking what they were planning to do. Probably, Teddy thought, because at this point, she didn't want to know. What had seemed like a small, serious problem had exploded into an entire can of worms, and he couldn't blame her for not wanting anything to do with any of it. At least she had the sense to know they couldn't just be ignored.

"All right," Ginny said, finally. "So the first thing is, find out more about our spray-painting pamphlet-happy fanatics, maybe shake them down and see if anything falls out."

"You are definitely cut off of those detective movies," he muttered, already knowing who was going to be volunteered for shakedown duty.

Penny sat above the humans, hidden from sight on top of the liquor displays, and cleaned her whiskers thoughtfully. She didn't understand much of what humans did, but they seemed to be chasing their tails on this, rather than their noses, despite everything she'd done.

She needed to talk to Georgie. Maybe the dog would have a better idea of how to get them to pay attention to the right things.

Silently as she came, Penny turned around in the cramped space and slid through the unfinished crawlspace that led to a small, decorative window. It was stuck open just enough to let one small cat through, an easy leap from a tree on the street—and she made sure that no squirrels or birds thought they could claim it.

The air smelled like decay and cold, the sun still high enough to reach over the buildings, but not casting any warmth on the ground. It was easier to move at dusk or night, but a cat did as a cat must.

The others at the shelter were counting on them.

12

Is this your first meeting? Welcome!"

The woman standing at the door, handing out pamphlets and greeting people as they came in, had short faux-red hair that had been chemically treated too many times, and a face that had seen too much sun. Teddy took one of the pamphlets automatically, grunted at the greeting, and went inside the meeting hall—really just the basement of the local Y, set up with chairs in the center, a chalkboard at the far end where, he guessed, the speakers would be speaking, and a table at the far back that seemed to hold the inevitable snacks.

There were about thirty chairs set up, and half of them were filled. He'd expected to see earnest young people, straight out of college or maybe still students, but there were a number of older men there, too, and a few women clearly out of their twenties, scattered throughout. Most were white, a few were black, and at a quick scan none of them looked either poor or wealthy, not that you could tell much from people's clothing around here. Although Ginny probably could.

It made sense, though. Worrying about the animal population was a middle-class thing.

The slogan "Free to Breed" was written on the chalkboard, and a tall woman was standing by it, talking intently to two younger people, a boy and a girl, definitely college-aged, who seemed to be hanging on to her every word.

Teddy had agreed to come scope the meeting out, to see if their vandals let anything slip, see what he could pick up by watching them in their native habitat. Ginny had suggested it was because he was better at reading people—although she was getting better, he would give her that—but he had agreed without too much argument because he had some small sympathy for the group.

Not the unrestricted breeding—he didn't think that was smart for anyone, human or four-foots—but being against the way that humans tried to regulate animals . . . yeah. He would, under pressure, admit to being Penny's human, and that she was his cat, but the idea of putting a collar on her and chipping her, of claiming ownership and control over another creature, still bothered him a little. He knew he had issues, he was okay with his issues, thank you very much.

So, yeah, he'd volunteered to come and scout out their vandals and see what was up. And part of him hoped really they weren't the guilty parties in the shelter case.

Then the room settled and the tall woman got up and started to speak. By the time she introduced their guest, a doctor of something-or-other specializing in "wild psychology," Teddy had decided that everyone in the room might not be criminals, but they were definitely wackos.

Not spaying or neutering house pets was just the start. They not only wanted animals to be free to breed; they wanted animals in the zoos to be freed, too. Teddy wasn't a big fan of cages, but he was pretty sure he'd read somewhere that most endangered species survived only because of the breeding populations in major zoos, worldwide.

Also, turn them loose *where*? He didn't think giraffes or rhinos would fare well in downtown Seattle, although the thought of a lion pride roaming the Market had a certain sick appeal, especially on high-tourist days.

Shaking his head slightly, he tried to make himself comfortable on the folding chair and turned his attention to the crowd. He didn't think any of them would be holding up signs saying, "I broke into the shelter and stole money and/or knocked the bookkeeper over the head," but you never knew what people would admit to if they didn't know you were watching.

The woman on the business end of the desk glanced at the papers in front of her, and then looked sternly at Ginny. "You have permission to show me these?"

Ginny had learned not to squirm under direct interrogation by the time she was eleven. "We were asked to look into some financial irregularities. How was left to my discretion."

Wendy raised an eyebrow but didn't push. Ginny breathed a sigh of relief. Technically, nothing she had said was a lie. But it wasn't exactly truthful, either. Tonica would probably disapprove, but Tonica wasn't there.

Wendy made a noncommittal hrmm noise and went back to studying the ledgers Ginny had printed out for her. There was a plate shoved to the side of her desk, with the remains of dinner long since cooled. Ginny knew that the other woman had done her a favor, meeting with her tonight, but she still had this urge to push for a response. She sat on it for another ten minutes, then asked, "Well?"

"Mallard, this isn't like doing a crossword puzzle. It's going to take me some time. Chill. Better yet, go home and I'll call you when I have something." Wendy had been her CPA for almost a decade; they'd long ago given up on any pretense of business politeness. They were sitting in her office downtown, the quiet hum of other late workers barely audible on the other side of the door.

"How long do you *think*?" Ginny asked.

Wendy scowled at the papers, and then looked up over the rims of her glasses at Ginny. "If there's anything obviously fishy, I'll know soon enough. Tomorrow, probably. Or Wednesday, if something else more urgent comes up. Or is there a time frame you need them by? Is the IRS waiting to swoop down on someone?"

"No." Ginny shook her head. She wanted an answer, she wanted to get this job moving again, but unlike the investigation into the bookkeeper's death, this wasn't a life-or-death matter.

Except for the animals who might not have a home for much longer, if the shelter lost funding. Ginny thought of Georgie, looking at her with those big brown eyes, just a half-grown puppy being held in someone else's arms, and set her jaw. Nobody else might care, the founders might want to sweep it under the table, but she *would* solve this.

Penny would rather have been curled up in the Busy Place, watching her humans, staying dry and warm. But there were still things that needed to be done. The old hound let her in through the hole in the gate again, touching her briefly with his nose in greeting. It was last walks of the night for the shelter dogs—most of them were taking advantage, chasing an old tennis ball around the court, while one of the humans watched, occasionally throwing a new ball in to even the score a little.

"Been a little crazy around here," the hound said. "One of the night-humans died."

"I know," Penny said, settling down next to the dog and watching the activity in the courtyard. "You hear or smell anything that night?"

"Not like the bad smell," he said. "Nothing smelled wrong. But someone was here, yeah. Sometimes humans come in, do things."

"Who? And do what?"

The hound shrugged. "Humans. Two voices, thumping, sometimes. Sometimes one voice, talking. That's all we could tell. Humans do odd things. Maybe the cats know more; you should go talk to them."

She could, and she would, but it wouldn't do much good. Cats didn't pay as much attention to unclaimed humans as dogs did, and if they'd heard something they would have sent word. Still, leave no corner unmarked.

Leaving the dogs to their play, she slipped into the building proper, following her nose to where the cats were kept. There were only seven cats in the shelter: several had been adopted over the weekend, and no new ones had been brought in. Three of the cats were kittens; they were curious about this stranger walking freely, but their brains were more focused on food and play than remembering anything useful, and they were sleepy-tired this late, ready to curl up in a pile while the elders spoke.

The other four cats came to the front of their cages when Penny called to them, paws sliding underneath the wire rims, ears forward-alert.

"Took your time getting here," the silver tabby said.

"Dogs take more coaxing, to get something useful out of them," Penny replied. "And none of you were coming forward, either." They had less chance, less freedom to roam, true, but she knew that wouldn't stop a cat determined to leave. "What do you have?"

"You know about the night-human dying."

"Yes."

"The dark smell was back, a couple days ago." The little black and white female crouched low and kept her voice down. "All over the big man and his things."

"But not the other man," an orange male added. "He didn't come here, but the dogs said he smelled like cat, and okay things."

"That was my human," Penny said. "He came here to investigate."

There was a rattling noise, like someone coming in through the door. Penny pressed against the wall, ready to flee if needed, but whoever it was passed on by without walking down the hallway.

"That's the only new scent," the silver tabby said. "There was yelling last night, but there's always yelling."

"Always?" Penny had found that humans didn't yell more often than they did, and when they did there was something to pay attention to.

The silver tabby hit the back of her cage with her tail, causing a hollow thump. "They're just on the other side," she said. "When they talk it's a rumble. When they yell, we hear. And they thump, too. Two of them, but last time it was three. But they weren't the dark smell."

Penny's own tail twitched, and she groomed her whiskers to give her time to think. The shelter inmates were so focused on the dark smell, and how unhappy it made them, they didn't think about anything else. If it didn't smell wrong, it didn't connect. Penny, though, was making connections.

After a year of the Busy Place, she knew how humans worked. When a place was open, there were people. Noises, and voices and smells and activity. Then they turned out the lights and everyone went away. No noises. No voices.

Why were humans coming back, yelling and thumping, when the lights were out?

The shelter cats couldn't give her anything more, so she found a place in the main area, the faint reassuring smell of Georgie still lingering in the carpet, and curled in an alcove behind a plant, watching through half-slitted eyes as the humans did their things, and then turned out the lights and left. She waited a little longer, and then slid out from her hiding place, stretching and scenting the air.

You had to look for it, faded and not-fresh, but the dark scent lingered. Unpleasant, and unnerving. Like the others, her hackles rose instinctively. She padded over to the door where the dark scent came from, and pushed at it. The door didn't move. She had already tried to find other ways in, from the outside, but it was better built than the other wing; there was no access. Even the humans had lingered outside, unable to go in, even when they poked at the wall and considered the door.

Penny considered the scent, and decided that she didn't really want to go in there anyway. Instead she crossed the space again and put her paw to the groove in the wall, shoving the door aside and sliding into the office behind, where the cats had heard thumping, and the night-human had died. Humans thought they hid things, but the scents gave them away. If Theodore had a better nose, he wouldn't waste so much time looking.

Inside, her whiskers twitched almost immediately. Not a dark scent, but something like it. Heavy and musky and not-usual. Anything not-usual needed to be investigated, to make sure it wasn't connected to the dark scent.

Not in the larger space: that smelled of normal human sweat and skin, food, dust, metal. Usual things. Farther inside. Somewhere else. She moved under the desks, ears alert to the hint of anyone else nearby, whiskers twitching almost unconsciously, the tip of her tail crooked over and quivering.

Not the first office, smelling of dust and blood: she backed out of that one hastily. The night-human had died there. Not even the faint traces of Theodore and Georgie's human in that space recently could erase the death-smell.

The second office was larger. No blood. Less dust, more green things, the faint tinge of alcohol, perfume, and there, the musky scent. Faded but definite . . .

She went inside and breathed in deeply, letting the smells hit her, and categorizing them one by one. Hunger and anger, boredom, excitement . . . all the things humans smelled like, but something else, too. Something different.

Then a memory kicked in; she had smelled this before. On Theodore, and on Georgie's Ginny, although never at the same time. And the smaller female at the Busy Place, too, more often. It smelled like their own scent then, too, which was why she hadn't recognized it at first.

Sex.

Someone had gone into heat here.

An hour into the talk, Teddy's knees ached from sitting in the wooden folding chair, his butt was numb from the same cause, and he was just about ready to gnaw his own arm off to escape.

Scanning the crowd had been even more boring than listening to the crazy talk about "innate better nature of animals" or the "gross evil of curtailing the natural desire to procreate." They were all either intent on the speaker, or head-down, playing with their phones or tablets, sending off emails or texting or posting to Facebook, who knew. None of them seemed particularly guilty, or suspicious, or even interesting.

And then there was a shuffling behind and to his left, as though someone had come in late. Teddy tried to look without being conspicuous, then said the hell with it and craned his neck to check out what was going on. From the glares, the guy in the third row, at the far end, had just arrived. Teddy frowned. The guy looked vaguely familiar, but . . . It took a minute, then his bartender's memory caught up with his eyesight. From the shelter . . . what was his name? Williams. Scott Williams.

Teddy's frown deepened. The shelter's volunteer vet was a right-to-breeder?

A round of applause caught Teddy by surprise, and he joined in automatically, twisting back around in his seat and trying to look as though he'd been paying attention all along. People started to get up and move around, starting conversations, so he assumed that the crazy-speaking part was done. Time for Kool-Aid and cookies, he supposed.

He stood up and stretched, using the movement as an excuse to look around. Williams had stood up as well, moving to the front of the room as though he was going to congratulate the speaker. That took cojones, after showing up at the very end of the speech, but Teddy supposed that in the crowd of people already doing the same thing, it would be easy enough to fake knowledge—and for all he knew, the same guy said the same thing every meeting.

He'd been right: the back table he'd noted before now had cookies and what looked like a coffee urn set out on it, and people were slowly beginning to drift toward it. He could probably get more useful gossip out of them then . . . but the risk of Williams recognizing him was too high. Teddy might be able to explain away his being there, but it could get dicey, and too many people would be paying attention.

Coincidences happened: Williams's being here might

have nothing to do with the graffiti, nothing to do with the missing money. Teddy wasn't willing to take that chance. Not before he ran this new information past Ginny, anyway.

He reclaimed his jacket, nodded at the woman at the door, who wished him a good evening, and texted Ginny as he walked up the stairs and out into the street, telling her to meet him back at Mary's.

Back in the basement, Williams was intercepted before he could reach the speaker by two other attendees, a man and a woman. The greetings were not friendly, their body language aggressive, as though they were trying to keep him away from someone—or something.

"Why are you here, Scott?"

He tried to make an end-run around them, and, when blocked, gave in less than gracefully. "Look, I just need to—"

"You don't need to do anything," the man said, cutting him off.

He let out an exasperated sigh. "I'm not your enemy. I'm not their enemy. If I were, you'd all be in jail by now."

"We haven't done anything illegal."

Williams gave the woman an incredulous glare. "Seriously?"

"Whatever you need to ask, you can ask me," the man said, not letting the two of them get into an actual argument.

Williams set his expression and shook his head. "No."

"It's me, or nobody. We're not going to let you harass anyone."

"Since when is asking questions harassment? I thought that was reserved for, oh, I don't know, yelling slogans and stopping people from entering or leaving their cars. Or painting slogans on private property?"

"Picketing is our right," the woman said. "And we have a permit for the pamphlets. It's all perfectly legal."

"And defacing private property? What's next, guys? Smashing more windows? Destroying property? If this escalates, you're the ones who lose. If my clinic is damaged . . ."

"We're not here to hurt anyone," the man said. "Just to make our point."

"Your point . . ." is insane, he wanted to say, but bit back the words.

They all stared at each other for long seconds, while the woman he'd wanted to speak to fell into conversation with someone else, turning and walking, not toward the refreshments area with the others, but toward the back of the hall. They paused and then, still talking, left together through the emergency exit.

"Damn it," Williams said, not quite under his breath. "Fine. You tell her . . . tell her what I said. If you're doing anything more than pamphlets, stop. Now. Believe me, you're not going to be helping your cause."

"Like you care about our cause," the man said. "You—"

"Stop it," the woman said, although it wasn't clear which

one of them she was talking to. Possibly both. "You're going to start yelling, and I won't have it."

"Whatever. I tried." Williams threw up his hands in a classic expression of disgust and turned to leave the building.

"Scott!" the woman called after him.

He stopped but didn't turn around.

"Be careful."

He made a scornful, dismissive gesture over his shoulder, and left.

"Do you think he knows?" the man asked quietly.

"No. If he did, he would have gone to the police already. But be careful. He's right about one thing: getting caught won't help us at all."

When Tonica arrived at Mary's, Ginny was already sitting at her usual table near the front window, a half-empty martini glass at her elbow, and her tablet in front of her.

"No Georgie?" he asked, sliding into the chair opposite her, indicating the greyhound and the shaggy black mutt tied up outside, but no shar-pei.

"I got home to discover that she'd eaten something that didn't agree with her." Ginny made a face, and waved a hand in front of her nose to illustrate. "I was afraid I'd get a ticket for air pollution, if I brought her out."

She gave him points for not laughing.

"Is that normal for dogs?"

"Sadly, yes. Or at least, not unusual. But at least I don't have to deal with a litter box."

As though summoned by the mention, a small gray tabby wound herself around Tonica's ankles, asking to be picked up. He obliged, giving her damp fur an absent scritch behind one ear before offering up his own news.

"No litter box here, either. Best of both worlds." He changed the subject before she could bring up the topic of responsible cat ownership again. "And speaking of shared worlds, guess who showed up at the meeting tonight?"

Normally a challenge like that would rouse her interest—or her irritation, because there was no way you could actually *guess* something like that with any hope of accuracy. Ginny wasn't in the mood for games tonight, though: after the noninformational meeting with Wendy, she'd gotten home to a message from last week's date, calling to cancel their plans for this weekend with an excuse that was both vague and unapologetically lame. She understood about cancellations, and it wasn't like they were an item or anything yet, but he could at least have put some effort into the excuse.

"Not in the mood, Tonica. Who?"

"Scott Williams. The shelter's on-call vet."

"A vet's antineutering?" That was the craziest thing she'd ever heard. Or in the top ten, anyway. Her brain started to hum over the possibilities.

"I don't know. He showed up late: the speechifying was almost over. Maybe he was there to check out the opposition, or . . . The shelter side was the one that was vandalized, so maybe he was there . . . no. He didn't look mad, or even pissed-off."

“Did he see you there?” If he was a member, or somehow connected, and he saw Tonica . . .

“No. Like I said, he came in late, and I figured it was better to slip out before he did see me.”

“Smart.” She knew it sounded grudging, but Tonica just grinned, and half turned to get Jon’s attention, pointing to the tap to order a beer. “So what do we know about Dr. Williams,” he asked, “other than the fact that the animals at the shelter didn’t seem to like him much?”

She was just about to answer when her phone rang. She looked at the display and then pushed the tablet across the table. “Look for yourself,” she said. “I’m taking this outside, where it’s quieter.”

Outside, the chill air had shifted to cold rain, and people were moving quicker, some carrying umbrellas, more just ducking their heads and trying to pretend that the drops didn’t bother them. She leaned against the slight overhang, wishing she’d thought to grab her jacket, and answered the phone.

“Hi. I didn’t expect to hear from you so soon. What’s up? Did you find anything?” She could see Tonica through the plate glass window, first trying to figure out how to work the touchscreen, then sorting through the sheet she’d opened for him. Ginny allowed herself a smirk: Tonica might be better educated, and might come from more money, but when it came to technology, her sixty-three-year-old mother could manage better.

“What? No, wait, back up.” She listened intently, making mental notes as the CPA explained what she’d found.

When she came back inside, her face was set in grim lines, but there was a sparkle in her eye.

"The books were cooked."

Tonica did a double take that was almost funny. "What?"

"The books. Okay, not cooked, exactly. There were improprieties." Ginny was more or less parroting what Wendy had told her. "She started looking over the entries, and discovered the dead guy had made notes, things he was seeing that didn't look quite right. He hadn't gone anywhere with it yet, just starting to connect the dots, but someone had been embezzling, and not just a couple thousand dollars. Maybe a lot of money, over a long period of time. She said it was really well done."

Tonica leaned back in his chair, and ran his hand over the top of his hair. Not for the first time, she envied him the relative lack-of-fuss of his brushtop.

"Shit," he said. "That's going to complicate things."

Understatement. "If it's the same person. It may not be. In fact, it probably isn't. I mean, someone who's been gouging the shelter for a long time isn't going to risk stealing relatively small amounts of cash, right?"

"Even if it's not the same person, whoever it is will have a vested interest in us not poking around or finding anything." He drank half of his beer in one gulp, and then put the glass down on the table with a hard thump. "So we've got a thief, an embezzler, a dead guy, and animal rights graffiti artists who may or may not be vandals, thieves, and killers. Even at double what we're getting paid, Gin, it's not enough."

"Do you think we should give up?" She leaned forward, her elbows on the table, and rested her chin on her folded hands. "It's a legitimate question. This is not what we signed on for, you're right. Este and Roger would probably hold the door open for us. And I have other clients I need to deal with, and . . ."

"Gin Mallard, giving up?" He meant it to tease, she thought, but the words stung.

"Normally when a job spins out of parameters, I negotiate an increase in my fee," she said tartly. "That's not going to happen here; I doubt they're even going to be able to pay us, if they're being squeezed dry, and Nora . . . I doubt she even has the original fee, honestly."

"So?"

"So."

They stared at each other, and Tonica blinked first. "For the puppies."

"And the kittens," Ginny added.

"Hell, we always knew we weren't going to get rich doing this." It had been more about the mental challenge than anything else. "On the plus side, hey, nobody's threatening us with bodily harm."

"Yet," she said direly, and waved for a refill.

"Yeah," Tonica said quietly. "Yet."

13

Ginny Mallard wasn't the sort to shirk from doing things that had to be done. But so far that morning, she'd had to deal with doggy vomit on the hardwood floor, deflected a panicked email from a client she wasn't scheduled to work with for another two weeks, but who had suddenly decided she had to have things done *now*, and her favorite mug's handle had broken when she picked it up, spilling coffee all over her pajamas.

And then her mother called with an update on the Thanksgiving Situation, and a side run by her stepfather, who suggested that they all run off to Hawaii for that week instead—and not tell her aunt and uncle.

By the time Ginny had dealt with her parents, showered, and actually gotten to drink her second mug of coffee, she was in no mood for anyone else giving her grief. Not even her dog.

"Georgie, come on."

The dog, usually more than happy for a walk, lay on the floor and looked up at her mistress mournfully.

"I know, baby, you feel like crap. But you need to walk."

She had called the vet, and then double-checked half a dozen pet care sites to confirm the advice, and they'd all said the same thing: make sure Georgie got exercise, and as many chances to empty her system as possible—preferably out the back end, rather than throwing up. That, and change her diet to a brand that, of course, cost twice as much as what Ginny had been buying.

"If I'd known you were going to be a fart machine, I'd . . ." Ginny paused. "I'd have taken you home anyway," she admitted. "But seriously, this had better be a passing phase, and I can't believe I just made that pun. Georgie, come *on*."

The dog got to her feet with a sigh, and went to where Ginny was waiting, letting the human attach the leash to her collar and lead her out the door.

"How's the kid feeling?" Tonica was waiting outside, looking far too awake and alert for someone who had still been in the bar, matching a group beer for beer, when she left around eleven o'clock. To have gotten here by ten, he had to have been up well before his usual time.

"She feels fine," she said. "How she smells is another thing entirely."

He looked down at Georgie dubiously. "And in my car . . . oh hell, we can leave the windows open, I guess. That the evidence?" and he nodded at the folder in her hand.

"Yeah. Scans of the relevant pages from the ledger, Jimmy's original notes, and Wendy's notes on those notes. I'll pick up the originals this afternoon, and return them . . . assuming everything goes well."

"So what's the plan, boss?" He didn't mention that he'd originally claimed lead on this, and she didn't bring it up.

"The plan is to lay out what we've discovered, and see what happens. Missing money, the possible connection to the antineuter group, the evidence of embezzlement. Then we tell Este to take it to the cops, come clean, and it's entirely possible that they come out like a sterling silver victim, tarnished but polishable.

"They can't try to sweep this under the rug the way they did the theft, not all of this. And once it's out in the open . . . well, if they're lucky the thief will get scared away, decide it's not worth the increased risk, and the spray-painting loonies are likewise deterred by police presence, and they hold that fund-raiser in the dead guy's name, like they planned, and replace the missing money that way." The entire thing made her mouth taste icky, but there wasn't anything else they could do, not really. Wendy had made that clear to her on the phone the night before: This was too much for them. Way too much. And once they knew it was this big, they were obligated to say something.

"For lack of cash, a shelter was lost," Tonica said, softly. "Damn it."

"Maybe not," Ginny said, but she didn't feel too optimistic, either.

Georgie took that opportunity to release some pressure,

and both humans winced. "You sure you want to bring her along?" he asked, breathing into his hand.

Ginny shrugged. "Comic relief? Or canine protection, if anyone snaps and tries to blame us. We may need both. I can't imagine that this is going to go well."

Not going well, Teddy decided half an hour later, was a slight understatement.

Nora hadn't gotten in yet, the receptionist told them cautiously when they arrived, but Este was, and would meet with them as soon as she finished the morning staff briefing. He didn't imagine that meeting was going to be a lot of fun, even if she didn't mention anything about the missing money.

While they waited, they'd brought Georgie out to the dog run area, Ginny hoping that the chance to roughhouse with other dogs would work whatever was bothering the shar-pei out of her system. Having been exposed to the unhappy flatulence twice on the walk down to the shelter, Teddy was all for working it out somewhere he wasn't. And he supposed other dogs wouldn't even notice; they seemed to delight in disgusting smells.

The staff meeting ended promptly at 10:30 a.m., but when Este came out to meet them, she didn't lead them to the office where they'd met previously, but through the opposite door, into the clinic wing.

"Ah, I'm not sure . . . ," Ginny started to say, exchanging

a glance with Teddy. He shrugged: the vet only came in on the weekends, right? So they should be fine. Or not.

Este indicated the battered sofa and chairs of the waiting room. "Please excuse the surroundings, but everyone came in this morning for our meeting, and even with the door closed, the walls in the office are not particularly thick. There has been enough upset lately, I would rather these discussions not fall within general knowledge."

"That's . . . probably wise," Teddy said, and then sat down and shut up. Ginny sat next to him, with Este presiding in a straight-backed chair, as regal as any queen.

Ginny took the lead, laying out what they'd learned, in as gentle a manner as she could, telling her about Wendy's findings with the ledger.

When she had finished, she leaned back slightly and let Teddy pick up. Este was so pale, he felt like he was kicking someone when they were already down, but he went on, telling her about seeing Williams at the antineuter meeting.

The guy had been with them since the beginning, based on the photos they saw. Hearing all this couldn't be easy, or pleasant.

"The evidence we've gathered isn't conclusive," Ginny said when he was finished, "and we don't want to accuse anyone. But there *is* evidence, and we can't ignore the fact that they all point to Dr. Williams being involved in at least part of what's been going on here."

"No. Absolutely not."

Teddy had thought she would throw them out then and there, blaming the messenger for the message. But Este Snyder was of sterner material than that; he recognized the tight-lipped, drawn-cheekbones signs of a woman steeling herself to deal with unpleasantness: he'd seen it enough growing up.

"While I am not happy that he has any connection whatsoever with those . . . lunatic vandals," Este said, "the fact is that simply attending a meeting—and you admit that he was not there for the entire thing—isn't cause for suspicion. He might have been there for much the same reason as you, after all. He has seen firsthand the damage they do, maybe he wanted to confront them directly."

Teddy had to admit that she had a point. And his own observations that the animals didn't like him seemed too silly to even mention. He wasn't too fond of his own doctor, and he *knew* why the guy stuck him with needles and looked in his ears.

Almost instinctively he looked over his shoulder toward the door at the far side of the room, but it remained closed, the receptionists' cubby dark. They didn't have the usual Plexiglas window, just an open space. He supposed there wasn't much need for it. He'd never understood why doctors' offices had it, except to keep sneezes at bay.

"At least ask him." Ginny was pushing, despite Este's clear reluctance. For the first time, he regretted the fact that they weren't, actually, investigators. Going directly to the suspect and asking questions themselves would have avoided this scene, but the book he'd gotten, *Investigation for Morons*, had been clear on what they could and couldn't do, and actual direct questioning of a suspect was in the "do not." And yeah, they could have gone in all casual like, but if he clammed up and called a lawyer, and sued them for harassment? Ginny and he were both in the service industry—something like that could cost them jobs, for the rest of their careers.

"Absolutely not."

Teddy narrowed his eyes, looking at Este. Something in her voice . . .

"Methinks the lady doth protest too much."

"What?" Both of them turned to look at him, Gin with confusion, Este with a seriously scary glare.

He'd been glared at by pros in his life. Este was good, but not that good.

He addressed himself to Ginny, intentionally putting Este out of the conversation for the moment. "She doesn't want us talking to him, she won't confront him about the missing money . . . there's more than just protecting the shelter here. She's protecting herself."

It was a guess, but he was used to trusting his instincts on things like that, the way a person stood, and looked, and the tone of their voice. Was someone drunk? Violent? Crazy? Lying? Were they dangerous, to him, to themselves? All the things he'd learned to see, and decide on, in a minute's turn.

He might be wrong, but he didn't think so.

"Ms. Snyder." Ginny Mallard, when formal, was scary-cold. "Is there something about Dr. Williams that we should know about? Something relevant to the investigation?"

Este licked her lips, and some of her fierce certainty faded.

"He . . . knows some of the people involved in that group. He's not a sympathizer, but he knew some of the members, from other, less . . . radical groups. I suppose he went to ask them to back off."

Teddy hadn't hung around, so he couldn't say for certain, but it was a reasonable explanation. Ginny looked at him, her eyes asking for an opinion, and he shrugged slightly, and then nodded. It made sense, and since they had no real proof the graffiti was tied in to the missing money anyway . . .

"There's no need to question him about what happened in the office," Este went on. "He wasn't involved in . . . any of the things going on."

"But he did have access to the main office?" Ginny asked, picking up the fact that Este had brought up the office, when they'd been talking about something else.

"I mean he— Yes. He did." She would have lied if she could, Teddy could tell from her expression, her body language, but she'd spoken without thinking, stressed into an incautious outburst, and once caught, she knew better than to backtrack.

"Because . . ." Ginny prodded her to finish.

"They were having an affair," Teddy said, still watching Este's face. "And they were using the office as their meeting place. Safer, more secure than a hotel, somewhere she controlled, where they both had a reason to be at any time, and nobody would question it."

Ginny Mallard wasn't exactly a prude, and she'd seen and heard enough of people's private lives, working as a concierge, that it was hard to shock her. But Tonica's comment left her flat-footed and maybe, just maybe, a little horrified. Not about the affair, and not at the fact that Este obviously liked younger men, but that they did it in the office . . . There wasn't even a couch!

It made it incredibly difficult not to visualize that small office, the desk covered with papers, and imagine . . . No. Not going there. Think of anything other than that. Especially since she hadn't gotten any in months.

"How do you know that he's not responsible?" she asked instead. "If you gave him access to the main office, trusted him here when everyone else was gone . . ."

"He didn't steal the money," Este said. "I did."

As conversation stoppers went, that one was damned effective. Ginny realized that her mouth was hanging open, and shut it with a snap. On the sofa next to her, Tonica wasn't doing much better.

"You . . . what?"

"I stole the money. Jimmy . . . he came in one night he wasn't scheduled, my own fault for giving him a key, and letting him know the security passcode." Este drew herself up, and then exhaled. "He heard us, listened in like a little sneak thief, a voyeur. Listened and took notes and the next morning called me to set up lunch, said he had something we needed to talk about. I thought it was about the books, of course, so I said yes."

"He blackmailed you? Threatened to tell Roger?" That was cause enough for murder.

"He threatened to tell everyone. I spent most of my life arranging other people's public faces. I know what bad PR can do, even to someone as far out of the spotlight as I am now. A scandal—and an older woman with a much younger man is still a scandal, believe me, even at our age—would do no good, and possibly much harm. The shelter . . . this was our dream. A scandal could destroy it. And Roger . . . we've had our problems, but you know about his illness, his heart isn't good. I couldn't . . ."

"So you took the money to pay him off." Tonica shifted, leaning forward to stare at her. "And got Nora, who is in no way qualified to be handling these things, to take care of the money. And then Nora, not being as dumb as you thought, hired us to investigate. . . ."

"I asked Nora to take over before . . . before everything. She was the best choice for it. . . ." Este almost smiled. "She proved she was the best choice, by realizing that something was wrong, despite my best efforts to confuse the issue."

She had said something about it being a mistake to give the assignment to Nora, Ginny remembered. That was what she had meant.

"But I couldn't dismiss you without raising even more questions—and keeping you close allowed me to know where you were going."

"And now he's dead," Ginny said bluntly. "You know this makes his cause of death suspicious—and you the prime suspect?"

Este blanched, and her hands pressed down against the arms of her chair as though she were trying to hold the furniture down. Either she hadn't thought of that, or she hadn't thought they'd be tacky enough to mention it.

Ginny was feeling distinctly tacky just then. Also seriously irritated.

"Did you kill him?"

"No! God, no."

Ginny looked at Tonica, who was studying the older woman, and saw his head tilt forward, barely a nod of his chin. He believed her.

Tonica was their body language specialist, the people-reader. She should trust his take—but Ginny wasn't convinced. Logic said Este was the prime suspect, and prime suspects lied. She had already lied to them, over and over again, and had been cheating on her partner to begin with, so not the world's most truthful person—although she supposed she could see where Scott Williams was more appealing than Roger.

People behaved badly. This was not news. But how badly?

"So the thing we were hired to solve is now officially solved, if not actually fixed. And I'm not sure it even matters, because even before then," and Ginny tapped the copies of the records, "you were being stolen from. That leaves you still shy, what, twenty thousand dollars out of your budget, over the past few years?"

"Twenty thousand. Dear God. And no, I can't replace that." Irritation replaced the fear in her voice. "No wonder we were always scraping by, budget-wise, no matter how many donations we got. How the hell did we miss it?"

"My accountant took a look at your records, and says your bookkeeper was trying to unravel that, but it was really well done. Very subtle." Ginny paused. "He may have been crap as a human being, but Jimmy was good at this job. And he didn't like mysteries."

Hard to imagine a blackmailer being conscientious enough to unravel another person's theft, but maybe he didn't like competition. Or wanted to take notes for his own use. Who the hell knew, and the guy was dead, so they couldn't ask him.

"There are only so many people working here," Tonica said, leaning back again. "And only half of them have access, assuming you weren't handing out keys to every good-looking male. So who was cooking the books?"

"And who killed Jimmy?" Ginny asked. "Because at this point, I'm not buying the utter coincidence of a blackmailing, about-to-discover-embezzlement bookkeeper's having-a-stroke, dying alone thing anymore, are you?"

Neither of them were, based on their expressions. Then Este's expression changed again, looking over their heads, her eyes widening just enough to show real shock. "Roger?"

For a guy on the other side of sixty, Roger was pretty fast with the gun. Tonica had only just started to get out of the sofa when the weapon was pointed at him, the dark metal looking ominously, well, ominous. Ginny wished briefly that they'd let Georgie come in with them—the dog had already proven herself against one gunman before—and then she started looking for something within reach she could use as a weapon.

He'd come in through the clinic itself: nobody in the front office would know he was in there with them, assuming anyone even knew *they* were in there. And these old warehouses were solidly built; odds were nobody would hear the gun going off, either.

"I knew, when you said you were meeting with them, that it would all come out," Roger said, his gaze only on Este. "Finally, it would all come out."

"You *killed* him?" Este sounded more than surprised; she sounded horrified.

"You *slept* with him?" Roger replied, his tone mocking hers, although—weirdly to Ginny's ears, not unkindly. He sounded more . . . resigned.

"You were the one cooking the books," Ginny said, everything clicking in place with a firm snap. "Sliding money out would be easy for the guy who was handling the finances, paying the bills, and nobody would ever know—until you got sick and had to be replaced."

"Why?" Este had stood up, but not moved, staring at her partner. "Why on earth would you do that? If you needed money, all you had to do was ask!"

"It wasn't about the money," Roger snarled, the amiable façade cracking under his fury. "It was about *you*. Screwing him, here, in the office."

"What?" She stared at him. "You haven't been interested in sex for years, even before you got sick!"

"That didn't mean you should sneak around, in *our* office!"

"I so didn't need to know this much about other people's sex lives," Ginny said, not quite under her breath.

"You've been having this affair with Williams for how long?" Tonica asked. "Two years? Three?"

Este nodded, her gaze still locked with Roger's.

"Same time he's been fiddling with the books," Ginny said. "Tit for tat?"

"You were going to destroy it all," he said to Este, the words so carefully enunciated, they might have had actual edges. "Everything we worked for, so you could play cougar, and scratch your itch."

"So you were going to destroy it first," Ginny said, standing up—slowly, not wanting to freak him out, but not able to sit there passively. If she could move a foot away, he'd have to cover both of them with one gun, and they'd have a better chance. Maybe. "And then what, blame Williams for it? Or Este?"

Robert shrugged, but his hand holding the gun never wavered. "Didn't know, didn't care. I told you, it wasn't about the money. It was a fixed routine. Every time she met with him, I took a little more out. It seemed fair play."

It was, Ginny had to admit, a logical sort of revenge: if she stopped, so would he. Sick, but logical. She could almost admire the cold-blooded beauty of it.

"And now?" Tonica could have been asking the guy if he wanted another beer. But she saw how his hand was resting on the arm of the sofa; he wasn't anywhere near as cool or calm as his voice sounded, but braced to explode into action if need be. The older man wouldn't stand a chance—except for the gun.

Guns trumped muscle just about every time. Her self-defense teacher had told them that, back in college.

"You going to kill us, Roger?" she asked, trying to keep his attention on her, so if Tonica tried anything, maybe he'd have a few extra seconds to move. "Like you killed Jimmy?"

"I didn't kill him!" Roger seemed to finally register what they were talking about, and looked dismayed at the thought that they could think he'd murder someone. Considering he was holding a gun on them, Ginny wasn't reassured. "I found the gun, on my way in that night. Someone had thrown it in the alley behind the dog run. I picked it up; it wasn't safe to leave there."

"You just picked up a gun and walked into the shelter? Are you an utter idiot?" Este was beside herself.

"What was I supposed to do, leave it there for anyone to find? And then I saw the light on in my office and all I could think was that someone was in there, poking around in the books—"

"You knew we'd hired someone to do them!"

"I didn't know he worked at three in the morning!"

"What were you even doing there at three in the morning?"

Ginny was pretty sure that the two of them had forgotten anyone else was in the room. Which would be great—she had no problem with two adults working their issues out by screaming at each other, except one of them was still holding that damn gun.

Time to do something about that.

The difference between shooting a guy and surprising him with a gun so he had a heart attack was something for lawyers and judges to figure out, but looking at the way Roger was holding the weapon, Teddy was pretty sure he was telling the truth about the gun not being his. He was also pretty sure that the only way Roger would hit anyone with a bullet would be by accident.

Never mind that an accident would be just as deadly as intent, in the relatively small space of the waiting room. He wished they'd taken Georgie in with them: a man this nervous would probably wet himself if a dog—even a sweet dog—growled at him.

Or maybe not, considering that the guy helped found an animal rescue shelter.

"There's a way out of this that doesn't involve a gun." Ginny was stepping forward, her hands out to her side, her voice shaky but calm. Teddy wanted to yell at her—what the hell did she think she was doing, you don't irritate a guy with a gun! But he was afraid to say anything, afraid to even breathe, trying to identify all the ways this could possibly—probably—go wrong.

But Roger took a step back, even though he was still aiming the gun at them, and seemed to be listening. Maybe she could talk him down after all.

"Right now, everything's a terrible, tragic accident," Ginny went on. "Nobody was intentionally hurt."

Something brushed his ankle, and Teddy twitched instinctively, then looked down, somehow not surprised to see a cat winding her way around his legs. He *was* surprised to recognize Penny. She rested her head against his calf and looked up at him with those pale green eyes, like she was expecting him to do something.

He had just enough time to wonder how the hell she'd gotten here, how she'd found them, when a low growl filled the room, making everyone stop dead. For a moment, he had the crazy thought that Penny had somehow gotten Georgie out of the waiting room, but it didn't sound like Georgie.

It didn't sound like a dog at all.

Across from them, Este had gone ashen, her eyes looking to the left, but her entire body gone very still.

"Nobody move," Roger said, his voice the kind of calm that made smart people break out in a cold sweat. "Nobody . . . move."

"That's not a dog," Ginny said, as the growl sounded again, and this time it was definitely in the room.

14

There was a third low growl, this one ending with a weird kind of sneezing sound, and Ginny suddenly knew what was in the room with them: a cat. A *big* cat, deep-chested and muscled. She could feel it behind her, pacing along the wall, large, menacing, and nasty. She pictured it as a sabertooth, with glowing red eyes and drool, just waiting to pounce. Even if she'd wanted to jump and run, even if Roger hadn't warned against exactly that, her body would have refused. Instinct froze her, still and silent as a mouse, hoping against hope the beast would choose someone else, or better yet, go *away*.

Someone, she didn't know who, it might even have been her, let out a whimper, barely audible, and like a trigger being pulled, all hell broke loose. The leap was silent, but she could hear it, her nerves screaming at her body to *move move move*. She saw Roger turning, the gun he'd just been pointing at Este dropping lower, then rising to aim it at her—no, behind her—even as the door left ajar by his entry banged open, slamming against the wall with a sound like a gunshot.

"Don't shoot!" Alice cried, panicked. "It's valuable, don't shoot it!"

The noise and the plea were just enough to make Roger hesitate. The cat, however, had no such consideration. Ginny's muscles finally unlocked enough to let her slide to the floor, her only instinct to get out of the way, to be less of a target. Something brushed by her, and the cat's scream was matched by a human cry of pain, not hers, too deep to be hers, was she hurt? Then there was a bellow that could only be Tonica entering the fray, with a woman's voice calling out again, "Don't shoot it don't hurt it!"

And then another scream, this one fainter but no less fierce, and something launched itself over Ginny like an arrow, long and lean and . . . furred?

Ginny rolled over on her side in time to see a smaller cat, housecat-sized, land claws-out on the larger animal, her tail bottled and her ears flat.

"Penny," Ginny whispered in shock, with no idea of how she could recognize the fierce warrior as the same smooth-coated cat who rubbed against her ankles, but she knew the tabby as easily as she would know Georgie. Fear was a sour taste in her mouth, watching the much smaller animal cling to the larger cat's neck, hissing like some cartoon that wasn't funny at all.

The tabby didn't have a chance; the larger animal shook her off easily, and Penny landed on the floor, hard, and didn't move.

Before the larger cat could recover enough to attack or flee, the vet tech was there, on her knees in what looked like the stupidest move ever, and stabbed the animal with a hypodermic needle. She stayed there by its side, either batshit crazy or just too exhausted to move. Her eyes were wide, her chest heaving as though she'd been running a sprint. Ginny could relate: she felt like she needed a paper bag to breath into, herself.

The cat—a tawny spotted beast a little larger than Georgie—struggled to get back on its feet, and then collapsed.

Ginny exhaled, coughed as her lungs demanded more air—now!—and was finally able to look around the room, to see what the hell had happened. Roger was down on the ground, on his hands and knees, his shirt ripped and bloody. Tonica was flat on his back, holding his arm to his chest, but she couldn't see any blood. Their chairs were knocked over and scattered across the floor, her chest was heaving as though there weren't enough air in the room, and she could feel bruises starting to form everywhere.

"What. The. Fuck?" Este's voice came from behind the sofa, where she, smarter than the rest of them, had ducked the moment things went to hell.

Ginny stared at the cat—a cougar? No, the markings were all wrong, spotted, and it was too small—and nodded. "Yeah. What she said."

"That's an ocelot," Este said, moving around the sofa cautiously now, staring at the cat. "A wildcat. What the *hell*?" The look she turned on the vet tech was venomous, and Ginny instinctively scooted back a few inches until her back was up against the coffee table, its out-of-date magazines and candy jar somehow unmoved by all the action.

The vet tech swallowed nervously, but with the evidence on the floor in front of her, the syringe still in her hands, there wasn't any way she could deny responsibility.

Tonica had managed to sit up, and he nodded briefly to Ginny, to tell her he was all right. In the chaos, Roger had dropped the gun, and Ginny managed to overcome her distaste for the thing long enough to draw it to her, sliding it under the coffee table where nobody could get to it easily.

Penny, apparently unharmed, crawled into Tonica's lap and draped herself over one thigh, calmly grooming her paw with no sign of the hissing weapon she'd been minutes before. The three of them waited there, catching their breath and letting the others unravel what the hell was going on.

"You miserable bitch," Roger said, and it wasn't clear at first who he was talking to. Then he went down on his knees beside the cat, checking to see if it was still breathing, and the glare he shot the vet tech made it clear. "Este, stop gawping like an idiot, and call the cops."

"But . . ."

"I don't give a fuck about the bad publicity," he snarled. "I want this bitch arrested. For animal abuse, if nothing else."

It seemed that, once you'd had a dead body on your premises, a second call to the cops got quick attention, especially if you mentioned there was a wild, if currently sedated, animal involved. With the cops came an officer from the Seattle Animal Shelter and, surprisingly, Scott Williams.

It took the cops about thirty seconds to secure the scene, considering that nobody was in any shape to move. "Do we need a paramedic?"

"No, we've got this," Williams said, and then, realizing that they were talking about the human injuries, flushed.

"We're fine," Roger said, clearly still angry, brushing off the officer trying to check his wounds. "How is the cat?"

Right after that, Ginny and Tonica were hustled out into the parking lot, where a patrolman took their statements and then seemed to forget about them. Alice was escorted to the first patrol car, her hands fastened behind her back, even though as far as Ginny could tell she hadn't offered any resistance at all. She was crying and glaring at people all at once, which took some doing.

The ocelot was taken out on a stretcher a few minutes after that, Williams carrying one end, the animal control officer at the other, talking into a headset all the while. Este and Roger were nowhere to be seen, presumably still inside, giving their own statements. As owners of the shelter, they'd have some serious explaining to do.

"I wonder if Roger was telling the truth," Ginny said, still a little dazed from the events. "If Jimmy was poking around in the books, Roger would've known; he'd be the only one who would've known. If he came back from medical leave and saw Jimmy's notes . . . it would make sense to threaten him, maybe even plan to kill him. If he did have a heart attack because of Roger's actions, does that make it manslaughter?

"I still don't get . . . what the hell was all that? Keeping wild animals in the clinic? Why?" Tonica sounded bewildered, totally not listening to her.

"They're in demand as pets," Ginny said, switching gears. "I read something about it a while back, or saw some documentary, I don't remember. Mainly by people with more money than brains. At a guess, she was smuggling them in using the shelter as a cover, or maybe just holding them for someone else to sell. The latter, probably."

"Jesus." Tonica was starting to focus a little more. "That's illegal, right?"

"Very. I don't know if that cat was an endangered species or not, but . . . at the very least, you're supposed to have a license to handle wild animals, I'm pretty sure."

"Jesus," he said again. "I bet the gun was hers. If she was part of a smuggling ring . . . but then, why did it end up in the alley?"

"I don't know. Talk about bad timing . . . If the money hadn't gone missing, and Nora hadn't called us in, nobody would have known, probably."

"Yeah. We fixed everything, didn't we?" Tonica shook his head. "For the first time in a very long time . . . I need a drink."

"I need to get Georgie," Ginny said, more worried about immediate concerns. "Do you think—hey!" and she accosted Williams, who, after helping to load the cat into an emergency vehicle, had come back to stand, staring at the wall of the clinic as though the faded graffiti would give him answers. "My dog, she's inside, in the dog run."

"I'll let the cops know," he said. "I think they're going to close the shelter, at least for a couple of days while they go over the office again, but for now, everyone's staying where they are, so she's fine. Georgie won't get put back in the kennel, I promise."

Ginny didn't much feel like trusting anyone, but she didn't have a choice, right then. The cops weren't letting anyone back into the building unless they actually worked there.

"It's my fault," Williams said finally, still standing there.

"What?" Tonica turned to look at him, frowning. "What was?"

"All of this, maybe." He sighed, raising his hands and then letting them drop again, not looking away from the remains of the graffiti. "I knew something . . . I knew something wasn't right. With Alice. There were supplies missing I couldn't account for, things that didn't feel right. And I knew the shelter wasn't paying her enough, especially for the hours she put in. She was here too often late at night, and the clinic . . ." He shrugged. "You saw the graffiti. We were being hit by a group of . . . extremists, who wanted to shut the spay clinic down. I guess I thought she was part of that, trying to sabotage us from within? It didn't make any sense, but all the pieces were there, and I was trying to put them together. . . ."

He laughed, the sound lacking any humor. "Right pieces, wrong shape."

"Wild cats smell different from domestic," Tonica said, and Ginny knew him well enough now to hear the click-click-click of things fitting in his head, too. "That's why the animals reacted to you that morning; it wasn't you, it was the gurney."

"The gurney, and maybe my lab coat, too. Things that were left in the clinic . . . It wasn't the first time I'd gotten those reactions, but I'd thought—I don't know what I'd thought. I'm an idiot. But I didn't have any *proof* that she was doing anything illegal, or even wrong. And I'd been the one to suggest her for the job. I felt responsible, I needed to be sure she was actually breaking the law, before I went to the police."

Tonica nodded. "So that's why you went to the 'Right-to-Breed' meeting, to find out if she was connected with them."

"What? Um. Yeah. I was hoping I'd be able to get something out of them, so I could confront her . . . but they closed ranks. She wasn't part of their group. People keeping wild animals as pets? Not their thing at all. They'd see her as even worse than us, I think. But they knew something was wrong—maybe they thought we were all in on it? I don't know, they're nuts."

Neither of them could argue that point.

"So she was using the clinic to store illegal animals?" Ginny asked, looking to confirm her theory—and as a distraction from worrying about Georgie, who probably thought she'd been abandoned, by now.

"Yeah. Looks like she was hiding them in one of the

cages we used to quarantine new animals before they were brought forward for adoption. Using the clinic as a front to smuggle exotic pets into the country. Stupid, stupid."

She didn't know if he was talking about the vet tech, or himself for not knowing, for not saying anything sooner.

"You were only here once a week," Tonica said. "She had plenty of time to do . . . whatever she was doing, and then clean up, after."

"Except you were here more often than that," Ginny said. "Late at night." For the sake of delicacy, she didn't reference *why* he was there then. "So you knew something was going on."

"Like I said, I had suspicions. And with the escalation of the extremists' actions, I was worried. . . ." He laughed a little. "I was worried that they were close to getting violent. So I brought in a gun."

That surprised both of them. "That gun was yours?" Tonica asked.

"Yeah. Legally registered, I've owned it for years. Never bothered for a concealed carry permit or anything, it was . . . I brought it in one night, and left it in the clinic. And then, last week, the day they spray-painted the clinic, it disappeared. I thought they'd gotten in, that she'd let them in, and they'd taken it." His eyes closed, and he exhaled, as though all the tension in him was just running out. "Maybe they did, maybe she did, and it fell out of her pocket when she was leaving, I don't know. Does it matter, anymore?"

Ginny was going to go into a rant about the dangers of

casual gun ownership and the actual wording of the Second Amendment, when a cop came up alongside them.

"Ma'am? I think this belongs to you?"

The cop was holding a pink leash, and at the end of it, Georgie looked up at her, blue-black tongue lolling as though today had been the Best. Playday. Ever.

Ginny sniffed a little and knelt down to hug her dog, getting a face-washing in return. "Yeah," she said to the cop. "Yeah, she's mine."

The rooftop was always a good place to be. You could see everything there, and humans so rarely looked up. And even if they did, what would they see?

Penny groomed her left paw, and then gave her tail a once-over. In the end, she'd practically had to lead their humans to the problem—or, more specifically, lead the problem to them. But once she had, they'd dealt with it admirably. She knew that the whirling lights and confusion meant that the problem was being dealt with. They made noise when they figured things out, both humans and dogs.

She turned her head and studied the humans again, her whiskers flaring with satisfaction. Everything was just as it should be. No more dark-smells would be coming into the clinic.

15

After another half hour of standing around, the cops finally let them go. Ginny had thought that she should go find Nora, talk about settling up the bill, but Tonica's reaction convinced her that now wasn't the time or the place. They'd headed for Mary's instead, leaving Georgie curled up asleep in her usual spot, with a black poodle for company.

Tonica walked in, and stopped dead, so that Ginny almost stepped on him. "Jesus, what a disaster."

"The case?" she asked, confused.

"This bar," Tonica said. He looked around Mary's and shook his head.

Ginny couldn't see anything particularly out of place or disastrous, but she wasn't going to argue with him.

"Teddy!" Stacy looked relieved enough to break into tears. "Oh God, I didn't want to call you but you're here, and help!"

Apparently, Stacy thought it was a disaster, too.

"What happened to Jon?"

"He quit," Stacy said. "And Patrick said he'd put an ad in the paper, that he was going to hire a bunch of people but none of that is useful now, and it's trivia night and it's going to get *insane* and help!"

Stacy was usually more put-together than this, but she was right, trivia night did get insane, with people coming in from all over the city to match their knowledge against other teams, and Berto, their trivia master.

"Did Seth come tonight?" Tonica asked, in a voice that suggested it would be best for the old man if he had.

"I called and yelled at him, and he came in. But he's not happy. I think he's going to quit, too." Stacy didn't wail, but her voice sounded like she wanted to.

"I got this," he said, sliding under the break in the bar, and taking up position. "Finish up that order, and then we can split the load."

Once he had order restored, Teddy worked his way down to Ginny's usual spot at the end of the bar, where she was nursing her first drink and keeping an eye on Georgie, who was eating dinner. Either Ginny had been carrying a can of food with her, or Georgie was eating some of Seth's best leftovers.

"If Williams had gone to the police when he first suspected—" She interrupted him.

"You mean, like we did?"

He acknowledged the hit. "Him saying why he was there off hours might've meant admitting why he was there, and then all the story between him and Este comes out, but he knew something was wrong, and—"

"And he just went in and tried to investigate by himself?" Ginny's question had a self-mocking tone that he acknowledged.

"The difference is, we're okay with giving the cops what we know."

"No, we're not," Ginny said, shaking her head. "We're obsessive and compulsive and we want to find the answer first."

"I'm neither obsessive, nor compulsive." But he had to admit that she had a point. They had first gotten to know each other going head-to-head on trivia night, after all. "You playing tonight?"

She looked exhausted, her face drawn and her mouth sad, but she looked up at that, and then down the bar to where the chalk scoreboard was already set up. "Yeah. Yeah, I think so. Let me take Georgie home and settle her, then I'll be back. We're gonna kick your team's ass, Tonica."

"Sure you are, Mallard. Sure you are."

He gave a quick scan down the bar, to make sure that nobody else needed a refill, or was lifting a finger to call for Stacy. She was right: with Jon gone and Seth sulking, they were short-staffed and overrun. If Patrick didn't hire someone soon, he was going to have a total revolt on his hands. But his comment about hiring a bunch of people . . . what the hell was up with that?

"So they're still calling the bookkeeper's death an accident?" Ginny asked, obviously not able to let the job go, even though they'd done what they'd been hired for, and more.

"Well, it was. Stroke or heart attack; just one of those things that happen, although at a really damn bad time. Tragedy, but no foul play."

"But . . ."

"Ginny. An affair, embezzlement-for-revenge, blackmail, and wild animal smuggling isn't enough, you want murder, too?" He shook his head. "I think that's taking overcompetitiveness to a new and bad level."

"Right. I know." She sipped her drink, and looked around the bar. "Uh-oh . . ."

Patrick had just walked in, and he had a look on his face that made her want to dive under the nearest table. It wasn't a bad look, in fact, it was open, happy . . . maybe even exuberant. That was what made it so terrifying.

"Teddy. Open a bottle of the good stuff."

For Patrick, that meant bourbon. Teddy went back behind the bar and pulled the bottle in question off the shelf—the small batch, not the crap they kept for mixing—and poured a glass.

"To me, and to my budding empire," Patrick said, toasting the bar, and then took a drink. "The bank approved the loan, the deal went through. Next year, we'll have a sister site in Fremont. And after that . . . who knows?"

"You're opening another bar?"

"I am." Patrick looked so proud, Teddy bit back the urge to yell at him that he should be dealing with the one he had, first.

"So those architects . . ."

"Were here to see what it was about Mary's that I like so

much. I'll be spending a lot of time at the new site, making sure they do it properly . . . and that means I'm not going to be able to give as much attention to Mary's as I usually do."

Teddy bit his tongue, hard.

"So I want you to take over."

He almost bit his tongue again, and carefully did not look over at Ginny. "What?"

"As manager. Run the place for me."

"You want me . . ."

"You think I didn't know you were doing the job already?"

That was exactly what he had thought, yeah.

"If I'm going to do this, I can't be paying attention to every little detail of the day-to-day running. I need a manager I can trust. Is that you?"

Responsibility. Teddy licked suddenly dry lips, and gave the bartop a pointless sweep with his dishcloth, buying time to think. He like being a bartender: coming in and then going home, not carrying anything of the job with him when he left. And it gave him the freedom to help Ginny, which he enjoyed, probably more than he should.

But it wasn't like he hadn't been doing the work anyway, because it had to be done, and worrying about it all the time anyway. And if he said no, and Patrick hired someone else, someone who didn't know Mary's, who didn't understand that they'd figured out what worked and what didn't . . .

He looked up and saw that Ginny and Stacy were talking now, leaning across the bar, heads together, Ginny's tablet between them. They could have been arguing about the proper way to make a gimlet, or looking at the new fashions, or discussing the details of wild animal trafficking, or . . . with those two, he never knew.

And beyond them, he could see Georgie through the window, sleeping where they'd left her. On impulse, Teddy looked up, and saw just the tip of a striped tail dangling over the edge of the shelving, twitching back and forth as Penny surveyed her domain.

Without realizing it, he'd made his choice already. It wasn't as though the investigating—*researching*—projects took that much time. . . .

Ginny looked over at him then, and raised her eyebrows. Clearly, she'd heard every word Patrick had said. Her expression was neutral, but the look in her eyes was a challenge.

Woman knew him too damn well.

Teddy nodded back at her, then turned to Patrick. "Yeah," he said. "It's me, yeah."

Above them, Penny's tail flicked once, then curled up in satisfaction.

Acknowledgments

Once again, to my on-site research team: Barbara Caridad Ferrer, Janna Silverstein, and Kat Richardson, who were always willing to check details against my imagination. Any missteps, mistakes, or misinterpretations are the work of the author, not her advisors.